BY COURAGE ENDURED

Recent Titles by Margaret Allan

BY FAITH DIVIDED *
BY HOPE UNITED *
DOCTOR DAVID
THE DOCTOR AT PARTRIDGE HILL
HIGHLAND DOCTOR
THE KISSING GATE
THE MAN FROM LAMB HILL
A PORTRAIT OF JAY
RETURN TO EDEN
A SMALL PARADISE
SON OF HAMISH
THE SONG IS ENDED
A WOMAN OF FAITH *
YESTERDAY'S NEWS *

* *available from Severn House*

BY COURAGE ENDURED

Margaret Allan

This first world edition published in Great Britain 2005 by
SEVERN HOUSE PUBLISHERS LTD of
9–15 High Street, Sutton, Surrey SM1 1DF.
This first world edition published in the USA 2006 by
SEVERN HOUSE PUBLISHERS INC of
595 Madison Avenue, New York, N.Y. 10022.

British Library Cataloguing in Publication Data

Allan, Margaret, 1922-
    By courage endured
    1.   Cameron, Andrea (Fictitious character) - Fiction
    2.   Women clergy - En gland - Yorkshire - Fiction
    3.   Remarriage - Fiction
    4.   Yorkshire (England) - Fiction
    I.   Title
    823.9'14 [F]

    ISBN-10 : 0-7278-6315-0

Typeset by Palimpsest Book Production Ltd.,
Polmont, Stirlingshire, Scotland.
Printed and bound in Great Britain by
MPG Books Ltd., Bodmin, Cornwall.

To the memory of MADELINE DAWSON SRN
1950 – 2003
A dedicated nurse and a woman of great courage

One

It was warm in the kitchen of Abbot's Fold Farm, but the view from the big window, which gave wide views of the moorland scenery, indicated that spring was still far away, even though the calendar bearing the logo of a local animal-feed supplier showed that the dreaded month of February was almost at an end. When she turned her head to the left, Julie was able to catch sight of the fast-thickening bodies of Dave's sheep huddling together in the fields closest to the farm, where there was shelter for them from the worst of the elements and where it was easiest for Dave to be on hand all the time when the lambing started.

An outbreak of barking from the two sheepdogs, Tyke and Brack, caused her to glance in the other direction to where the farm gate gave access to the lane that some distance away met with the summit of Abbot's Hill. There was a vehicle advancing along that lane. Not the vehicle Julie had been expecting to see: not the elderly Land Rover belonging to Dave. It would be too early for Dave to be back home yet from Nyddford, where he had gone to the auction mart. She hoped it would not be a salesman looking for an order. Dave had not left her any instructions about what to say to anyone like that. Also, time was rushing on and she needed to shower and change into her uniform as soon as she had the meal in the oven so that she could eat with Dave before starting her round of visits to the housebound patients who were unable to get to Nyddford Health Centre for the treatment they required.

The vehicle came to a stop outside the farm entrance and the driver got out to open the heavy gate as the noise from the dogs became more frenzied. Julie wondered if this would deter him from entering the farmyard. Then he turned and lifted his head towards the window where she stood, as though he already knew she would be there. Her heart sank when she recognized him. It was Matt Harper, and she certainly was not pleased to see *him*. Already Matt was through the gate and closing it again before stooping to stroke the heads of the two dogs, who welcomed him with waving tails. As she moved away from the window and made for the back door, the thought came into her mind that even though Dave's dog, and Jack's dog, gave Matt Harper a welcome, their two owners would have found it hard to do so. Dave would have been polite but cool towards the son of the man his mother had married a little over a year ago. Young Jack would have acted likewise simply because to him his father could do no wrong. If Dave didn't like anyone, nor did Jack! It was as simple as that. So it was just as well that neither of them was around when Matt made this unexpected visit to Abbot's Fold Farm.

'How are you, Julie darling?' Matt asked as they met in the back porch. He smelled of fresh air and expensive after-shave. His black hair was fashionably cut and his dark eyes sparkled as they met her own brown, vaguely troubled gaze.

'Surprised to see you, Matt,' she replied as she took a step back in case he intended to kiss her.

'But pleased, I hope?' There was laughter lurking round his mouth as he guessed why she had evaded him. 'I haven't come to take advantage of you while your husband is away at the auction mart in Nyddford,' he added.

'I didn't think you had,' she assured him hastily as he followed her into the kitchen. 'How did you know Dave was there today?'

'I ran into him at the bank and he said he was on his way there.'

'I don't think he'll be there for much longer. He'll be wanting to get back in time to eat with me before I start my rounds at two.'

Matt sighed. 'He's a lucky man to be sharing his meals, and everything else, with you, Julie.'

Something in the way he said this, the emphasis he placed

2

on the words *everything else*, brought a swift rush of colour to Julie's face. It was time, more than time, that Matt gave up on these reminders of how close *they* had been only a few months ago. She had to make that clear to him before he forgot himself and uttered such words in the presence of Dave, because the jealousy Dave had felt of Matt right from the start of their friendship did not seem to have diminished since their marriage.

'There are plenty of things other people would not want to share with me, Matt,' she began, purposely avoiding referring to him personally.

'I can't think of any,' he broke in before she could continue.

'There's my work, for one thing,' she reminded him. 'The unsocial hours: evening work and weekend work, and being called out sometimes at short notice.'

'I would have shared all that, gladly, as long as you were coming home to *me*. You know I would, don't you?'

Julie did not answer. Nor could she meet the pleading in his eyes. She could not get used to Matt Harper in this frame of mind. It was so unlike him. So different from that determined, self-confident man who had become part of her life less than a year ago when he had come back to North Yorkshire after spending some years in America. His father's critical illness had brought about Matt's hasty return, but as Ben Harper slowly recovered Matt had begun to take over the running of the Harper Farm Transport business, and to lay siege to Julie. She had been flattered by his attention, having at that time been in despair of Dave ever asking her to marry him or to move in with him at Abbot's Fold – though in fact Dave *had* suggested that when Jacob's Cottage, where she was then living, was needed by the holiday-makers who had booked it months earlier, he could provide her with a room in his home.

It was the way Dave had offered her the room that had provoked her angry refusal. The offer had been made as though he was offering to take an extra animal into his care rather than begging the woman he loved to come and share his home and his life. So she had blown her top with Dave and made haste to Nyddford in search of a house that would be just large enough for herself and a pet cat or dog. While she had still been in that angry mood, Matt had pressed home his advantage by inviting her out more and more often, and since Matt was not only good-looking but also very good company, their friendship had soon flourished. Until Matt made it clear that he wanted much more than friendship from her . . .

'Is he making you happy, Julie?' Matt's voice broke into her wandering thoughts. 'Because if not I'll soon—'

'Yes! Yes he is,' she hurried to reassure him, all the time listening for the sound of Dave's Land Rover turning into the lane. Dave would not be best pleased to find Matt had been here with her while he had been away at the auction.

'I could have made you happy too, and given you an easier life than you have here. You would not have had to combine your nursing career with all the cooking and housework you have to do now,' Matt reminded her.

'Don't go on, Matt, please,' she begged. 'You know we went through all that last year. I told you then that I knew what I was taking on.'

'It's not just the work you have to do though, is it? It's having to cope with Dave's kids as well. I don't suppose Jack is much of a problem, but by all accounts Carla is more than a handful for anyone to deal with,' he persisted.

'She'll grow out of it. Most of them do,' Julie said with an attempt at a laugh. They *were* having problems with Carla, which she hoped Matt had not heard about.

'You ought to have been looking after your own children, Julie. You would have been, if I'd had anything to do with it.'

Julie laughed again, determined now to move away from where this conversation was taking them. 'There was hardly time for that to happen during our short engagement, was there?'

'That wasn't my fault,' he said. 'Just because Susanna decided to follow me over here and turned up at the Golden Fleece that night—'

'Perhaps you ought to have asked Susanna to stay here and marry you,' Julie broke in.'After all, that was what she came for, wasn't it?'

4

'No! It was not!' he replied vehemently. 'She came over to try and talk me into going back to America with her, to the position her father had lined up for me in his company. There was never any question of her staying over here. In fact she wasted her time in coming, as I told her at the time. So there was really no need for you to get all upset and go rushing off like you did. It was *you* I wanted, Julie, not Susanna. You *must* believe that.' It was Julie he *still* wanted, but if he told her that, she would probably send him on his way with some hard words. He had told himself that he must let her go, especially now that she had married into the family of his father's new wife; but every time he met her, either by accident in Nyddford or at a family meal at Ford House, the same strong attraction for her surged inside him that he had felt for her when he first came back to Nyddford. The force of that feeling had made him stay on instead of going back to America, and Susanna.

'Don't go on, Matt, *please*. I told you that night that I had made a mistake in ever thinking I could marry you,' Julie interrupted before he could say anything to bring even more embarrassment to her than she was already experiencing. 'If it had not been so, I wouldn't be married to Dave now.'

'I don't believe you really love him, and I'm not so sure he loves you. If he had loved you, he would not have kept you waiting so long for him to make his mind up about marrying you.'

'That was because he believed he had nothing much to offer me except all the problems that go with farming these days, and with bringing up someone else's children,' she added. This last was a mistake, she was soon to discover.

'I think you married him because you were sorry for him and his children. Because he was a man on his own trying to cope with the farming crisis and two teenage kids at the same time. Once his mother had moved out of here, when she married my father, he would be struggling to manage, and there you were, living close to him in Jacob's Cottage, seeing it all happening and feeling sorry for him. Sympathy isn't the same as love though, is it, Julie?'

'It is in my case,' she said sharply. 'Yes, I was sorry for

5

Dave, but I would never have married him only for that reason. I'd been in love with him for a long time.' She paused; then, seeing the doubt that still lingered in his face, she took a deep breath and told him the rest. 'I was in love with Dave when he married my friend Jill. I would have married him then if he had asked *me* instead of her. You see, I knew Dave first; I went out with him first. Then I introduced him to Jill, who was my friend when we did our nursing training together.'

Matt found this difficult to understand. 'You can't mean that you actually waited all these years for Dave Bramley!'

Julie nodded. 'Yes, I do.'

'Surely you must have made other relationships during those – how many years? If Carla is sixteen, and they were probably married for a few years before then . . .'

Dave and Jill had been married for only a few months when Carla had arrived, but Julie was not going to share that with Matt. Instead she said, 'I did meet other men during those years, and I kept hoping I would meet someone who would mean to me what Dave had meant, because I didn't want to go on being in love with my friend's husband. Only none of them ever did. That's really the way it always was, and still is, Matt.'

'So Dave knew that when his mother married my father and moved to Ford House, you were here on his doorstep, waiting to take over from her?' Matt's strong, square face bore a scowl as he expressed his understanding of the situation.

'No! He had no idea of how I felt about him. In fact he thought—' Julie broke off abruptly then, because she had no intention of telling him that Dave had thought she was in a relationship with Matt long before her brief engagement to Matt had been announced. What she wanted was to end this pointless discussion as soon as possible. 'I need to get ready for work, Matt; I'm on duty at two,' she told him briskly. 'You didn't say why you called today; was it for some special reason?'

'I came because I wanted to see you,' he said quietly.

'But you'll see me on Saturday when we come to Ford

House for supper. Dorothy said she had asked you to be there, as well as us, to celebrate your father's birthday.'

Matt sighed. 'I won't see you alone then, will I? Dave will be there, and his children, as well as his mother and my father. It won't be the same.'

'It can't be the same now. You have to accept that or—' Even as she began to utter the words, Julie heard the sound of Dave's elderly Land Rover chugging along the lane and coming to a halt outside the farm gate. Dave must already have seen Matt's vehicle parked just beyond the gate, so he would be aware that they had a visitor. He would be aware of it, but not pleased about it if he had recognized the almost new people-carrier as belonging to Matt Harper.

'That sounds like Dave home. I'd better put the vegetables on to cook. I'll see you on Saturday at Ford House.'

Julie turned away from him and made for the cooker, so Matt had no alternative but to leave. She watched as he strode across the yard, his burly figure clad in the sort of expensive country clothes and shoes that went with his position as partner in the Harper Farm Transport business. His gear was in sharp contrast to that of Dave, who wore a rubbed dark-coloured fleece on top of his jeans. The two men met and exchanged a few words before Matt strolled on to pass through the gate and close it after him. Dave paused only for long enough to speak to the collies and silence their welcome before barging into the house with a thunderous scowl on his face.

'What was he doing here?'

The question was not unexpected, but Julie hadn't had sufficient time to think up a believable answer for it. Instead she busied herself at the cooker with her back turned to her husband.

'I asked what he was doing here?' Dave said again.

Julie went on stirring the gravy as she answered. 'I think he was just passing this way on one of his business calls, so he decided to drop in and say hallo.'

'He'll be saying hallo to you on Saturday night, won't he? Couldn't he wait until then?'

Hot colour that had nothing to do with the warmth coming

from the Aga rushed into Julie's creamy skin. 'It was just a friendly call, as he was out this way. That's all,' she protested.

'I hope you're not going to encourage him to make a habit of doing that.'

Irritation surged up inside her, but she took a deep breath and said calmly, 'I think you know I won't be doing that, Dave.'

He sighed as he moved across to the sink and turned on the tap to wash his hands. 'I've got enough to worry about without having to wonder if your old flame is waiting for every chance to come up here when I'm out of the way.'

'It's not like that, Dave. You know it isn't!' she responded sharply.

'Isn't it? I've seen the way he looks at you sometimes when we're at Ford House.'

'You're imagining things.' Her voice was even sharper this time.

'I'm not!'

'Surely you can trust me, Dave? After all, it was you I married . . .'

'He hasn't found anyone else, has he?'

'I don't know. He may have,' she added hopefully, because anger with Dave was building inside her and she was determined to keep it under control.

'The sooner he does, the better, as far as I'm concerned. I just don't like him hanging about around here.'

Suddenly her anger erupted. 'That's enough, Dave! You have to trust me when you are not here, the same as you have to trust me when I go out to see a male patient who lives alone.'

'That's different!'

'How do you know?' She was trembling with the heat of her emotion now.

'They're old, aren't they?'

Her irritation subsided as she choked back a laugh when she recalled the elderly, though still handsome, retired army officer who enjoyed gently flirting with her. The posy of carnations on the oak dresser had been waiting for her on her last visit to him. Dave had assumed they were a gift from a woman patient. When he stopped being so jealous, she would be able to share with him some of those lighter moments her job brought into her life. Not yet, though. Her marriage was not stable enough for that.

'We'd better get our meal, or I'll be late,' she told him as she went to take the casserole out of the oven.

At Ford House, that beautiful stone dwelling set on the outskirts of Nyddford, Dave's mother, Dorothy, and her husband of a little over a year were also sharing a meal. Dorothy waited until they had finished their main course and were dawdling over their dishes of apple crumble to voice her concern. Ben would probably think she was worrying about nothing, but then Ben did not know her Dave as well as she did.

'Come on, Dorothy love, tell me what's bothering you,' Ben said while she was still wondering just how to lead into the subject.

'How do you know anything *is* bothering me?' She smiled as she asked that question. There were still times when she could hardly believe her good fortune in having married Ben Harper at last after the long delay brought about by the tragic death of her son's young wife, which had meant her postponing her marriage to Ben and moving into the farmhouse to look after Dave and his children.

'Because you haven't been giving your full attention to anything I've been saying to you since you came back from seeing your friend at Far Moor.'

'Oh, I'm so sorry, Ben! Did I miss anything important?'

He chuckled as he answered her. 'Obviously nothing as important as the matter on your mind since you came back from Far Moor. What is it? Is Mary Gray not well? Or is her son's wife suffering from depression again?'

Dorothy shook her head. 'No, it's nothing like that. Mary's fine, and so is Belinda.'

'Well, what is it? It's not you, my darling, is it? You're not feeling ill, are you? If so, why didn't you stay at home and let me call the doctor?' The good-looking face beneath the thatch of thick, silver hair was full of Ben's anxiety.

9

'No! No! It's nothing like that, Ben. I'm perfectly well.'
She managed a laugh to prove it. Her face sobered again as
she sought for the words she needed. They came out in a
rush. 'It's Matt I'm concerned about.'

'Matt!' In his relief Ben let out a shout of laughter. 'I don't
think you need waste any time worrying about Matt. He's
more than capable of looking after himself.'

Dorothy bit her lip, and hesitated before replying. It was
going to be so difficult. Perhaps she was worrying about
nothing, after all.

'So what has my son done to bring that frown to your
lovely face, my dear?' Ben's voice was gentle. He loved her
so much, and had loved her for so long – even when she
had been married to her first husband, Jacob Bramley.
Sometimes he believed she had loved him too during the
years of Jacob's illness, but she had been loyal to her marriage
vows and her Christian faith and kept her feelings to herself
until the death of their partners had freed them both.

'I might be worrying about nothing.' She spoke her
thoughts aloud. 'It was just that, as I was driving up to Far
Moor Farm, I thought I'd drop in at Abbot's Fold on the
way with some cakes for Carla and Jack. Only when I was
about to turn into the farm lane I saw Matt's car was there.
So I backed out and went straight on to see Mary.'

Ben was puzzled. 'Why did you do that?'

'Well, I can't help but be aware of how Matt still feels
about Julie, and I knew Dave would be down at the auction
mart in Nyddford at that time. I didn't want Matt to think I
was spying on him. Or for Julie to think I didn't trust her.'

'You surely don't think Matt and Julie are getting involved
again?'

'I don't *want* to believe that, but Matt doesn't seem to go
out and about like he used to . . .'

'That doesn't prove anything except that he's beginning
to settle down at last.'

Dorothy's eyes were still troubled. 'I've seen the way he
looks at Julie sometimes. As though he's still very attracted
to her.'

Ben was silent. His spoon lay idle in the dish, even though

10

apple crumble was his favourite pudding. All at once he saw the problem as Dorothy saw it. Julie would not need to give Matt any encouragement to arouse jealousy in Dave's mind. Because Dave still had a huge chip on his shoulder about how little he had been able to offer Julie compared to what Matt would have been able to give her. Dorothy had told him as much at the time of their marriage. Matt was handsome, and successful. He was also used to getting his own way in most things. His mother had given him too much when he was a boy, Ben thought. Certainly Ben was sure *he* had never made that mistake. After all, the reason Matt had gone to work in America rather than staying in Nyddford to work for Harper Farm Transport was that Ben would not allow him to put so many of his own ideas into the business. They had clashed head-on about that, ending with an almighty row that had kept Matt in America until Ben's critical illness last year. Those years had done a lot for his son, Ben had to acknowledge. Some of his business ideas were good ideas now. It was not a good idea for him to be still pursuing Julie, though, when she was married to Dave. Nothing good could come of that. He'd have a word with the lad as soon as possible, even though Matt wouldn't like it.

'I can't discuss this with Matt in the office this afternoon when his secretary is around; I'll give him a ring at home tonight and have a word about it. So stop worrying, my dear, and finish your meal,' he said.

Would those words from his father be enough? Or would Matt tell his father to mind his own business? Unease filled Dorothy as she carried the dishes from the table and went to make their coffee. She could only offer up a silent prayer that both men would keep their temper and there would be no clash of wills that might endanger Ben's health.

Matt ate alone in the lounge bar of the Abbey Inn with a copy of the *Yorkshire Post* open before him. His attention was on neither the business page of the newspaper nor the hearty steak baguette that he had ordered with his single glass of lager. He was still back in thought with what had been said in the kitchen of Abbot's Fold Farm. He knew he should not have gone there today. It was a bloody stupid thing to do when he knew what Dave Bramley's reaction would be if he found out, but he had not expected Dave to be back from the auction so early. Plainly, Dave had been in a black mood when they had come face to face in the yard of his farm. His curt nod had shown no welcome, his brief words of greeting no warmth. All Matt could hope now was that Julie would not suffer because of his visit.

Julie should not have been there in that kitchen cooking a big meal for Dave before starting her hours of driving about the icy roads of the dale to carry out her nursing duties. She should not have been there to cope with Dave's children and their problems. She should not have been there at the end of the day to share Dave's bed. Where Julie ought to have been was in *his* new, luxurious home, waiting to have a couple of children of her own before it was too late.

When he reached that thought, a chill ran down his spine. What if Julie was already expecting a baby? If it had been so, he would surely have heard about it by now from Dave's mother. Before it happened he must try to make Julie realize that she had made a colossal mistake in marrying Dave Bramley. It would not be easy, but he was a man who enjoyed a challenge.

Two

In the big living room at Nyddbeck Manse Andrea and Bill were snatching a precious few minutes alone together in their too-busy day. Andrea had just answered a telephone call that brought a request for a funeral service from someone she didn't know – someone who was not a regular attender at either of her churches. She had arranged to go and see the close relative later that afternoon to offer words of comfort and find out what the wishes of the relatives were about things like which hymns, if any, were to be used during the service and whether there were to be spoken tributes from family members. There was a fervent hope inside her that they would not insist on anything too unsuitable in the way of songs. She never ceased to be amazed at the choices made by some people for these events. An outrageous choice could sometimes provoke at the least a plainly audible 'Oh no!' from some of those present, if not outspoken criticism. Yet she had always held a firm belief that the wishes of those who had lost a loved one must come first, rather than her own preferences.

'Is it anyone we know?' Bill asked as Andrea took her seat again on the sofa next to him.

She shook her head slightly, so that the curtain of silky black hair moved from her right shoulder just far enough to touch his chin. 'No. They've only been living here since the Boltons left. They bought the Mill House and are opening it as a guest house soon. I don't know much more than that about them.'

'I think Carla's made friends with them,' Bill said thoughtfully. 'I've seen her around the Mill House a couple of times when I've been walking Lucky that way.'

13

At the sound of his name, and the magic word 'walking' Lucky leapt to his feet and wagged his long, plumed chestnut-coloured tail. To make quite certain they knew he was all for the idea of walking, he added a couple of barks.

Andrea and Bill laughed together. 'Not yet, Lucky. You've got your timing wrong,' Bill told him. At which Lucky gave a disappointed sigh and flopped down again on to the sheep-skin rug before the fire with his head on his paws and a reproachful look in his eyes.

'I could do with a breath of fresh air,' Andrea decided as she drained her coffee mug. 'Too much paperwork this morning, plus two hospital visits, adds up to a sluggish brain just now. I need to be alert at the meeting tonight to settle some of the changes we are going to have to make at Nyddford while the roof is being repaired. So I think I'll walk to the Mill House to see Paula Price about the funeral instead of going in the car.'

'You'll need to put your boots on, darling, because there's a lot of ice about,' Bill warned. 'It was quite bad when I took Lucky out this morning and there's been no let-up since then.'

'I'll be careful,' Andrea promised as she reached across to kiss him before moving to the door. 'You worry about me too much.'

'That's because I love you so much.' Bill drew her firmly into his arms as he spoke and began to stop her next words with a kiss that set her heart pounding. 'I was just having lovely thoughts about something we could do on a winter afternoon where you certainly wouldn't need to wear your boots,' he murmured.

Andrea sighed. 'Oh, Bill, I'm so sorry. You know I'd much rather be with you, don't you?'

It was Bill's turn to sigh as he let her go reluctantly. 'It's the timing of these calls for help that I have problems with. The callers seem to know when I've got you to myself for a while and I'm about to take advantage of you, don't they?'

Now Andrea laughed. 'Don't get sorry for yourself, Bill Wyndham! I'll be back within the hour, and you can always console yourself in my absence by catching up on your own work.'

Bill stretched out to full length on the roomy sofa and put his feet up. 'I'm far too comfortable to want to drag myself over to the studio, my love. I'd much rather wait here for you to come back. Within the hour, you said?'

Andrea hesitated. 'That's what I hope, but I don't know what sort of person Paula Price is – how she's coping with this and what sort of help she might need.'

'I'll see you when I'll see you, then. We won't wait up for you, will we, Lucky?'

Andrea threw him a kiss as she closed the door on him. They looked so comfortable there in the dying afternoon light, the man she loved and the dog who had gone to lie beside him with a paw placed possessively on his chest. One part of her longed to stay with them, but the other part of her mind was already reaching out in thought to that unknown woman whose need of her presence at this time must be her priority. Five minutes later, having changed her red sweater for a dark-blue clerical shirt and her white collar of office, she was walking as fast as she dared along the icy surface of Beck Lane, leaving behind her manse and her little stone-built church, the long row of ancient cottages that had once housed farm workers and market gardeners and now belonged mainly to city commuters and weekenders.

On the right of her now were the Monks' Steps, which led up the long incline to Abbot's Moor. It was down these same worn steps that centuries ago the monks had walked from the abbey to give comfort and help to the people who lived in Nyddbeck then. There was no visible sign left of the building they might have used, except for a scattered collection of huge stones; but Andrea sometimes felt that they had left behind a blessing for her, because it was here in this place that she had been able to come to terms with the two tragedies in her life and find new happiness with Bill.

The beck was wider and faster flowing now beneath tall horse chestnut trees, which had provided a thick carpet of fallen bronze leaves for her to walk more safely on until she reached the wooded garden and the large stone house which had once been the dwelling for the owner of a thriving flour mill. Andrea had never been within the grounds of the Mill House before, although she had been invited there when the Bolton family held their farewell party before leaving for America, when Mr Bolton's months of a teaching exchange at Nyddford High School had ended. It had by all accounts been a spectacular barbecue enjoyed by all – except perhaps Carla Bramley, who had been heartbroken at the prospect of losing her boyfriend, Josh Bolton. There had been fireworks and fun for all ages, but Andrea had missed it because of a church meeting. Now the grounds were utterly silent and quite beautiful under a glittering white carpet of frost.

As she lifted her hand to press the doorbell, she was already sending up a quick prayer that she would be able to offer the woman who had asked her to come the right sort of comfort. It seemed a long time to her before her second pushing of the bell brought a beam of light and the opening of the huge carved-oak door.

'Oh! I'm so sorry to keep you waiting,' the young woman who was facing her said breathlessly. 'I was out in the back garden putting food for the birds and listening for the sound of your car. Do come in. I'm Paula Price.' She held out a hand – a very cold hand – and Andrea took it firmly in her own warm fingers.

'I decided to walk here as I hadn't had time to go for a walk this morning. Everything looks very beautiful under the frost, doesn't it?'

'Yes,' Paula agreed. 'My father loved days like this.' Her voice stumbled as she came to the end of the sentence, but she collected herself rapidly and opened a door to her right and held it for Andrea to enter a room that sent out an atmosphere of warmth and welcome.

'You've got an open fire – how lovely!' Andrea exclaimed. 'My parents have one in their home in Scotland.'

'Dad loved his open fire, and we thought the guests might enjoy it too. When they start coming, that is.'

'Of course – you haven't been here long, have you? I hope you're settling in without too many problems?' Andrea said as she sank gracefully into the armchair closest to the fire.

Paula Price sighed. 'We were settling in so well until Dad

picked up this chest infection and became so ill that he had to go into the cottage hospital at Nyddford.' She bit her lip as emotion threatened to spill over. 'I don't know where he picked it up, because we haven't been into any crowded places. There was far too much to do here, with all the decorating and the gardening that we wanted to do before we opened at Easter.'

'There have been quite a lot of chest infections about since Christmas. I've been kept very busy hospital-visiting some of my older church members,' Andrea told her. 'It must have been very hard for you, having to travel to Nyddford to visit your father every day when you had so much to do here. Have you anyone else to share things with? Any other family member nearby?'

Andrea did not miss the shadow that crossed the pretty but tired-looking face. Or the too-long interval before the answer came. She must not ask any more questions of that sort, she decided.

'No. There was just Dad and me.' As the answer came, there was another biting of lips and a hint of tears before the girl said in a rush, 'I'm sorry we haven't managed to get to your church since we came here. I feel awful asking you to come here now, when we haven't done so, but I just didn't know what else to do.'

Andrea smiled at her, liking her honesty. 'You did the right thing, ringing me, Paula.'

'I saw your name and phone number on the church notice board when I was taking Dad for a walk one day.'

'So your father was already not too well when you came here?'

'He was quite badly visually impaired after an accident, so he needed help. That's why I gave up my job in London and we came here to open the guest house.'

'A very big change for you, then,' Andrea said thoughtfully.

'Yes. In every way.' Paula Price pressed her lips firmly together to stop their trembling. 'But there was nothing else I could do. I couldn't leave Dad to cope on his own while I was working in the restaurant until late in the evening.'

17

'What made you choose Nyddbeck? Do you mind me asking that?' Andrea added quickly.

'It was because Dad spent his childhood and early teens here. He used to say how happy he'd been here – what a lovely childhood he'd had in North Yorkshire. So when he was well enough to travel after the accident, we came up on holiday and stayed in Nyddford. While we were there we saw this place advertised, so we came to look at it and I fell in love with it. I've always wanted to own my own restaurant – I'm a chef, you see. Only I didn't think I'd end up having to do it all on my own.'

'You'll need help, won't you? It's quite a big place, isn't it?' Andrea said thoughtfully.

'Yes. That's another problem I'll have to face. You see I thought – someone – a friend – would be coming with us. Only he backed out at the last minute.'

Pain flickered momentarily in the luminous grey eyes as Paula Price shared that with Andrea. Then the pointed chin lifted proudly as she went on. 'I'll be able to cope, though, without him. I'm quite determined to make a success of this place.'

'I'm sure you will. We get a lot of tourists here from Easter to the end of October, and some hardy walkers all the year round. There are the locals too, who like to go out for meals.'

A thought struck Paula and she voiced it swiftly. 'I'm so sorry, I ought to have asked you if you'd like some tea or coffee, Mrs Wyndham. Which would you prefer?'

'Neither, thank you. I had some coffee with my husband just before I came to see you. My name is Andrea, by the way. That's what most people here call me. Now, shall we talk about what sort of service you would like for your father, Paula?'

Which is what they did for the next half-hour or so before Andrea said she must be going. At the door when she left Paula Price thanked her as they shook hands again.

'You've been so kind, Andrea. So helpful,' she murmured.

Andrea smiled as she answered. 'I'm here to do that. It's why I was ordained. One reason why, I should say. I'll be in touch with you again before the service, and you've got my phone number, so I hope you'll ring me if there's anything I can do.'

'Thanks, I will.'

As Andrea made her way carefully back to her manse, and Bill, there were silent prayers in her mind for the girl who had come here to make a new life, as she herself had come almost two years ago, only to find that tragedy awaited her. Her own deep faith plus Bill's friendship, then his love, had helped her to come to terms with what had happened and move on to happier times. The girl she had left behind in the Mill House had more to come to terms with than the death of her father, who had been only fifty-five, Andrea was certain. There was something else she had not spoken of, or maybe only hinted at. A broken relationship, maybe, which was also causing her great pain. So she must keep praying for Paula Price, and try to think of ways in which she might help her to become integrated into this small but friendly community. That must wait, though, until after the funeral of her father. Paula Price must be given time to grieve, but her situation must not be forgotten because of all the paperwork, meetings, sick-visiting and service-planning that took up so many of her hours every day. Sometimes even on what was supposed to be her day off.

Those days off shared with Bill were what helped Andrea to stop feeling guilty about the time Bill lost from his painting because of the help he gave her. 'Oh Lord, thanks again for Bill,' she murmured to herself as she glanced across Nyddbeck village green to where rays of light cast out by a Victorian lamp standard illuminated the lychgate where Bill had kissed her for the first time as the millennium bells had rung out from her little church and fireworks had lit up the sky to welcome the new century.

As she came to the packhorse bridge that spanned the beck, more light beamed out from the lamp at the gate of her manse. There was a man standing there looking out for her – a tall man, who began to walk down to the bridge to meet her; a man who had shared a problem with her soon after her arrival, and a few months later had opened his arms and his heart to her while she had shared with him what she

19

had been unable to share with anyone else – the fact that her first husband, Ian Cameron, had fathered a child with Beth Barclay even though he had refused to have another child with *her* after the death of their three-year-old son.

Bill was very close to her now. Bill, the well-known artist, the accomplished musician, the very special man who now shared her faith as well as her life. Would *their* child be an artist, or a musician? Andrea was not absolutely certain yet about this child. It was too soon for her to be sure. Too soon even to share her hopes with Bill, because if she did so, Bill would urge her to slow down and do less work. She could not do that when there were so many people needing her help and support. So she would keep her dawning hope a secret from Bill for the time being.

'I was getting worried about you, darling,' Bill told her as they came close enough to clasp hands while Lucky barked his welcome and raced backwards and forwards across the frosted grass that ran down to the edge of the water. 'So I decided to come and meet you. Or rather, we did,' he added as the dog came to lick Andrea's hand.

'Oh, Bill, what would I do without you?' she whispered as she reached up to kiss his eager mouth.

Bill laughed as they moved on towards their home. 'Work yourself into an early grave, I guess; but I don't intend to let you do that, my love.'

'Things are a lot easier for me now I have you, and some regular help from Jane Lindsay with my ironing and house-work,' she assured him.

Bill laughed as they left the icy chill of outdoors behind them and entered the warmth of the manse. 'I've got to admit that I find Jane a great help too, especially with the ironing of my shirts. Mrs Ramsbottom was a superb housekeeper, but she wasn't too good at ironing shirts.'

'You could have always done them yourself, Bill,' Andrea told him with a laugh. 'I'm glad you decided to keep Annie Ramsbottom on to look after your studio when you moved in with me. I think she has a struggle to manage now she's on her own.'

'I'm glad she agreed to stay on, because I really need

Beckside to be kept immaculate so that the people who are interested in buying my pictures aren't put off because the place is scruffy.'

He paused, uncertain whether or not to tentatively broach the piece of news that he would have to share with Andrea sooner or later. It had better be later, he decided when he had taken a closer look at her face and seen the faint lines of strain mirrored there. She could have had a difficult time with the young woman who had just been bereaved. It did happen sometimes, when death came suddenly and unexpectedly to someone who was not old and had not been ill for long. So he would save what might be unwelcome news for Andrea until later, when her meeting was over and they had shared a meal and were relaxing together.

'How are things with you, Jane?' Andrea asked a few days later, after taking in the sight of the neatly folded casual clothes laid out on the dining table and the many shirts and blouses Jane had placed on hangers.

'Oh, fine thanks, Andrea, really fine.' Jane's voice was bright, but she had lost more weight, Andrea thought.

'Brendon tells me the choir rehearsals are going well,' Andrea went on. He had also told her that Jane had an outstanding voice, which he intended to make certain would be used for solos.

'Yes, they are.' Jane's face lit up and became beautiful rather than pretty. 'Brendon is so encouraging that we all want to do our best for him.' She hesitated, then went on 'He thinks I ought to have some private singing lessons. You know, on my own.'

'Do you mean with Brendon? At his home?' Andrea was not sure this would be a wise move. She guessed that it might cause some jealousy among the other female singers whose voices were not as fine as Brendon May believed Jane's to be. There was also some concern in the back of her mind that Brendon might be getting *too* interested in Jane Lindsay.

'Oh no! He thinks I need specialist training from an expert. He says there's a very good singing teacher in York who could be right for me, but of course the lessons would be expensive. I might not be able to afford them.'

'What does Tim think to the idea? Is he in favour of it?' He would have to be, since the fees would be costly.

'I don't know. I haven't talked about it to him yet.'

Andrea was surprised to hear that, but was not going to say so. She knew that Tim's affair with his fellow teacher had ended with Donna Dawson's death a few months ago, so she had hoped, when Jane spoke of family outings and meals with Tim sometimes, that they were living together again. Maybe they were not?

'Perhaps you ought to mention it to Tim,' she suggested. 'I expect he'll be pleased for you and want to help you.'

'I haven't told him yet because we might not be able to afford the lessons.' Jane bit her lip then went on, 'You see, the flat where Tim is living now is quite expensive, and there's the mortgage on our house to pay as well.'

'Oh, I thought—' Andrea stopped.

'You thought Tim was back living with us again, I suppose.' Jane completed the sentence for her. 'Because I talk about him sometimes when I'm here. Only we aren't. Tim is still living in the flat he rented when Donna's place had to be sold. It's just her dog, Darcy, who came to live with us.'

Andrea stifled a sigh of disappointment. 'I'm sorry, Jane; I didn't mean to embarrass you,' she began.

'He wants to come back to live with us, but I'm afraid to let him,' Jane confessed.

Andrea was more puzzled than ever. 'Why, Jane? If you still love him, and your children miss him so much . . .'

Jane's eyes were downcast as she folded the last item and switched off the iron. 'Because I'm so afraid I'll have to go through all the hurt again. I mean, if it happened once that Tim fell in love with someone he cared for more than he cared for me, it could happen again, couldn't it, Andrea?'

'You were not living in Nyddford then, though, were you? You were hundreds of miles away, living with your parents, weren't you?' Andrea pointed out quietly. 'So Tim was probably quite vulnerable because he was missing you so much.'

Jane folded the ironing table as she took a long moment

to answer. 'That's what he said. He told me he joined the Nyddford Ramblers and became friendly with her while they were walking at weekends. Then one day she told him about her illness and how frightened she was. He said she cried then, and he felt as if it was Kerry who needed him because she was feeling alone and frightened of what was going to happen.'

'So it began as pity,' Andrea said thoughtfully, 'and just went on from there.'

'That's what Tim said, but I've found it hard to believe him. You see, I came here with such high hopes because it was the place where we had wanted to live ever since we came here on honeymoon. I expected everything to be wonderful once the house was finally finished and I moved here, but it wasn't like that. I knew quite soon that there was a problem, but I thought it was just that Tim was having to work too hard, with having a lot more meetings to go to in the evenings than he had in the school in London. I was devastated when I found out the truth. You know how badly I handled that, Andrea, don't you? If you hadn't come out to me that night, I don't know what would have happened . . .'

'That's all in the past now, Jane. So you must try to put it behind you and think about your future. Yours and your children's,' Andrea said firmly.

Jane did not meet her eyes as she answered. 'I can't seem to do that. It's as if I don't have any self-esteem left. When Tim comes to the house, as he does so often, I can't seem to believe that he really wants to see me as well as Kerry and Elliot, even though he's told me he'd like to come back and live with us.'

Andrea offered up a silent prayer that she would find the right words to help put this young family back together again. 'It could be that if you don't take him back he'll come to think you don't love him any more, Jane,' she suggested. 'That wouldn't be true, would it?'

Jane shook her head. 'No,' she whispered. 'What I'm afraid of is that if I took him back and then he found someone else he fancied more than me, I'd have to go through it all again. I don't think I could cope with that, even for the children's sake. So what can I do, Andrea?'

It was a question so often voiced to Andrea by people lost in despair, and one that was almost impossible to answer when the decision must come from those most closely concerned. So, as always, Andrea knew she must be cautious about giving advice too hastily. Yet she must say something to this girl who so plainly needed help.

'Maybe you would be best to have patience, Jane. To just give yourself, and Tim, more time to grow together again as you need to. In the meantime, I'll be praying for you both. You can be sure of that.'

'Yes, I know, Andrea. Maybe it was the prayers the children placed on the prayer tree that sent Tim back for them. They're quite sure it was,' Jane told her.

Andrea smiled as she recalled the misspelt but heart-rending message scribbled by Kerry and corrected by Elliot asking God to send their daddy back to them. 'You don't need a leaf from a prayer tree to ask for help, Jane. All you need is faith.'

With these words Andrea left Jane to reflect and made for her study to catch up on some of the paperwork that was the least favourite part of her work.

Three

Carla knew she ought not to have got off the school bus down in the village instead of staying on until it reached the summit of Abbot's Hill, because now she would be late home and Dad might start asking the sort of questions she would find it hard to answer. He would never understand about the longing that came over her every now and then to go to the place where she and Josh had been so happy together. She just knew he would never understand about that. So she must not spend too long in the woods around the Mill House – just long enough to remember how wonderful it had been when Josh had made love to her there for the first time. Then she would have to race up the Monks' Steps and run across the moor to Abbot's Fold, and hope to get in through the old dairy door and up to her room before her dad realized she was late home and started asking those questions.

If she managed to do that, he would probably think she had been upstairs in her room doing some of the homework that was necessary now that she was staying on at school until she was old enough to begin her training for nursing. A career in nursing! That was what she had made her mind up to do a few months ago, even though it meant staying on at school. Julie had said it would be worth it. In fact Julie had talked her dad into agreeing to it. Which seemed to Carla to be almost a miracle, because not only would she be doing what her mum had done, and what Julie was still doing, but qualifying as a nurse would make it much easier for her to go and work in America one day. She would be able to work near Josh, and she would have those important letters after her name. Julie had said those letters would earn her respect as well as a good salary.

Josh and his family would be proud of her then. Much prouder than if she had taken any old job in a hotel or restaurant, as she had once planned to do.

Josh had been all for the idea too, when she had phoned him and told him of her change of plan. 'That's just great, Carla honey! Really great!' he'd said. Carla had loved the sound of his voice, which she had missed so much since he went back to the States with his parents.

'Hi there!'

The woman's voice with its southern accent startled Carla so much that she swung round too sharply and the backpack containing her school work caught the woman's shoulder.

'Ooh! Sorry! I didn't know you were there.' Panic crept over Carla as the thought came to her that these woods might be private and she was trespassing. She had no idea whether or not that was the case. It could be that the woman was also trespassing. Carla didn't know her by sight, yet there was something in her voice that was vaguely familiar.

'I think we've met before, but maybe you don't remember, as you were feeling quite ill at the time. It was a few months ago, when I came to look at the Mill House with my father.'

When the woman said that, Carla knew why her voice had sounded familiar. Shame washed over her as she recalled their meeting inside the Mill House. What a state she must have been in when this woman had first seen her lying fast asleep in the bedroom that had belonged to Josh when the Bolton family had been living there. Then there had been the moment when she had woken in severe and frightening pain and staggered on to the first floor landing with blood all over her arms and legs. She had been so afraid at that time – so terrified of what her dad would say if what she feared was true, that her love-making with Josh had resulted in a pregnancy which could wreck her own life and Josh's.

'You drove me home. Or rather to Julie's house in Nyddford, didn't you? Thanks for doing that. I was in an awful state, so I hope I didn't spoil the inside of your car.' It was not easy to say the words, but Carla knew they had to be said, because the woman had been so kind to her and she couldn't remember if she had said thanks at the time.

'You didn't, but even if you had, I couldn't have left you in the house on your own. Could I?'

Carla hung her head and stared down at the ground. 'Some people would have done,' she muttered; then lifted her head and went on. 'I know I ought not to have been in there. Not after Josh and his family had gone.'

'Was Josh a friend of yours?'

'He was my boyfriend. He *is* my boyfriend, only he's back in America now.'

'So he must be the son of the American people who were renting the house before we bought it? The agent said they had been here for some months on a teaching exchange.'

'Yes. I used to come here a lot with Josh.' Carla's voice faltered as the memories washed over her and brought a lump to her throat.

'So you'll be missing him now?' the woman said gently. 'I know the feeling . . .'

Carla was surprised to hear that. 'Do you?'

'Yes, I have someone I miss too,' Paula Price said wistfully.

'Did they have to go away?'

Paula took her time about answering. 'No. I was the one who had to go away. It was my choice.'

Carla was puzzled. 'Why did you do it then?'

Paula sighed. 'Because I had to. I had a responsibility to someone else.'

'Do you mean you had to come here?'

Paula nodded. 'Yes, or to somewhere like this.'

'Couldn't he come too?'

'He wasn't willing to. It wasn't the way he wanted things.' As she added that, Paula wondered why she was telling the girl all this.

'Do the woods belong to you now, if you've bought the Mill House?' Carla wanted to know. 'If they do, I suppose I shouldn't be here. I mean, they could be private now.'

'I don't mind you being here, especially if it helps you. Though I'm a bit worried about how you are going to get to Nyddford now it's getting dark.'

27

Again Carla was puzzled. 'I don't need to go to Nyddford. I've just come from there on the school bus.'

'So you don't live there in Nyddford? I thought, when Dad and I took you home, that you did . . .'

Carla swallowed. This was getting too complicated. 'No. I live at Abbot's Fold Farm on Nyddmoor. I asked you to take me to Nyddford that day because Julie lived there. She lives with us now that she's married my dad.'

'How will you get to Nyddmoor? Will there be a bus?'

Carla shrugged. 'Not at this time. I'll walk home.'

Paula was appalled. 'You mustn't do that. It won't be safe, in the dark.'

Carla shrugged off her concern. 'I'll be fine. There won't be anyone up on the moor at this time. If I go up the Monks' Steps, it won't take me long.'

Paula made her mind up quickly. 'You'll be there quicker if I take you. Come on, we'll get the car. Then you can tell me the way.'

'There's no need.'

'There is, or I'll be worrying about you walking alone on the moors.'

'In that case I'll walk up Abbot's Hill,' Carla responded.

'If you do, you could be hit by a car. So I'll be even more worried about you. I expect your parents would be too if they knew.'

Suddenly Carla made her mind up. She might as well accept the lift, because that way she wouldn't be quite so late home. 'Thanks a lot,' she said. 'I have got quite a lot of homework to do tonight.'

When they were in her car and turning up Abbot's Hill, Paula Price asked Carla what she was called, and where she lived.

'I'm Carla Bramley and I live at Abbot's Fold Farm. You turn right at the top of the hill into the lane. You could drop me off at the bus stop there and I'll walk the rest of the way.' There wouldn't be any questions asked then about who had brought her home, and why, Carla decided.

'If you're quite sure. I don't mind taking you right to the farm.'

28

'Won't someone be waiting for you? Didn't you say your dad was living with you?' They were slowing down at the bus stop when Carla said that.

'Yes. Dad did live with me. We were going to run the guest house together; that's why we bought the Mill House. But he died a few days ago.'

Carla wished now that she hadn't asked about him. 'I'm sorry,' she blurted out. 'It must be awful for you, like it was for me when my mum died.'

'Not quite as bad, because you must have been very young to lose a parent, Carla.'

'It's better now we've got Julie living with us. She's a community nurse, like my mum was and like I'm going to be.'

'That's a good thing to aim for. I'm a chef,' Paula Price told her. 'I worked in a London restaurant until I came here to open my own guest house and restaurant. My name's Paula Price. Take care now, Carla.'

Carla was out of the car and lifting a hand to wave as Paula turned the vehicle about in the parking bay ready to drive back down the hill. As she walked quickly along the lane towards the lights of home, Carla found herself thinking still of the woman who must be quite alone now in that big house set on the outer edge of the village. Maybe Paula Price would be needing some help at the Mill House if it was going to be a guest house – someone to change the rooms round as she had been helping to do in Jacob's Cottage ready for the tourists who rented it. She wouldn't mind doing something like that at weekends. Maybe she'd call and ask Paula Price about that one day soon . . .

'Why do you have to go somewhere else to live, Daddy? Why don't you stay with us all the time now, like you did in London?'

Pain pierced Tim Lindsay afresh when Elliot asked the questions, not for the first time, as he reached for his leather jacket and prepared to leave the house in Nyddford Gardens, which had been the dream home for him and Jane before things had begun to fall apart between them. It was almost

29

impossible for him to answer those questions. How could you ever manage to explain to an inquisitive four-year-old that it was because his daddy had behaved so badly to his mum that, even after he had said how sorry he was, she still felt unable to either trust him again or forgive him for what he had done. You could not tell such a small child, as you might have been able to tell someone older, that you had behaved so bloody badly that all the good years shared with his mum had been forgotten and only the recent traumatic times were remembered. Tim looked again into those trusting eyes that were so like Jane's and felt shame envelop him.

'Why, Daddy?' Elliot persisted. 'Kerry and Darcy want you to come and live here again. So do I. Why don't you?'

At the sound of his name Darcy barged into the living room from the hall, where he had stationed himself behind the front door when Tim had picked up his leather jacket. He broke into the troubled silence with a series of ecstatic barks, for which Tim was profoundly thankful, since the barks brought Kerry in from the kitchen to ask if they were all going for a walk. Tim was very glad of that interruption.

'It's too late for you to go walks, darling. It's nearly your bedtime, and I have to go home and do some marking of books ready for tomorrow,' he told her.

'I could come and mark books with you while Mummy puts Kerry to bed,' Elliot decided. He was already on his way to get his own little outdoor fleece.

'Don't want Mummy to put me to bed. Want you, Daddy!' Kerry, overtired, was getting weepy.

'I'll do that tomorrow night when I don't have so much marking to do. I promise, my precious.' As he spoke, Tim gathered his little daughter into his arms and hugged her. Love for her, and for Elliot and Jane, overwhelmed him so that he was hardly able to hide his emotion from them. A single tear began to escape and trickle slowly down his cheek. Because his arms were full, he was powerless to check it.

Kerry placed a tiny finger on it. 'Why are you crying, Daddy?' she asked.

Tim looked away from her to where Jane waited in the

open door to take the child from him. He was unable to answer her for the lump that seemed to be blocking his throat. All he could do was pass Kerry hurriedly over to Jane – so hurriedly that the child began to protest. Then he walked away from them so fast that he stumbled over the threshold and almost fell. Since the door was still open, Darcy followed him, barking excitedly. Elliot raced after the dog, shouting fiercely, 'Sit down, Darcy! Sit! At once!'

Darcy ignored him and ran ahead, bouncing off the edge of the pavement, still wagging his tail and barking madly. It all happened too quickly then: Elliot's warning cry, the sound of squealing brakes and Darcy's yelp of pain when the collision came. There was a moment of silence as Tim, Elliot and the shocked motorist stared down at Darcy's black body spreadeagled on the road – Darcy's very still black body.

Then Elliot screamed. 'Darcy's dead! He's killed!'

'Be quiet, Elliot,' Tim ordered. 'Go indoors to your mum. At once!' he added when the boy stayed where he was.

Trying hard not to cry, Elliot went back to the gate where Jane waited for him. Jane felt sick with fright. For one awful moment she had thought it was Elliot who had been hit by the vehicle.

'I want to stay with Darcy. I want to look after him,' Elliot protested.

Jane put an arm about him. 'The vet will look after him. Daddy's going to take him there now, so you must be a good boy and go to bed.'

'I want to go to the vet with Darcy as well.' Tears were pouring down Elliot's face now.

'You can't do that, Elliot, because I'll need to put Darcy into the back seat where you usually sit,' Tim told him gently.

'I could sit in the front beside you—'

'No, I want you to stay here and look after Mummy and Kerry till I get back. Will you do that for me?'

Reluctantly, Elliot agreed, but not until he'd watched Tim and the motorist begin to lift his dog from the ground.

'I'm going to take Kerry up to bed right now, and you as well,' Jane said.

'I want to see Darcy again too,' Kerry wailed.

31

Jane felt like crying too, because she had become very fond of the lanky black retriever since Tim had brought him for the children. Yet when she had first learned that the dog had belonged to the woman Tim had gone to live with, she had been determined not to keep him. She had tried so hard not to like Darcy. She had even tried to hate him, because he had been part of that affair which had devastated her life and that of her children. It hadn't worked, because she had found herself thinking of how much Darcy must be missing the young woman teacher who had died. Darcy had looked so forlorn sometimes when the children were out at nursery school. Then, one day when she was indulging in one of the weeping sessions that came over her at times when she was alone in the house, Darcy had come to lean against her and put his sad face on her knee. She had found herself putting a hand on his silky head and finding comfort in stroking it. Now there was an ache in her heart for the poor creature whose short life might already have ended, but she must put a brave face on before the children or they would never be able to sleep.

'You must both go to bed while Daddy takes Darcy to the vet to find out how much he's been hurt,' she told them.

'I wanted to go with him,' Elliot said dolefully.

'Me as well,' Kerry added in between sobs.

'Daddy says there won't be room in the car for you as well as Darcy,' Jane reminded them. 'If the vet can make Darcy better, he'll bring him back to you.'

'What if he can't? Darcy might be—' Elliot broke off as he heard something. It was more of a whimper than a bark, but it was enough. 'It was him! He's not dead! He's just hurt, Mummy!'

Then there was the sound of Tim's car engine springing to life. A huge surge of relief hit Jane. 'That sounds like Daddy taking Darcy to the vet now. So I want you both to go to sleep.'

'Will Daddy bring him back tonight?' Elliot wanted to know.

Jane hesitated. She didn't want to lie to the children. 'If he's well enough to come home; but he might have to stay in the doggy hospital for a while.'

'Will we be able to go and see him and take him some-thing nice to eat like Grandad did to me when I was in hospital?' That was Elliot again. He never gave up.

Jane sighed. 'I expect so. I hope so. Goodnight, and God bless.' She bent to kiss them both.

'We'll write a message to God on the prayer tree and ask him to make Darcy better,' Elliot said sleepily. Kerry was already asleep.

'Yes, that's a good idea,' Jane whispered as she closed the bedroom door.

For a long moment then she stood on the landing, wondering what she would say to them if Darcy did not recover. How she would help them to come to terms with the loss of their beloved pet. Before she went downstairs to set about clearing the chaos left by them in the living room she found she was asking God to send Darcy safely back to where he now belonged, in her home and in her heart.

Four

Paula found she was unable to control her shivering as the time for the funeral drew closer, even though she had turned the central heating full on. She moved restlessly about the Mill House from the hall to the lounge, from the lounge to the dining room and from the dining room to the kitchen, giving the flower arrangement in the hall yet another twitch, checking that there were clean towels in the cloakroom and plenty of coat hangers in the porch just in case any of her father's long-unheard-of relatives turned up for the service after reading of the event in the *Yorkshire Post*. In the kitchen fresh scones waited to be warmed, along with savoury pastries she had cooked that morning. There was a huge pan of home-made soup waiting there too because a few of her dad's old friends from London were due to arrive, and one or two of her own close friends.

'We'll have the church as warm as we can for you, Paula,' Andrea Wyndham had assured her on her visit yesterday to go through the final details of the service with her. 'Do try and eat something warm first, if you can. I know it's not easy at such a time, but it will help you to cope.'

What would she have done without Andrea's support and help, when all her friends were in London and there was no longer Gareth to lean on when things got tough? There had been no one else she could call on here in this village where she was still a stranger to most people.

Except, perhaps, for the girl called Carla. She had been surprised last night, or rather in the late afternoon, when she had answered the ring on the back-door bell and found Carla there with a small bunch of anemones clutched in her chilly hands.

'They're for you,' the girl had said in a rush as she thrust the flowers at Paula. 'For looking after me that time.' She had stopped, then gone on again hurriedly. 'You know when I mean.'

'Oh Carla, how kind of you!' Paula had been deeply touched. 'Would you like to come in?'

Paula had sensed the hesitation before the girl said, 'Only for a few minutes. I expect you have a lot to do. Ready for tomorrow, I mean.'

'There's not much more I can do now. Everything is done, except for the food that has to be finished off tomorrow morning for the people who come long distances to be at the service.'

'Where will they come from?' Carla had wanted to know.

'Some will come from Surrey: the people who worked with Dad in his garden centre. Until the accident, that is. Some of them became close friends and were planning to visit us here.'

'Don't you have anyone up here who'll help you, like my gran and Julie did when Mum died?'

Paula had wished the girl had not asked that question. 'Not that I know of,' she'd said. 'It's a long time since Dad lived up here.'

'Did he live in the village?'

'No. His father farmed somewhere between here and Nyddford, but he lost touch with the family when he decided he wanted to be a gardener instead of a farmer and went to work at one of the big stately homes.'

Carla had considered this, then given her verdict. 'I expect he was right to do that because my dad says there's no future in farming these days and nothing but problems and setbacks.'

'Oh, he was right to do it, though not for that reason, Carla. You see he did well at the stately home and was sent to college by his employers. Then later he bought a run-down garden centre and built it up into a good business. He opened a little coffee shop that I helped my mum with until I went to catering college.'

Then had come Carla's final question – the one that was hardest to answer: 'Where's your mum now, then?' The

35

girl stopped with a gasp before going on. 'I'm sorry! Is she—'

Into the silence that followed, Paula had said at last, 'I don't know where she is. She left us while I was still at college.'

'You mean – she just disappeared?' Carla had been shocked.

Paula had hesitated. 'She left a note explaining that she had had enough of spending all her life working at the garden centre and was going to do what she really wanted to do.'

'I'm sorry! I shouldn't have asked. It's just that I felt worried about you being here on your own in a strange place . . .'

Her words had brought swift emotion to Paula. 'Oh Carla, that's so kind of you. I'm not used to having someone worry about me now.'

'I could come and help you to clear up tomorrow after all your visitors have gone. I mean on my way home from school,' Carla had offered then.

'I don't know for certain whether anyone *will* come back here for refreshments . . .'

'I'll call in case you need me.' With that Carla had departed as suddenly as she had appeared.

What was appearing now, Paula was able to see through the huge window that looked out on to the drive, was a gleaming black hearse followed by a single black limousine. It was time for her to say her final goodbye to the father she had loved so dearly.

It was late when Tim came back from his visit to the vet. So late that Jane was getting really worried about both him and Darcy. He came back alone, not letting himself in with his own key but ringing the front-door bell and waiting for Jane to invite him in. Dismay engulfed her then.

'Is he –?' she began, but could not go on.

Tim shook his head. 'He's not too badly damaged, but he did need some surgery, so they felt he'd be better to stay with them for a few days.'

'Poor Darcy,' she whispered. 'What a thing to happen just

when he was beginning to settle down with us. The children were so upset, but they're both asleep now, thank goodness.'

'I suppose I ought not to have asked you to have him here,' Tim began hesitantly. 'But I couldn't keep him in the flat I've got now, and I knew Donna would have been very upset at the thought of him going into a dogs' home. I wasn't thinking straight at the time or I'd have realized that it was unfair of me to ask you to take him. I'm sorry about that. If you don't feel you can take him back, I'll try and find him another home as soon as he's fit.'

'Oh no! You mustn't do that,' Jane broke in. 'The children would be heartbroken. They love him so much, and he's so good with them.'

'Yes, I know,' Tim said slowly. 'But you're the one who'll have to cope with him until he gets better and you might not be prepared to do that.'

'I am,' Jane broke in again. 'I've become very fond of Darcy and he seems to like me.'

'In spite of . . .'

'What happened wasn't Darcy's fault, was it?' she challenged.

Tim could not meet her eyes. He stared instead at the photograph on the bookcase that showed Elliot and Kerry on either side of Darcy out in the back garden. 'No,' he muttered. 'It was my fault. I'd give anything to put the clock back.'

Before Jane had time to reply to this the door from the hall burst open and there was Elliot, his hair sticking up in spikes about his rosy face, his pyjama jacket undone and his feet bare as he stared about him in search of his dog.

'Where is he, Daddy?' he wanted to know. 'Why didn't you bring him home? Couldn't the vet make him better?' His distress was plain to see. Jane felt her heart sink as she looked ahead to the scene that was about to erupt and the sleepless night that could follow.

'Calm down, Elliot,' his father said gently. 'Come here and sit with me, then I'll tell you what's been going on.'

Fighting back his tears, Elliot did as he was told.

'Mummy's going to make you some hot chocolate while

I tell you what the vet said. Then you must go back to bed before you wake Kerry.'

'Yes, it's very late and you're both at nursery school tomorrow morning,' Jane reminded him; but he was too busy cuddling up to Tim by then to take notice, so she left them and went to the kitchen to put milk in the microwave to heat. She was battling against tiredness by then and longing to be in her own bed, so she hoped Tim would soon settle Elliot down and go back to his own flat. There was a fear inside her that if he did not go soon, she might find herself saying he could stay the night. She was not ready for that, yet.

When she came back into the room a few minutes later with Elliot's chocolate and a large mug of coffee for Tim, it was to find the pair of them sound asleep on the sofa. Lines of weariness marked Tim's face so that he looked older than his years while Elliot looked younger than his. Her heart ached with love for them both as she put out the light and made her way up the stairs to her lonely bed. In spite of her exhaustion she could not get to sleep but spent restless hours wondering why, since she loved him so much, she was not yet able to trust Tim again.

As Bill looked down into Andrea's sleeping face in the harsh light of the early March morning, he felt his adoration of her envelop him afresh. On the heels of that came the concern about her that kept creeping back into his mind more and more often. Even in slumber the lines of strain around her forehead and beneath her eyes were there to see. He must insist that Andrea saw a doctor as soon as possible. Because he could not even consider doing what Miriam, his agent, wanted him to do until Andrea was looking much better. It might be the fact that she was simply working too hard in an effort to cope with the burden of constant sick-visiting, which was worst at this time of the year, while she was also getting deeply involved with plans for the Nyddford Church Festival of Talents. Andrea was enthusiastic about this in the hope that it would swell the funds needed to top up the hefty repair bill that would follow when the work on the roof was completed, and also perhaps bring more local people into the church.

Bill was sure she would not ease off without a warning from her doctor, because she certainly had not taken seriously his idea that she should take a break from her work at the cottage in Scotland that he had bought her for a wedding present. Hadn't she put him off this by promising to do that as soon as all the arrangements for the festival were finished? Was it just tiredness that was making Andrea look so ill? Or was it some terrible disease waiting to take her away from him just as their life together was beginning? This last thought was so terrifying that Bill was only able to push it away from him with difficulty before Lucky, who seemed to have a built-in timer where his daily walks were concerned, reminded him that it was time they were out of the house. Bill managed to quieten him before he could rouse Andrea from her promised extra hour of sleep, because today there were no school assemblies for her to start her day's work with. Soon he and his dog were on their way through the village.

Bill's concern about Andrea's heavy workload resurfaced when he reached the lychgate of Nyddbeck Church and remembered that, as well as all the more mundane things such as meetings and paperwork that had to be fitted in today, there was also a funeral service in this church for a man who had only recently come to live in the village. Bill had only spoken to this man once since he had come to live in the Mill House with his daughter. That had been when he had set up his easel close to the beck so that he could paint the old bridge and the village green with the beautiful little church in the background. He had noticed, when the man stopped his slow, hesitant stroll to watch him painting, that he appeared to have problems with his sight. So Bill had stopped work and asked if he could help him. That was when he had learned that the man from the Mill House had loved drawing and painting the flowers from his own garden centre until an accident there had cost him most of his sight.

Walking on, enjoying the crispness of the frosty air, into Church Lane and passing his own studio at Beckside before going from there up the Monks' Steps to the start of Nyddmoor, Bill found that, as usual, Lucky was pulling ahead, eager to be free of his lead for a short time. There was a brilliance about the sky this morning, a kind of stark beauty in the scenery that pushed all else out of his mind except the wish to sit down right now and capture it on canvas before the light changed. It was all to do with the sight of the shining slate rooftops of Abbot's Fold Farm just visible from the hollow where they nestled, protected from the worst of the winds that scoured this region in the winter months. Beyond them in the distance the towering ruined arches of Nyddmoor Abbey could also be seen. It was breathtaking, standing there on this great roof of Yorkshire, taking in the full glory of what God had provided, and what those monks of centuries ago had added to the landscape.

Lucky was oblivious to such delights. Once set free he gave fruitless chase to a rabbit; then, when he spotted a pheasant pecking about in the heather, he soon sent it into startled flight. There were no sheep about up here; they were all in the pastures close to the farmhouse, ready for the lambing which was imminent, so he was able to allow the dog the freedom he loved while he strode swiftly along the well-worn sheep tracks, relishing his own brief spell of freedom from his worry about Andrea.

It was as the sheep track he was traversing took him nearer to the farmhouse that his fear about Andrea returned. From where his feet came to a stop while he called the dog to him he was able to see down into the yard of Abbot's Fold Farm, and watch Dave's wife crossing the yard to where her car was parked. The thought came to him then that Julie might be the right person for him to share his concern about Andrea with, since the two women were such close friends. So, having clipped the lead on to Lucky, he broke into a run, at the same time calling Julie's name. Julie looked upwards then and answered his wave with one of her own.

'Have you time for a quick word?' He watched his breath, fast after the moorland run, drift away on the frosty air as he went over the stile that crossed the drystone wall and dropped into the farm lane.

'Yes, if you really do make it brief, Bill. I'm on duty at the health centre in half an hour.'

Julie looked her best in her nursing uniform, Bill thought as he came face to face with her over the farm gate. The artist in him admired the look of shining cleanliness, coupled with the vitality in the glowing brown eyes and the rosy cheeks beneath her neat brown hair.

'It's about Andrea,' he began without preamble. 'I'm terribly worried about her.'

Instantly the smile faded from her face. 'Why? What's wrong, Bill?'

He hesitated. 'I'm not quite sure. It's just that she seems so exhausted; yet she won't ease up and take a break from work as I've asked her to.'

Julie sighed softly. 'I know what you mean. I've noticed myself that she's rather on edge. I suppose it's the worst time of the year for her, as it is for me, with so many older people being ill and needing visits. To say nothing of all the extra funeral services in her case.'

'So what can I do about it, Julie? Without being told I'm talking rubbish, I mean.'

'That's not so easy to answer, Bill,' she said ruefully.

'I have to do *something*,' Bill went on. 'I can't just stand by and watch her getting thinner and thinner and more and more exhausted because she often doesn't even get a proper day off.'

Julie took a long moment to consider this before answering. 'I suppose you could try pointing out to Andrea that if *she* doesn't take a proper day off, you don't get one either.'

Bill shrugged. 'I did go down that road a few days ago, but we ended up very much at odds with one another. So I decided I'd chosen the wrong tactics.'

Julie sighed again. 'It's always going to be difficult, almost impossible perhaps, for you to make Andrea realize that if she doesn't look after her own health, she won't be able to do her job properly.'

Bill agreed. 'Yes, Andrea doesn't see it that way at all. She has a closed mind on that subject. Hasn't she?'

'I suppose if she were not like that, she wouldn't be in

41

the right sort of job, would she? I mean, being a church minister isn't like any other profession, is it, Bill?' Julie answered thoughtfully.

He nodded. 'That's the sort of answer she gives me when I try to reason with her. I thought you might be in a better position to talk sense into her – being a nurse as well as her closest friend.'

'I wish I could—' Julie broke off then as Dave's dog came towards them, followed by Dave himself. Instantly there was an outbreak of barking from the two animals that made further talk almost impossible. 'I'll have to go, Bill, or I'll be late. I'll try and talk to Andrea as soon as I can. I'll try to drop in and help her with the drama club tonight so I can bring up the subject then.' It wouldn't be easy, but it was all she could think of to try and set Bill's mind at rest.

'Thanks! Thanks a lot. I won't delay you any longer.' Stopping only for long enough to give her husband a hasty greeting, Bill dragged his dog out of range of Dave's Tyke, who did not tolerate other dogs, and went back over the stile on to the moor, where he was soon out of hearing as Dave spoke to Julie.

'What was that all about?' Dave wanted to know, having ordered Tyke to 'lie down and be quiet', which the dog instantly obeyed.

'Bill's worried about Andrea because she's working far too hard. He asked me if I'd try and talk to her about it, and I said I would.' Julie didn't miss the frown that deepened on Dave's thin, high-cheekboned face. Was another black mood descending on him?

'Why can't he talk to her about it himself? He'll have more time to spare than you will,' he said morosely, confirming her fears.

'He has done, but she won't take it on board. That's why he asked me to help.'

'So you'll be going back to Nyddford again tonight after you finish your work there to help at the church drama group?'

'Yes.' Julie was unlocking her car now and throwing her bag into the back of it. A new thought came to her then. 'I might be better to stay down there instead of coming home.'

42

'What about the meal?'

'It's shepherd's pie, already in the freezer. I'm sure Carla can manage to cook the vegetables to go with it, and there's an apple crumble to follow. I'll leave her a note.' Julie spoke quickly, eager to be on her way.

'Where will you eat?' The frown grew worse as that question came.

'I might get fish and chips and eat them at my cottage, as it's empty this week.' The cottage Julie had bought, with the help of a mortgage, near the health centre in Nyddford was being let as a holiday property for part of the year. Dave had wanted her to sell it, but she had said she was not ready to do that yet. Though she could not have explained why.

'Or is it an excuse to go and spend some time with Matt Harper? If so—'

'Don't be ridiculous, Dave! How many times do I have to tell you that I'm not interested in Matt, other than as a member of your mother's family? You have to trust me, otherwise we—'

'It's him I don't trust!' Dave broke in 'Ever since I caught him here last week when I was away at Nyddford..'

Julie was losing patience with him now. 'It wasn't my fault that Matt called that day. I didn't ask him to come. You need to put that visit out of your mind, as I have, and let me get on with my work while you get on with yours. I'm going to be late as it is, without having to stand here and tell you yet again that you really can trust me when I'm out of your sight.'

On that last word she dropped into the driving seat, slammed the door with unnecessary force and without a backward glance or a wave to him roared away along the farm lane at the sort of speed she did not normally employ on such narrow roads.

Dave remained where he was for some time, listening to the sound of the racing engine with his heart thumping while he awaited the noise of metal making contact with drystone wall; but the feared sound did not come. He shook his head then and rubbed a hand over one thick, dark eyebrow as the thought came to him that if Julie had come to grief, it would have been his fault. His wife had a calm disposition; it was only when provoked by his own unreasoning jealousy that she lost control of herself.

The trouble was that he still could not believe that Julie belonged to him now – that she was in his home as well as in his heart, and that she had chosen him instead of Matt in spite of all the advantages Matt could have given her.

'I've acted like a bloody fool, again, Tyke,' he said as he clicked his fingers to call the dog to him so they could take another look at the ewes that were due to drop their lambs at any time now. 'I'll drive her away if I'm not careful, and it'll be my own damned fault.'

Tyke nudged his master's knee with a strong black muzzle and murmured his sympathy deep in his white-ruffed throat. His master was always right, to him. He followed, wagging his plumed tail, as Dave went to deal with the tasks that belonged to this day and this place.

Five

Paula shivered in spite of the long, thick, midnight-blue coat which she had decided to wear for the service in the little village church. Ahead of her was the coffin bearing her father on his last journey. It was covered with the spring flowers that he had loved best and grown so successfully. She was surprised by the quantity of floral tributes to be seen – so many that they would not all go on the oak casket but were carried into the church to be placed around it. She was amazed by the number of people gathered there in this unfamiliar building, but also touched and proud of this evidence that her father had been so highly regarded that those present had travelled such long distances for the service.

Her fingers shook as she picked up the prayer book and bent her head. She had thought there would be no tears left now, but they were there forcing their way out of her eyes as prayers were said and her father's favourite hymns were quietly sung. Loneliness threatened to overwhelm her as she listened, because they had been so close in recent years, she and this father who had survived a serious accident only to lose his life to an illness which many much older people would have recovered from. The injustice of it had troubled Paula so often in recent days. Now it came over her again as the service proceeded. Suddenly she longed to be out of this building, away from this village where she and her dad had come with such high hopes of making a new life together. Her shoulders began to shake with the effort she was forced to make just to stand still and not lose control in front of all these people.

Andrea, standing only a few feet away from her, was acutely aware of Paula's distress – so much so that she cut short her oration and signalled to Bill that they would move on to the final hymn. Paula, hearing it with overwhelming relief, was able to regain control of her emotions then and take her place to receive her father's friends in the porch. It was bitterly cold there too, but there was warmth of spirit to be gained from the handclasps, the hugs and the voiced tributes of both people she knew and people who were strangers to her.

'Please come back to the Mill House for some hot food,' she said, time and time again, to the people she knew had travelled from the south that morning. Then she was meeting the people who had hung back inside the church until last. There were not many of them, but some bore a striking resemblance to her father. It would be hardest of all for her to face them, but it was something she had to do.

'I'm your uncle – Tom, your father's elder brother,' the first one told her as he held out a large, work-worn hand to grip her own slim fingers firmly. He was a stern-looking man, she thought.

'I'm Paula,' was all she could think of to say in reply.

'Your mother's not here then? Or is she . . .?'

'She's not here. I don't think she knows about – about Dad.' Oh, it hurt so much to have to say that. She waited with dread for the next question to come, but before it could do so another burly man was shouldering his way to greet her.

'Out of the way, our Tom; don't keep the poor lass hanging about in the cold any longer. I'm sure she'll be glad to get back into the warm, won't you, love?' he said. 'I'm your dad's brother Ted. I'm glad to meet you at last, though I wish it could have been at a better time than this.'

There was kindness rather than curiosity in the man's steady gaze that Paula found herself responding to by allowing her hand to remain in his until the next man took his place. This was a younger man but with the same square face and the same thickly marked black eyebrows as the two older men possessed, and as her father had also worn. Tears pricked her eyes again as she remembered, and she became lost for words.

46

'I'm Daniel. This is my aunt Jean, and my cousin Alison.'

This time there were kisses from the two women, and more concern for her voiced. 'You look cold, love. Don't hang about here any longer than you have to. Andrea gave your dad a very nice service, didn't she?' That was the woman called Jean speaking.

Paula nodded, struggling once more with the lump in her throat, before she managed to say, 'You will come to the Mill House for refreshments, won't you?'

'Yes, of course we will, as long as we're back in time for milking,' came the response.

So this part of her father's family were still carrying on with traditional farming. Why hadn't her dad kept in touch with them? Why had he hardly ever spoken of them to her? Why had he not contacted them when he had come back to live in the district? The questions only teased her mind for a moment before Andrea was there, leading them all to the place where there was a newly dug grave waiting in the little church-yard. Then at last it was over and people were drifting away.

'Thanks for everything, Andrea,' Paula said then. 'Will you come back with us for some refreshments?'

Andrea hesitated. 'I don't think I'll have time today, Paula,' she decided. 'But I'd like to come and see you another day, if I may.'

'Yes, I'd like that.'

'I think your aunt and uncle are waiting to give you a lift,' Andrea told her then.

Paula turned her head towards the lychgate where vehicles were parked and saw that the younger of her father's brothers was holding open the passenger door of his estate car.

'I don't know any of them,' she said hesitantly. 'They're strangers to me. I suppose they saw the announcement in the *Yorkshire Post* . . .'

'Perhaps it's time for you to get to know them, now that you'll be living so close to them?' With that, Andrea moved away and went back into the church to join Bill, who had been playing the organ today because Brendon May was teaching at Nyddford High School.

Apprehension slowed Paula's footsteps as she began to walk towards these unknown relatives. She was not normally shy with strangers, having worked in her father's garden centre and in a couple of large hotels, but there were so many strangers here that she was not sure whether she could cope with them all at once. Yet it was something she would have to do now that she had invited them. At least, by the look of the number of waiting vehicles, some of her dad's friends intended to come back with them, so maybe they would help her over the awkward bits. Like having to try and explain her mother's absence . . .

Julie was aware of hunger stirring inside her as she waited to be served in the small shop that had tempted generations of tourists, as well as the locals, with that tiny window display of enticing golden-glazed pork pies and other savoury pastries. Those delicious eatables sent out a rich aroma that made her long to sink her teeth into one of them, but she would have to wait her turn in the queue and then wait until she got back to her cottage to do that.

She had almost changed her mind about staying on in Nyddford to eat when she had finished duty and gone back to Abbot's Fold for her high tea, until there had been a call on her mobile as she was about to leave Nyddford Health Centre. The call had been from Andrea. It had left her even more worried about her friend than she had been after her brief chat with Bill earlier in the day. Before that call came she had almost decided to postpone doing as Bill had asked and turning up at the church drama-group meeting to try to talk to Andrea about Bill's concern for her health, because she hated being at odds with Dave. She knew he would be displeased with her if she didn't get back to Abbot's Fold until late in the evening when he had told her he wanted to get in some early nights before lambing kept him out of bed more than in it for a few weeks. Since listening to what Andrea had said during that call she knew she simply *must* take the chance of having a few words with her as soon as possible. Andrea had sounded so unlike herself – so at the end of her tether that Julie had been alarmed. The few words she had said kept repeating themselves in Julie's mind, making her more and more uneasy: 'Could you possibly help me tonight with the drama club, Julie? Please! I know it's short notice for you, but I'm so worried that we don't get the Easter drama right. There's so little time left, and I'm so terribly tired that I don't think I can cope with all the young people if I don't have some help.'

It was the first time Julie had ever heard Andrea express any doubts about her ability to cope with anything in her ministry. Her voice had been so strained. She had sounded so absolutely desperate. That was why Julie was standing here in the queue of customers waiting to be served by the plump, cheerful man in the crisp white coat. As she exchanged greetings with him while he wrapped her pork pie and sausage roll, she could see through the window that Matt Harper was walking across the pavement towards the shop. Had he seen her in there or was he just intending to come and buy his own food? She must get out of the place before he arrived, because after what he had said at their last encounter she had made her mind up to avoid being alone with Matt in future.

'You're going without your change, nurse!' the pork butcher called after her as she made a dash for the open door of his establishment.

She turned back to pick up the coins from the counter, and realized that she was too late to miss meeting Matt. He was there blocking her escape, his broad shoulders filling the narrow doorway, the spicy aroma of his expensive after-shave mingling with the scent of warm meat pies, his eyes sparkling with gladness at the sight of her.

'Julie! I didn't expect to find you waiting for me among Yorkshire's finest pork pies!' he teased. 'Do you come here often?'

'Only when I don't have enough time to go home to eat,' she replied, hoping this would indicate that she was in too much of a hurry to stay and talk to him.

His face brightened even more when he heard that. 'If you're pushed for time, you'll do better to come and eat with me rather than go back to your own house. Unless you've managed to find a parking place anywhere round the square even though it's market day?'

'I haven't,' she said without thinking, and immediately regretted it.

Matt laughed. 'That makes this my lucky day. Wait a moment till I get my pies, then we'll go to my place together.'

'But—' Julie intended to protest that she wanted do her paperwork while she was eating, but Matt was already placing his order and at the same time sharing a joke which brought a hearty laugh from the butcher, who had known him since his boyhood. So she could do nothing but wait for Matt, and hope that no one who knew them both would see them together and relay the information, even in the most innocent way, to someone else who would send it on via the rural Chinese whispers system in the direction of Dave. Maybe she was worrying about nothing and her brief engagement to Matt had now been forgotten. Though she wouldn't dare bank on that. The sooner she and Matt were away from the crowded market square the better, she decided, as she began to move swiftly in the direction of Matt's home.

'I thought you might be trying to run away from me,' Matt told her breathlessly as he caught up with her. 'I couldn't let you get away with that.'

'This is not a good idea, Matt,' she began.

'What on earth do you mean, Julie darling?' His shoulder was touching her own now as they walked side by side along the narrow footpath.

'You know very well what I mean! Us being seen together.' She did not look at him as she said that.

That made him chuckle. 'Why shouldn't we be seen together?' he challenged. 'Now that our families are united in marriage. My father being married to your husband's mother makes it all quite above reproach, doesn't it?'

'Not to Dave! No it certainly doesn't.' Immediately she had admitted it she wished the words unsaid.

'So Dave's still not sure of you!' There was elation in his voice.

'I don't know what you mean!'

'I'm quite sure you do, Julie.' He laughed again, then added, 'Anyway, as it happened, we didn't run into anyone we know, and we're almost there now.'

Yes, they were within sight of Matt's elegant modern house set on the outskirts of the market town. The house he had bought very quickly in the hope that she would share it with him. When they reached the gate, Julie hesitated, glancing at her watch.

'I don't really think I've got time to come in, Matt,' she began.

'Where do you intend to eat your pork pie then?' he demanded. 'It's hardly the day to have a picnic on the river bank, is it?'

As he spoke, the brisk, chilly wind whipped Julie's brown hair across her eyes while she sought desperately for an excuse to get away from him without hurting or offending him. 'It's just that I was going to catch up on a bit of paperwork while I ate at my cottage,' was all she could come up with.

Matt was ready with his answer. 'When we've eaten, I'll drive you down there so you can do your paperwork before you have to go on duty again.'

'Oh, I'm not—' Too late she realized she had told him too much.

He was urging her along the drive to his home by now. 'So where are you going, still wearing that very fetching uniform? I was always turned on by women in uniform – though not by traffic wardens,' he added with a grin. 'So where are you going, lovely Julie? After you've shared your lunch with me, that is?'

'To help Andrea with her youth drama group.' He was opening his front door as he spoke.

'I didn't know you were involved with that sort of thing.' He held the door for her to precede him into the house.

'I used to help with it sometimes before I married Dave. I don't have as much time now, but I'm going to help tonight because Andrea is a bit stressed out.' She was following Matt into his spacious kitchen, which gleamed with newly installed stainless-steel appliances.

51

'Don't *you* ever get stressed out with all you have to do? I'm sure you must.'

He was facing her again and subjecting her to such an intense stare that she was feeling uneasy about being here alone with him when she knew how strongly he felt about her. She ought not to have allowed herself to be talked into coming here. This thought made her step back from him and lean against one of the cabinets, still clutching the paper bag containing her food.

'I'm no more stressed out than any other woman who has a full-time job as well as a home and a husband to look after,' she argued.

'Plus someone else's teenage children,' he reminded her.

'My *friend*'s teenage children,' she hit back.

'And your friend's husband! How convenient for Dave to have you there when his mother married my dad and he found he couldn't cope with Carla and Jack. Especially Carla.'

It was quietly said, but there was no mistaking his meaning. Hot colour flooded Julie's face as she heard it. 'It wasn't like that!' she protested. 'I told you once before, I knew Dave long before he married Jill; in fact I introduced them because I was going out with him then.'

'Why didn't he marry *you* then instead of her?'

Julie would not answer that one. The question had brought old hurts to the surface. If she replied honestly to it, she might give Matt even more cause to think she had made a mistake in marrying Dave. So she would change the subject right now.

'If we're going to eat together, do you mind if we get on with it, Matt? Otherwise I won't have time to stay.'

'OK, if you insist, but I haven't given up on you yet, Julie, and I'm not going to.' As he spoke he was plugging in the coffee-maker and reaching into the fridge to bring out a bottle of wine and some cheese.

'You'll be wasting your time. I'm married to Dave, and I'm going to stay married to him,' she insisted.

'I never waste my time, Julie. Not wasting my time was an American habit I brought back here with me,' he said crisply as he opened the wine.

52

Julie ignored that remark and set about finding plates and cutlery for them both. Half an hour later, after they had eaten at the kitchen table while discussing less emotive local affairs, she was ready to make her escape.

'Thanks for sharing this time with me, when I know how busy you are,' Matt said as she rose to her feet. 'There's really no reason why we shouldn't do it again, is there?'

Julie did not reply to that. Instead she thanked him briefly for the wine, refused his offer of a lift to her cottage, and left vowing to herself that she would not come back here unless Dave was with her. That, she knew, was very unlikely to happen.

Back at the Mill House, with the ordeal of the funeral service behind her, Paula began to enjoy meeting again some of her father's old friends as she served them with coffee or whisky and passed round the hot savoury pastries she had made. It was comforting to hear them share with her their memories of her dad from before his accident as well as the concern they had felt for him after it happened. They even managed to smile together at some of his experiences with the customers from his garden centre.

With the other people present, the ones who had not travelled so far to pay their last respects to her dad, it was not so easy to hold conversations because she simply did not know anything about them except that they mostly bore the same surname as her dad and herself. While those who had come from the south were still in the Mill House, these other people seemed to remain in small groups talking quietly among themselves, halting only when Paula approached them to offer more food or drink. Yet some of them had spoken very kindly to her at the end of the service, she recalled. She just wished she could remember who they all were, other than her dad's two brothers. They had said they would need to be back in time for milking, so she must conquer her shyness and make a real effort to spend some time with them before they were forced to leave.

As though sensing this need, some of the people she knew, the husbands and wives who had to make long journeys home that night, were beginning to say their farewells to her with kisses, handclasps and entreaties for her not to lose touch with them now she was living so far away.

'We'll come and spend a holiday up here when you're open for business,' said more than one couple. 'You know where we live, so do send us your brochures.'

'Will you be able to manage this place on your own?' asked one of her honorary uncles. 'It'll take some managing. Especially the garden.'

'Yes, it will,' Paula agreed. 'I'll need to get some help with the garden now that Dad's not going to be here with me.'

'I expect there'll be local people willing to come and do the heavy work for you, in an area like this,' someone else reassured her before leaving.

By early afternoon she was seeing them off, watching five cars heading away from the village before turning back to face the few people she had until today never met.

'Harry must have been very well thought of to bring all these people up from the south today,' the uncle called Ted began.

'Yes, he was. His friends were wonderful when he had the accident,' Paula told them. 'They even came every day to see what they could do to keep his garden centre going for him until he was fit to get back to it.'

'What sort of accident was it?' the woman called Jean wanted to know.

Paula swallowed her distress as she recalled being sent for while she was preparing party food at the restaurant. 'A tree that had become unstable in the autumn gales last year fell and caught him on the head. His sight was badly damaged. That was why he sold the garden centre to his manager and we came here.'

Ted shook his head sadly 'Poor Harry! What else could he do when all his life had been given to horticulture rather than agriculture. That was what took him away from the family farm in the first place.'

'We were hoping he'd be able to see well enough after more treatment to restore the garden here. It was why we decided to buy the Mill House when we came to look at properties in the area,' Paula told them.

'Why didn't you get in touch with us then, love? We'd have been pleased to put you up while you looked round.'

That was warm-hearted Jean speaking. Ought she to call her Aunt Jean, Paula wondered. 'I think Dad was afraid he might be a nuisance with not being able to see properly. He was very sensitive about that.'

'But we're family!' came the reply.

'So ought I to be calling you Aunt Jean?' Paula wanted that cleared up quickly.

The older woman laughed. 'Not now, love. If you'd been a little girl, it would have been different, but you're – how old?'

'Twenty-six, Jean, and I'm a fully qualified chef. That's why we came here: so I could open this place as a guest house and small restaurant with Dad helping as much as he could.'

That brought another laugh from Jean. 'I'll need to watch I don't burn the dinner when you come to see us then. Which I hope you'll be doing soon,' she added more seriously.

Paula became aware then that others in the small group had stopped speaking to one another and were listening intently as she replied. 'Yes, I'd like to do that.'

Then someone else was asking a question – one that was not so easy to answer. 'What happened to your mother, Paula? We never got to know when she died.'

Paula took a long time to answer. 'She isn't dead. Not as far as I know. She decided to leave Dad a few years ago. We lost touch with her after that.'

'Didn't she even want to keep in touch with *you*, Paula? Her only daughter. Or have you got brothers and sisters who couldn't be here today?'

'No, I was the only one. It was just Dad and me after she left. Now it's just me.' Paula held her head high as she told them that, but inside she was hit by a desperate loneliness that she had never before experienced. Always before there had been Dad, and then for a few years Gareth. Now there was no one of her own any more.

'You're not married then? Or anything?'

Paula turned to answer the speaker: the man who had introduced his aunt and cousin.

'No. Not now. I was engaged, but it didn't work out. So I'm on my own.'

There was a long moment of silence while glances were exchanged between the older men and women until someone broke into the silence with a couple of words. They were words that Paula did not quite catch. The man called Ted – her father's younger brother, Paula thought – interrupted them to speak sharply as his glance swept round them all.

'Not now! It's time we were on our way or we'll be late with milking.' He moved forward to take her hand after ushering them all firmly out of the room ahead of him, before saying to her, 'We'll be there for you if you need us, Paula, just as Harry would have wanted. Now go and put your feet up and get some rest. You've had a bad time lately. I wish we'd known what was happening so we could have helped you. Take care now!'

She went with them to their estate cars and Land Rovers, and endured another round of kisses from the women and handshakes from the men before they drove away to the farms she had never visited or even heard of. As the sounds of their departure grew fainter and left only the silence of the garden about her, she found herself wondering what it was that Ted Price had stopped some member of his family from telling her. It was probably nothing important, so why should it, and those glances the family members had exchanged at the time, refuse to be banished from her mind as she went to gather up used glasses and empty plates?

Six

'When will Darcy come home?' Elliot asked again.
'When he's better,' Jane said wearily.

'When will he be better?' Elliot never gave up.

'I don't know. Soon, I hope.' The vet's bills were draining their already strained budget. Jane could see that the chances of them being able to afford the singing lessons that Brendon May felt she ought to have were getting slimmer. Yet she was as anxious as the children were to see their pet back home with them.

'Can I go with Daddy to see Darcy today?'

'Me too! I want to see him with Daddy,' Kerry chipped in.

'We'll have to see what Daddy says when he gets here,' she told them. 'Why don't you both go and play in the garden until then?'

'It's not the same without Darcy,' Elliot complained. 'I like to throw the playbone for him to fetch back.'

'So do I,' Kerry added.

Jane sighed as she heard that. All she could hope was that today would be the day when Darcy was fit enough to come home. He had been at the vet's for three days since his collision with the car. It wasn't just that she was worrying about the expense of his treatment: she missed him too. There *was* a way to cut down on their expenses, she knew – a way that would please the children and Tim. That was to say Tim could move out of his flat and come back to live with them. He had wanted to do that a couple of days ago after he had spent the night sleeping on the sofa with Elliot in his arms when the accident to Darcy had just happened

She had been so tempted to agree, until over breakfast

Elliot had asked where Darcy had lived before he came to live with them. In that moment, as Tim struggled to find words that would answer the boy's question without revealing that the dog had lived with the woman who had taken Jane's place in his life until her death had ended their affair, Jane had known that it was too soon, that there was too much bitterness left inside her still for her to take Tim back yet, even though she loved him. It would not be fair to the children to take him back until she could trust him, because they had been forced to live through one separation from him and they would have to endure another if Tim let her down again. She could not risk that. So all she could do as Tim's car stopped outside the house was hope that this was the day when Darcy came home.

'Thanks a lot for coming tonight, Julie,' Andrea said as the teenage boys and girls began to jostle one another on a burst of noisy teasing as they made their way out of the church hall. 'You've been such a help. I don't know what I'd have done without you to keep them in order.'

'You'd have managed, as you always do,' Julie responded cheerfully. 'Anyway, I really enjoyed helping. It was fun!'

Andrea sighed. 'It's usually fun for me, but at present I'm finding it hard going because I'm so tired all the time.'

'That's because you're packing too much into every day; working too hard.' Julie paused, then went on, 'I'm not surprised Bill's so worried about you.'

Andrea attempted a laugh, which didn't quite come off. 'Oh, you know what Bill's like! He worries far too much about me. It's not as if I'm feeling ill.'

'If you *don't* ease off, you might start to feel ill,' Julie warned.

Andrea was tempted then to tell her that if what she hoped was happening proved to be true, she would ease off; but since she hadn't told Bill yet, she must not do that. Instead she changed the subject by saying, 'I keep wondering if Bill is considering going on another American lecture tour and is worrying about how I'll cope here without all the help he gives me.'

'What makes you think that? Surely he would tell you if it *was* on the cards?'

Andrea frowned as she replied, 'I keep expecting him to bring the subject up, but he doesn't.'

'Well then, maybe you're wrong.' Julie knew Bill would not want to leave Andrea if she was not well. Yet it might be important that he should take on another American tour, for financial reasons. She knew he must have dipped deeply into his finances to buy the cottage in Scotland that had been his wedding present to Andrea.

'There have been quite a few calls from Bill's agent lately – more than usual; and he's brought the more recent ones to an end quickly if I've been there.'

'I don't suppose he would even consider going over there if he thought you were not well.'

'No, but he might want me to go with him, as he did last time.'

'Well, why not go if he suggests it? At least for part of the time. It would probably do you good to get away for a while,' Julie reasoned.

Andrea sighed again as she began to stack the drama scripts back into her bag. 'I don't think I could do that. There'd be too much travelling and I – I just feel I couldn't face it.'

This was so unlike Andrea that Julie felt alarm stir inside her. Maybe there was something seriously wrong with her friend. Was that what Bill was afraid of? Julie made her mind up to risk speaking out.

'Why don't you make an appointment with Dr Grantley and let her check you out? Then at least you'll be able to set Bill's mind at rest, and mine!' Julie added.

Andrea shrugged off her suggestion. 'Oh, I'm not in pain or anything. I'm only feeling a bit more tired than usual. So stop lecturing me, please, Julie. Even though I do appreciate your concern,' she said as they made their way out of the hall to where their cars were parked.

Carla saw the estate cars and Land Rovers nosing their cautious way out of the Mill House drive as she got off the school bus at the end of Beck Lane instead of staying on until it reached the stop closer to her home at the summit of Abbot's Hill. Were they the last people to leave after Paula had served the refreshments that followed the funeral? She hoped so, because she didn't want to arrive while there were still any relatives and friends hanging about. So it might be a good idea for her to go into the wooded garden by the little gate that she and Josh had used so often to escape on their own from family barbecues when the Boltons had been living in the Mill House. As she pushed aside the trails of ivy and blackberry fronds that needed cutting back, she kept thinking about Josh Bolton and how much they loved one another.

During his long phone call from America on Sunday Josh had told her how much he was missing her and how much he wanted her to go and spend time with him during August. Of course her dad wouldn't let her go this year, but as soon as she'd saved enough money she would go even if he didn't like it. Maybe she would be able to earn some of that money by helping Paula Price when her guest house and restaurant were ready for opening. That was what her visit here today was all about, though of course she did want to make sure that Paula was all right after having to go through the trauma of her dad's funeral service. Carla had a clear view now, as she made her way through a vegetable garden that had not been there when the Boltons were tenants, of the curving drive and the front of the house. It was empty of cars, she saw with satisfaction, so she need waste no more time. Running to the heavy oak door, she took up the polished brass knocker and let it fall sharply three times.

'Oh, it's you, Carla!' Paula exclaimed as she hurried to open the door with a tray in her hand.

'I said I'd come,' Carla reminded her. 'You know – to give you a hand with clearing up after the – the service.' She couldn't bring herself to say the word 'funeral' because she could see that Paula Price had been crying.

'That was very kind of you. Especially when you've been at school all day. You'd better come in. Put your school bag on the hall table, if you can find room there.'

'It'll be fine on the floor,' Carla said when she saw the stack of condolence cards and letters piled up beneath a vase of flowers. She slipped off the dark-coloured fleece jacket that was the furthest she was prepared to go with school uniform now that she was over sixteen, and dropped it on to a chair.

'Do your parents know where you are, Carla?' Paula wanted to know. This didn't please Carla. 'I'm nearly seventeen,' she declared. 'I'm old enough to—'

Old enough to get into situations that were not easy to get out of, Paula guessed as she thought back to their first meeting here last summer when she had found the girl ill and afraid, lying in one of the bedrooms when she and her father had been exploring the upstairs part of the house. Carla had looked so desperately ill; yet she would not allow Paula to take her to her farmhouse home, which was so much closer than the place where she had asked to go in the market town of Nyddford. Paula had been so worried about her, yet had not been able to change her mind about going instead to her own home. She found herself wondering again what had been wrong with Carla that day.

'I just thought, with me being a stranger here and not known to your family . . .' she began.

'What difference does that make?' Carla broke in.

This was a very forthright girl. A girl who knew her own mind, Paula decided. She was also a very beautiful girl with her long blonde hair and huge blue eyes.

'Your parents might like to know who you're spending your time with.'

Carla changed the subject quickly. 'Some of your family must live around here, Paula. I recognized one of them when I saw the cars leaving as I got off the school bus.'

Paula was taken aback. 'Who was that?'

'Simon Price. He's in the sixth at Nyddford High.'

'And he was in one of the cars?'

'The last one. The Discovery.'

'Where does he live?'

'Ings Farm, halfway to Nyddford.'

'I don't remember talking to him,' Paula said with a frown.

'There were several of them, you see – the relations I hadn't met until today.'

'He wouldn't say much anyway. Simon's a real brainbox,' Carla declared.

Obviously Carla didn't think much of 'real brainboxes'! This thought made Paula smile as she asked the girl if she'd like some coffee.

'Yes, please; but I've really come to help you clear up, like I said I would.'

'We'll start to do that while I get the coffee going. I'll put the food away while you stack the dishwasher, Carla.'

Paula smiled again when she noticed how Carla's face had brightened at the mention of using the dishwasher rather than the sink.

'Oh, I wish we had a dishwasher at home. I hate washing up,' the girl told her as she began to gather up the cups and saucers, plates and glasses that were scattered about the big sitting room.

'I expect you'll get one, one day. Though you might not need one as big as this one.'

'I've asked Dad and Julie to get one, but Dad says we can't afford one with the state farming is in these days,' Carla responded morosely.

'I suppose there are things you need more urgently,' Paula reasoned. 'Especially if you have any brothers or sisters. Do you?'

'There's only our Jack,' Carla told her. 'He's nearly thirteen and he doesn't want to stay on at school as I do. He just wants to work on the farm as soon as he's old enough.'

'You're lucky to have a brother,' Paula said. 'I always wished I had one.'

'Jack's all right, I suppose, but he thinks more of his dog than he does of me. Though maybe that's because Brack is such a clever dog. Brack's brilliant. She's even better than Tyke, Dad's sheepdog.'

'I like dogs. I'm wondering if I ought to have one now I'm living here on my own.'

That statement put a new idea into Carla's mind. Impulsive as always, she immediately put it into words. 'If you had someone working for you, you could ask them to live here. They might not want as much pay if they were living here, because they wouldn't have to use buses or a car to get here.'

Paula stopped what she was doing to think about that. Then she said, 'I don't know that people are all that keen to live in where they work. It wasn't something I ever wanted to do.'

'Oh but I wouldn't mind at all. I'd much rather live here than at home,' Carla assured her.

'You're a bit young for that, Carla. I don't think your parents would agree to it,' Paula said with a frown.

'I'll be seventeen soon; then I'll be able to please myself where I live.'

Suddenly Paula saw where this conversation was going. How was she going to discourage the girl without hurting her feelings?

'I expect I'll have to live away from home when I start to train for nursing,' Carla began before Paula could think of anything.

'You'll be a wee bit older then, though,' Paula reminded her. 'That will make a difference to the way your parents feel. If you're thinking of nursing as a career, you'll have a better chance of getting good exam results if you stay at home, and you will need good results, Carla.'

Carla sighed, sensing that her plans for a quick move into the Mill House were not going to succeed. 'I want to earn some money so I can go to America to see Josh,' she admitted. 'I thought you might need someone here now that . . .' She could not go on and remind Paula why she would need help.

Paula smiled. 'I might be able to offer you some work when I get the restaurant going. A few hours at weekends, perhaps, waiting at table, after I've given you some training in the way I like things to be done.'

Carla was quick to answer. 'That would be brilliant! Really brilliant!'

'Let me see how quickly you can stack the dishwasher and get rid of all the rubbish; then we'll discuss it more over coffee.'

It was going to work out right, after all, Carla decided

with satisfaction as she collected crumpled paper napkins and cake cases. Once she was working here, she would make herself so useful that in no time at all Paula would be asking her to do more hours and work so late in the evenings that she would need to stay overnight. She liked Paula Price, and she thought Paula Price liked her. That was all it needed to bring her back to spending lots of time here in the place where Josh used to live instead of at Abbot's Fold with grumpy old Dad and busy Julie.

Julie gave a sigh of thankfulness as she switched off the engine of her car and got out of the driving seat to take in deep breaths of the cool night air. She was feeling the effects now of her long day working away from the farm. All she longed for was to sink into a warm scented bath and go to bed with a hot milky drink that would soothe her into seven hours of the sleep she so desperately needed. It wouldn't happen, though, because she knew Dave would want her to have supper with him and listen to his latest worries about the farm. His dog was already giving warning from his kennel at the side of the house that she had arrived. Julie stopped to give Tyke a quick stroke on his ears before going into the back hall, where Jack's collie rose from his bed to welcome her with a friendly lick of her fingers.

Dave looked up from the old sofa where he was dozing over his *Yorkshire Post* as she went into the kitchen. 'I didn't know you were going to be as late as this or I'd have gone to bed,' was all he said by way of greeting.

So he was wrong-side-out with her, Julie knew then. Of course he liked to get in a few early nights before lambing started. 'I didn't know, either,' she said. 'The drama group was late starting and then I had to hang about so I could speak to Andrea alone about how worried Bill was about her.'

'Surely it was up to Bill to talk to Andrea about that?' Dave said then.

'He already has done, but he said she just told him he was worrying about nothing.' Julie saw that the table had been set for supper, probably by Carla, so she went to switch the kettle on for the hot drinks. With Dave in this mood she would abandon her plan to have a hot bath and take a quick shower instead.

'Your supper's in the oven. I've already had mine. I couldn't wait any longer,' Dave told her.

'I'm sorry. Why don't you go to bed now and I'll come up later?' she suggested.

'I'll wait for you. I've hardly seen you all day,' he argued.

'It could be another hour. I've got a bit of paperwork to finish off before I go up.' She knew he was not going to like that even as she said it.

'I thought you were going to do your paperwork while you were having your lunch at the cottage? That's what you said this morning.' His voice was accusing.

Julie bit her lip. Yes, she had said that. She had meant to do things that way, until she had met Matt and been persuaded to go and have lunch at his house. If she had gone to her cottage instead, the paperwork would have been finished at lunch time instead of being only half done. Now she would have to find an excuse to give Dave, which she didn't like doing.

'I was late getting to the cottage. There was a long queue at the pie shop, and then I just ran out of time.' It sounded a bit weak. She waited for Dave to question it, and felt an enormous sense of relief when he did not. He was on his feet now and moving to the door into the front hall where the staircase led to the bedrooms.

'I won't wait for you then, if your paperwork comes first.' With that he closed the door on her with more force than he usually used.

Julie groaned as she heard him go up the stairs and into their bedroom, again with a noisy closing of the door. He was certainly in one of the black moods that came over him at times. It was probably her own fault for allowing herself to get involved with Matt at lunch time instead of doing as she had planned and going to the cottage with her paperwork, but Matt could be very persuasive. She would take good care not to let such a thing happen again, she vowed, as she went to take from the oven the dried-up meal for which she had no appetite.

It was simply asking for trouble, spending time with Matt when she knew how Dave felt about him.

Seven

'What did you say, my dear?' Ben asked sleepily.

Dorothy hesitated, unsure now of whether or not to repeat what worry had caused her to utter a moment or so ago.

'Well, let's hear it,' Ben prompted. 'Unless you've changed your mind.'

Still she was not certain how he would take what she had to say. Then, 'I suppose you'll think I'm putting two and two together again and making a dozen,' she began. 'But I can't help feeling a bit uneasy about what I saw this afternoon. I've been trying to decide whether or not to tell you ever since.'

Ben sighed as he answered her. 'Dearest Dorothy, you must know by now that I want to share *all* your problems, even if they don't directly affect me. Sit down beside me and let's talk about this together.'

So Dorothy laid aside the cross-stitch picture she had been working on, which was to be auctioned later in the year at the Nyddford Festival lunch, and joined her husband on the big chintz-covered sofa. As soon as she settled there, Ben's arm went round her shoulders so he could give her a hug, which made her feel instantly loved, cosseted, and cared for.

'Come on now, out with it, whatever it is,' he ordered.

'It's just that, as I was driving down the road where Matt lives this afternoon, I saw him and Julie going through the gate together.'

Ben waited a moment before saying, 'Why shouldn't they?'

Dorothy twisted her hands together as she answered. 'Julie was supposed to be on duty. She was wearing her uniform.'

'So?' Even as he asked the question Ben knew what

67

Dorothy would say, because he could not seem to convince her that there was nothing 'going on' between his son and her daughter-in-law.

'You know it's not so long since I saw Matt visiting at Abbot's Fold while David was down at the auction mart. I just don't like what's happening, Ben,' she went on. 'If David finds out, there'll be trouble. I know there will.'

Ben shook his head. 'Dave must know by now, since she married him instead of Matt, that it's him she loves.'

He had been very disappointed when Julie had married Dorothy's son, because he had been hoping, once he discovered that Julie and Matt were going out together, that Julie would marry Matt. When they had announced their engagement, he had been delighted. He had thought Julie would make the perfect wife for his son. She had all the qualities that would help Matt to settle back into the family business. He had been devastated when the engagement had proved so short-lived, even though he had managed to conceal this from Dorothy. Now he found himself wondering whether already Julie was regretting splitting from Matt. If that were so, Dorothy would be very distressed. He must put aside his own feelings and reassure her at once.

'I think you're letting your imagination run riot, my darling,' he told her tenderly.

Dorothy bit her lip. 'I'm just praying that you're right, Ben. I can't believe Julie would deceive David, even though I think she's being very unwise to spend time alone with Matt as she seems to be doing. You know what Nyddford is like for gossip! If David hears that Julie's been seen with Matt, he'll blow his top. There could be a broken marriage then, and more changes for the children to have to get used to. They've been through too many already.'

Ben reached out for her hands and held them tightly. 'I don't suppose anyone *did* see them together, except you, love. So stop worrying, please!'

Dorothy reached across to kiss him. 'I'll try to, but when you see Matt, will you have a word with him about it?'

Ben took a long time to answer. He hated having to deny this beloved woman anything at all, but this was going to be far more difficult to do than she realized. Recently they had been on such good terms, he and Matt, but that could all come to a speedy end if Ben tried to interfere in Matt's private life. It could be a disaster for both of them, and also for the family business if as a result Matt decided on going back to America to work for someone else. Ben was not prepared to run that risk, especially now that his doctor had advised him to ease off from work.

'Matt will almost certainly resent it if I do bring up the subject,' he told her. 'Yet I hate to refuse you anything that will ease your mind. If I do it at all, I'll have to choose my moment carefully, and I dread to think what the outcome will be.'

Instantly Dorothy was aware of alarm invading her. She wished now that she had kept her concern to herself. The last thing she wanted was for father and son to become at odds with one another in the way they had been during the years Matt had lived and worked in America. 'I shouldn't have asked you to do it, Ben. Please forget about it,' she begged.

He frowned as he answered her. 'I don't know that I can, now that you've put the doubts into my mind; but I won't say anything to him yet. Now, how about some tea?'

So the subject was shelved for the time being. Though it was not completely banished from Dorothy's mind.

At Abbot's Fold Farm lambing was now taking place, which meant Dave working the clock round and having little to say to either Julie or Carla at meal times. Julie could not help being on edge as she watched him struggling to keep awake at times and at others being all too ready to snap if meals were not ready when he came in. Only with Jack was he at ease, as the boy took every chance he had to go to the lambing pens with his dad to check over the ewes, to help with the difficult births or sometimes to carry the orphaned lambs into the warmth of the farmhouse kitchen, where they would be placed in a box close to the Aga and bottle-fed until they were strong enough to be fed by a ewe who had lost a lamb.

Jack was in his element as he handled the little creatures

69

gently but firmly, and always where Jack went his dog, Brack, would follow. Julie, who was not from a farming family but a medical one, was amazed at the obedience shown to the boy by the young dog, and remarked on this at breakfast one morning.

'The dog needs to be obedient or we can't keep her. Don't forget she's here to work,' Dave reminded her and Jack morosely.

'She'll do well in the junior trials at Nyddford Show. Wandering Joe says she will,' Jack said proudly. 'He said so yesterday, and he knows what he's talking about.'

Dave's frown deepened. 'Is he hanging about here again with that scruffy animal of his?'

'He's just passing through, Dad. Not staying this time,' Jack said hastily.

'I don't want him sleeping in our buildings.'

'He wouldn't do any harm. He doesn't smoke, so he won't set them on fire,' Jack declared.

'I don't want his dog anywhere near our lambs. You know how dangerous that could be. I'll have a word or two to say to him when I catch up with him.'

'Don't send him away, Dad!' Jack pleaded. 'He's not very well. He's got this awful cough.'

'Shall I have a word with him?' Julie offered. 'I might be able to persuade him to see one of the doctors at the health centre. If he's willing to do that, I'll give him a lift into Nyddford one day when I go on duty.'

'That'd be great! Really great!' Jack beamed at her as he spoke.

Dave was not so pleased with her. 'I would have thought you had more than enough to do, with the work here and your job, without getting involved with every tramp in the area,' he snapped.

He certainly was in a black mood this morning, Julie thought uneasily, and with Carla late down to breakfast it could get worse.

Jack was indignant when he heard what Dave said. 'Wandering Joe's not a tramp! He's an old soldier who fought in the war!'

70

'Why isn't he in a home of some sort then, instead of wandering about sleeping in other people's farm buildings?'

'He has a home of his own. It's near the abbey. He comes over this way sometimes so he can go and see some of his old army mates who live near Nyddford.' Jack was determined to defend the old man.

'Why can't he sleep at their places then?'

Jack was ready with his answer. 'Because they live in a sheltered something-or-other and there isn't room for him. In summer he has an old army tent they sleep in. Just him and his dog, old Archie.'

Why couldn't Dave let the subject drop? Didn't he realize how upset Jack was becoming? Julie knew that Jack and his friend Rob from Far Moor Farm liked to listen to the old soldier talking about his adventures when he was around Abbot's Moor. She could not see any harm in it. Joe was a clean and well-spoken person in spite of his shabby clothes, and she would make sure she persuaded him to take something for his cough whether Dave approved of her doing so or not. Yes, Dave was overtired, she knew, but so was young Jack!

'Don't worry about him any more, Jack. I'll look out for him,' she promised.

'Could you make some of that stuff for him that you gave me when I had a bad cough, please, Julie?' Jack begged now.

Julie smiled at him. Jack was such a good lad, so caring, so much like his mother had been. Dave ought to be proud of him instead of finding fault with him. 'Yes, I'll do that. It was just lemon and honey and glycerine, and I've got all those in stock.'

'I could take it to him after school.'

Julie waited, as she drained her mug of tea, for Dave to object, but he did not. Instead he rose to his feet as Carla came hurtling into the kitchen in a panic because she had overslept, so she got the benefit of her father's ill temper instead.

'What time do you think this is? You're going to miss the school bus,' he began.

'Not if I take my breakfast with me and eat it on the way.'

'That's not the way to start the day.'

'It is if I haven't time to sit down at the table.' Carla gulped down the orange juice Julie had poured for her, grabbed a piece of toast and a banana, and was ready for off. Jack was already on his way to the back door, eager to avoid having to listen to his dad having a row with his sister.

'If you'd been home at a reasonable time last night you wouldn't have slept in,' Dave began again.

'It was only ten o'clock, but I had some homework to finish in my room,' Carla defended herself.

'If you can't get your school work done earlier than that, you're going to have to stop going to this drama group.'

'I can't do that, Dad!' Carla protested. 'Not now, when we're doing this special play for the Nyddford Festival! I promised Andrea I wouldn't miss any rehearsals.'

After a glance at her watch, followed by a swift look into Dave's face, Julie made her mind up. 'Get your fleece on quickly, Carla. I'll take you down to Nyddford.'

'It's not time for you to go yet, Julie,' Dave objected fiercely. 'If she's missed the bus, it's her own fault.'

'I need to go a bit earlier today to collect something from the cottage,' Julie told him, on her way to the door. She had paperwork still to finish, because she had been so tired last night after Dave had stormed off to bed on his own that she had fallen asleep while filling in all the forms relating to patients she had seen that day. It would be better to catch up on that at her cottage rather than attempt to do it here when Dave was in such a foul mood. They would both be better off with some distance between them.

'What about dinner? Will you be back for it?' he called after her as she reached the back door.

'I hope so. I'll bring something with me.' With that she left him.

Dave watched her go from the open back door. He saw the way she crossed the yard with swift but graceful movements, the way she gave Jack an affectionate pat on his shoulder as the boy thrust his school bag into the back seat of her car and the way she helped Carla, and Carla's bulky backpack, into the front passenger seat.

He sighed deeply as she switched on the engine and moved off without looking back or giving him a farewell wave. No wonder his kids adored Julie. They were lucky to have her to care for them. He was more than lucky that she was willing to share in their upbringing and to put up with him and his bad temper. What had got into him last night to make him storm off to bed without her when he had been looking forward for so much of the day to her coming home and them having an early night? Looking forward to them making love. Until Julie had come in so much later than he expected, and looking so tired. He had lost control of his temper then, and spoken out of turn. That was why Julie had been so cool with him this morning that she had not even bothered to kiss him before leaving, and he could not blame her for that. 'I've acted like a bloody fool again,' he told his dog when he felt Tyke's affectionate nudge on his knee. 'I'll do it once too often, one day, and then she'll leave us, won't she?'

Tyke replied with a slow rumble deep in his throat.

'We'd best get some work done. At least we know what we're doing there.'

As he moved towards the field closest to the farm buildings with the two sheepdogs, his own and Jack's, at his heels, Dave could feel the first faint touches of moisture drifting down on to his face. When he raised his glance to the sky he saw with dismay the pall of low cloud hanging over the moor. There had been snow forecast on the late news last night for this side of the Pennines – now, even though March was almost over and lambing was just starting; snow that could bring disaster to his ewes and their lambs. He could only pray the snow wouldn't come.

Even as the thought came into his mind Dave accepted that, as he didn't find time to pray these days, he shouldn't expect miracles to happen for him.

'Can I stay at home and look after Darcy, please?' Elliot begged as Jane urged him to eat his breakfast so they wouldn't be late for nursery school.

Jane shook her head. 'No, you can't, Elliot. Hurry up and eat your cereal.'

'Why can't I? He's my dog, so Daddy says he's my respon-sable—'

As he stumbled over the latest long word he had taken a fancy to using as often as possible, Jane glanced at Kerry, waiting for the inevitable to be said.

'I want to stay and look after Darcy too! 'Cos Daddy said he was mine as well as Elliot's.'

Jane sighed. 'He doesn't need either of you to stay at home and look after him today. He'll be fine on his own now the vet has treated him.'

'But you said it was your day to go and help Mrs Wyndham with her ironing,' Elliot broke in.

'Yes, and I'm going to be late if you two don't hurry up.'

'But you can't leave Darcy on his own,' Elliot protested.

'Of course I can. He'll go to sleep while I'm out.'

'Suppose he wakes up and he's frightened?'

'He won't be frightened.'

'He might, because he'll be used to having all the other poorly dogs and cats and the vets and nurses around him now,' Elliot insisted.

Jane was losing patience with Elliot now. As she opened her mouth to speak sharply to him Kerry got down from the table and went to put her arms about the dog.

'I think he'll be lonely without us or the other poorly dogs,' Kerry said.

'I expect Daddy's lonely without us,' Elliot said as he left his seat to join his sister in the corner of the kitchen where Darcy lay on his blanket, wagging his tail.

'Why doesn't Daddy come home to live, like Darcy has done?'

It was Kerry asking that loaded question. She was catching up fast on Elliot now as far as asking the wrong sort of ques-tion was concerned, Jane realized with a sinking heart. How was she going to answer this particular question honestly?

'Because Mummy doesn't want him to,' Elliot broke in accusingly.

'That's not true!' The words seemed to come out of Jane's mouth before she could stop them. Hot on their heels came a burst of anger – anger with Elliot for making the declaration and anger with herself for opening her mouth without taking time to make sure her brain was on the same wavelength.

'Why doesn't—' Elliot began.

'Why don't you do as you're told? Both of you! We're late! We're *very* late, and I'm *very* cross with the pair of you. Now get your coats on fast, or I'll be sending that dog back where he came from.'

The silence in the moment after she had finished speaking was absolute, and alarming for her. She found herself unable to drag her gaze away from the stunned expressions on their faces. Then Kerry began to whimper. Elliot put his arm about her and said what he thought.

'If you do send Darcy back, I'll go with him. Because he's my responsable. Daddy said so!'

Jane blinked back the tears that were threatening. What had they done to their children, she and Tim? They certainly hadn't got things right yet. If they had, she would have found it possible to let Tim come back to her and his children after Donna Dawson's death, once he had said how sorry he was and asked her to forgive him. That had been months ago, and still she was holding back from forgiving him because she was unable to let go of the misery he had caused her. Why was she still refusing to take Tim back? Why couldn't she trust him again now that he had explained how he had come to drift into the relationship with his terminally ill fellow teacher and why he had felt unable to leave her when she'd been alone and frightened?

Andrea had told her that prayer, and patience, would help her. So Jane had prayed often in the sleepless hours, lying alone in her bed, hoping that one day soon the doubts and fears would all be gone and she and Tim could start again. Yet each time those doubts seemed to be receding something came to remind her of all those long, lonely months that she had been alone here with her children while Tim had spent all the time when he was not teaching with this other woman. Often the reminder was those times when she found herself wondering whether Tim would ever have asked her to take him back if Donna Dawson had still been alive.

Tim was taking Elliot to the football match on Saturday

afternoon and coming back to have a meal with them afterwards. He had told her when he rang to make the arrangements for that and an outing with Kerry and her on Sunday that he wanted to stay and have a talk with her after the children were in bed. His voice had sounded different when he said that – different in a way that made her uneasy about what was in his mind.

Had Tim grown tired of asking her to take him back? Was Sunday going to be the day when he asked her for the last time? Had he met someone else while she had been refusing him?

Eight

Andrea gazed out of the kitchen window, her busy hands stilled as the beauty of the landscape to be seen from there filled her with delight. Of course it was far too late in the winter for them to have snow, and it would bring problems to many of her flock who had to travel some distance to their work, or were farming; but right now, with the brilliant blue of the sun-filled sky making the snow-covered field sparkle, she longed to snatch a short time out of doors to enjoy the fresh air. Lucky would love it too. He had been sulking with his head on his paws and a melancholy expression in his amber eyes ever since Bill had departed with his painting gear just after nine that morning.

'Come on, Lucky. Walks!' she told him with a smile as she reached for the lead hanging on a hook above his bed.

Instantly, the retriever was on his feet with his long feathery tail waving enthusiastically. Andrea slipped on her fleece and changed her indoor shoes for flat-heeled boots before heading for the back door. Lucky raced ahead of her as soon as she pulled it open. It was then, before she had time to close and lock the door, that the sound of the phone brought her to a halt. For a long moment she hesitated, one foot already resting in the thin covering of crisp snow in her eagerness to be away from the house for the only opportunity she would have that day to get some fresh air. Only for a moment, though, because already conscience was kicking in. The call might be urgent; there were still a few cases of chest infection going the rounds in Nyddbeck and Nyddford, and some of those were people in their eighties who lived alone. There was Mrs Castleton and old Mr Hardacre . . .

'Hello! Andrea Wyndham speaking.' She was slightly

breathless as she spoke from bending to grab Lucky before he could bound away from her and over the wall ready to get into who knew what sort of mischief.

'Miriam Marshall here, Andrea,' the confident female voice began. 'I was rather hoping to talk to Bill.'

'Oh, hello, Miriam! I'm afraid Bill's out just now. Can I give him a message?'

There was a stifled exclamation. 'That's a nuisance. I thought I'd ring to let him know how the arrangements are going. He said he'd be around at this time.'

Miriam sounded quite put out. Had Bill really said he would be in at this time? If he had, he must have forgotten in his eagerness to get out with his painting gear.

'We've got snow here, probably the last for this winter, and Bill just couldn't wait to get out and start a new picture while the light was so right,' she explained. He had been in such a rush to get away that he had not said what time he expected to be back. So Andrea was not able to suggest another time for his agent to call.

Miriam sighed audibly. 'Oh, I suppose I'll have to contact him on his mobile then.'

'He's forgotten to take it with him,' Andrea told her. Or had Bill left his mobile phone behind on purpose so that his painting time would not be disturbed? She was not going to share that thought with Miriam.

This brought another sigh of annoyance. 'Will you ask him to ring me then, as soon as he gets back. I think it's time we got things finalized for the tour.'

'Yes, I'll do that,' Andrea promised.

Miriam had not even taken the trouble to ask her how she was, she reflected as she replaced the phone. Her former good spirits had faded away now and a small frisson of annoyance was coming to life inside her, not only against Miriam but also against Bill. So there *was* another American lecture and demonstration tour being planned, as she had half expected. Yet Bill had not shared that important news with her! They would need to talk about it when Bill got back from his painting. She did not like being kept in the dark about things that were going to affect her as well as him.

Resentment strengthened in her mind as she set off again with Lucky. By the time they had gone down the back-garden path together and reached the drystone wall that gave access to the field where she would walk uphill to the little copse, resentment had become anger so strong that she was careless in climbing over the wall and fell headlong as she landed on an icy outcrop of rock. For a moment she lay stunned and tearful as blood seeped through her trousers from her damaged right knee. Then fury took over and she expressed it loudly to the startled cows grazing at the top of the slope, and to the dog who stared at her with puzzled eyes.

'Damn! Damn! Damn!'

Lucky whined, his lead trailing in the snow, then moved closer and licked her hand.

'I'll have something worse than that to say to your master when he gets back. Something he won't like!' she told him as she struggled to her feet. 'Something he won't like at all!'

When Julie opened the door of her terraced cottage and stepped into the tiny hall, she could already feel the tension in her shoulders starting to relax. The house was warm from the background heating she kept going in between the holiday lets, and it was utterly, marvellously, silent. Julie was not willing to admit as much to herself yet, but Heather Cottage was at times her refuge from the turmoil that her role as Dave Bramley's wife could bring to her. It was a place she could escape to, when she needed to. This was one of the times when she *did* need to escape.

The first thing she did after dropping her bag at the foot of the staircase was to go into the small kitchen and reach for a mug to make coffee in the microwave. The second was to gather up the small pile of mail that had accumulated behind the door. It would mostly be advertising stuff that could go straight into the bin, she guessed. So she was surprised to find there was also a thick, square envelope bearing her name and the word 'Private', hand-printed. Her eyes widened at the sight of the card it contained, an expensive hand-made and very beautiful one showing a single dark-red rose. There were no words to indicate what the card was for. It was not her birthday, so what was it about?

Inside the card were a few lines of words penned in bold, unfamiliar handwriting – words that brought alarm leaping into her mind; words that ended with the signature 'Matt'.

It was great to spend time with you, darling Julie, though not as much time as I really wanted. We must do it again, soon. I know you are not happy, Julie. Not as happy as you would be with me. Remember, I love you.

Swiftly she pushed the card back into the envelope. She must get rid of it, though not here in this house, because if Dave ever saw it, there would be the sort of trouble that would split their marriage and cause immense pain to Carla and Jack. Also to Dorothy and Ben. How foolish she had been to allow herself to be talked into sharing her lunch hour alone with Matt in his new home, of all places! It certainly must never happen again. She would make sure it did not. Matt was quite wrong to say that she was not happy with Dave. Of course she was . . .

Because of her tight schedule of fitting in some visiting at the District Hospital in Harrogate with one or two calls on the way to see housebound elderly people, it was late after-noon before Andrea was driving back to her manse. By then she was tense with tiredness and her injured knee was sore and throbbing. The main roads were quite clear of snow, but the bends on Abbot's Hill and on Beck Lane were treach-erous, so it was with relief that she steered her car on to the drive, which Bill had just finished clearing and sanding. He was waiting for her in the kitchen with the kettle already steaming away and a couple of mugs at the ready.

'Bad day, darling?' he murmured as he moved across the room to kiss her.

She nodded. 'I've had better.'

'You look all-in. Go and put your feet up beside the fire,' he ordered. 'I'll bring you some tea in a couple of minutes.'

'I need to check the answerphone first.' Already she was turning away from him to do that.

'Can't it wait for a while?'

'I've been out since eleven. There could be something urgent on it.'

'Didn't you come back for some lunch, as you said you were going to do?'

'No. I was afraid if I didn't get to Harrogate before some more snow came, I might be late getting back and then late for the meeting tonight at Nyddford.'

'Do you have to be at that?'

'Yes. I'm chairing it.' This was said over her shoulder as she moved back into the hall where the answerphone was blinking at her.

Bill sighed. Andrea was driving herself too hard. He was seriously worried about her. Yet she would not heed his warnings. He stirred the tea he had just poured boiling water on, and listened as she began to answer the first call listed for her. When she had dealt with all that must be done right now, *he* would have some words of his own to say to her because he simply could not let her go on as she was doing, working herself too hard to be able to enjoy any more their life together in this lovely place.

It seemed a long time to him as he waited with the tray of tea and biscuits in the big, pleasant sitting room from where he could see the centuries-old stone bridge that spanned the beck, the row of cottages that faced it, and the beautiful outlines of the ancient chestnut trees, lightly burdened with fresh snow, which stood on the village green in close proximity to the little church that had brought Andrea into his life. Dear God, what would he do without her? How, now that she had taken over his heart and his life so completely, would he cope if she was taken from him? Fear swept through him before he could manage to push the thought away. It was fear that made him get to his feet and stride into the hall to speak sharply to her.

'Leave it, Andrea!' he said sharply as she began to press out yet another number to answer yet another message.

'I can't!' she muttered as she waited to make contact with the voice at the other end.

'Why not?' Unusually, Bill was losing his temper now and was unable to conceal that fact from her.

'You know why!' she retorted. 'It's what I'm here for.' Still she waited for someone to reply to her call.

'You're not here to kill yourself with overwork,' he hit back. 'You're here as my wife as well as being the area agony aunt!'

Andrea had heard enough. She slammed down the phone with unnecessary force and turned round to face him, flinging out the words that had been creeping in and out of her mind throughout the day. 'As I'm your wife, why haven't I been told about this next American tour you and your precious agent have been cooking up? Didn't I have a right to know about it, since it's going to affect me as well as you?'

Bill drew in his breath sharply, lost for words. He'd been waiting for the right moment to broach the subject of the tour. Waiting, in fact, until he thought Andrea was not looking so tired and ill. Only that time had not arrived, and while he had been waiting, Andrea had found out about the tour. That could only mean Miriam had phoned him while he had been out painting. What could he say to Andrea now that would not make the situation much worse?

'Aren't you going to answer me, Bill?' she was asking quietly now.

He sighed. 'I suppose Miriam phoned while I was out?'

'Yes. She wants you to ring her back. She says it's urgent that you both get on with the arrangements as soon as possible. How long has this tour been on the cards, Bill?'

'Just a few weeks.'

'Why didn't you tell me?' Her words were quiet but her eyes were accusing.

He sighed again. 'Because I knew you wouldn't like it, and because I didn't really want to go anyway,' he added.

'Then why *are* you going?'

This was not going to be easy to answer. If he answered her honestly, Andrea would not like what she heard. The truth was that he had almost emptied his bank account in order to buy and furnish the cottage in Scotland that he had given her as a wedding present. He had no regrets about doing that, but he was anxious to earn more money, substantial money, as soon as possible, and the proposed American lecture and demo tour would enable him to do that.

'Miriam thinks another tour will boost the sales of Howard's book; perhaps enough to justify a second edition. Which will help me as well as Howard.' It was not *quite* what Miriam had said, but it was near enough. As a result of his tour last year the sales of *An American in the Dales*, with Howard Barclay's quirky text enhanced by his own pictures of Yorkshire villages, dales and moors, had soared.

Andrea took a deep breath. 'I still don't understand why you've kept this to yourself for so long, Bill? Didn't you think I had a right to know?'

Bill hesitated. 'Of course, but I was waiting until you were not looking so tired and ill before I spoke to you about it.'

Suddenly, and inexplicably, Andrea had had enough of the subject. 'You'd better go and ring Miriam then, hadn't you?' With that she turned her back on him and moved towards the sitting room, where the tea he had made for her was cooling rapidly

Bill watched her go with pain tearing at his guts. She was tired, and not well, and he had let her down. 'Andrea,' he began; but she did not turn her head and look back at him. He knew then that he had really blown it, but could not think how to put things right. Since he was in no mood to talk to anyone else, and certainly not to the agent who had managed to start up the first real row he and Andrea had experienced since their marriage, he reached for the dog lead and silently signalled to Lucky that they were going out.

Paula stared again at the letter she had received that day from her father's solicitor. She had been certain at first that there had been a mistake. The middle-aged lawyer, who had been one of the customers at her dad's garden centre, had assured her when she had phoned him that there had not. 'I'm very sorry if this has been a shock for you, Miss Price. I had assumed you would be aware of what was to happen in these circumstances.'

She was calmer now, but still full of bewilderment at what was to happen. The problem was that, when she and her father had bought the Mill House between them, she had assumed, since she was an only child and her parents were divorced, that when he died she would inherit everything from him, including his half of this property. Now, thanks to this letter setting out the terms of the will he had made some time ago, she knew this was not to be the case. It seemed that she had to share some of her father's estate with someone called Daniel Price.

Was Daniel Price one of those strangers who had attended the funeral and come back here for refreshments afterwards? There had been several men among that clan, a couple in the same age bracket as her dad and two or three much younger ones. Someone in the group had been about to say something to her, she recalled, then been interrupted hurriedly and ushered away even more swiftly. What was it all about?

It was mystifying, and alarming, to find herself in a position now where she was no longer certain of whether she was going to be able to go ahead with the plans for this business, which had seemed at the time to be so straightforward. So much the best for her and her dad. The plans that had cost her Gareth's love. If she had known then that she was to share her inheritance with this other person called Price, she would not have decided to come here, once she had become aware of how strongly Gareth was against it. No, she certainly would not.

Gareth had been so much a part of her life in London. She had believed he would be a part of the rest of her life. He had given her so much support at the time of her father's accident and seemed to understand when their plan to marry and set up a small restaurant together had had to be postponed for a while. He had been shocked and furious with her when she had told him she was to come instead with her father to this place he had described as 'the back of beyond'.

How could she have acted any differently, though, once she had been told that her father would not fully recover from his accident – certainly not enough to be able to continue to run the garden centre that he had made so successful. In a mood of deep despair about his future he had sold this with amazing speed, and then become deeply depressed about his future until she had persuaded him to come to North Yorkshire for a holiday with her, close to the place where he had spent the early years of his life. When she had seen how happy he was there, it had seemed right to put her plans to be shared with Gareth on hold and find a place to live and work in North Yorkshire. The Mill House had seemed the perfect solution to the problem of providing her dad with a purpose in life – the renovation of the overgrown garden – while she set about transforming the house into a small restaurant with accommodation for tourists or business people.

Her dad had been so enthusiastic and so happy during the few months they had lived in the Mill House. Now he was dead, she had lost Gareth, and she could be about to lose the place she had already come to love. Despair engulfed her. She dropped her head on her arms and wept until she was exhausted.

Nine

As she went about her work that day, visiting some of her housebound patients in the more remote moorland areas, Julie found that she was unable to push out of her mind the card she had found in her cottage and the message it contained. Time and time again, as she traversed the narrow lanes and negotiated the many tight bends that could bring disaster to drivers who lacked the power of concentration, she would force those disturbing words out of her mind only for them to return when she was least expecting them. Once, when a lurch of fear hit her at the thought of what would happen if Dave ever discovered that Matt was still determined to enter into a passionate relationship with her, she lost control of her vehicle on an icy stretch of the moorland road and found herself off the tarmac and on the frosted moor.

'Oh God!' she muttered when she realized how close she had come to toppling herself and her car over into a deep ditch. 'What the hell am I doing this morning?'

She sat there for several minutes feeling her heartbeats thumping uncomfortably, then forced herself to relax for a few moments with her hands crossed over the steering wheel. The road, and the moor, were deserted and silent. All she could hear was the harsh croaking of a pheasant, who stared at her resentfully from where she had encroached on his grazing. The sound made her send a few words his way when she glimpsed his bright plumage bringing a splash of colour on to the dead heather.

'It's all very well for you, you handsome bird. You're not a jealous husband, or a man who fancies someone else's wife, are you?' She watched then as the bird soared into the brilliant blue of the sky, heading in the direction of the abbey ruins, which were now plainly visible ahead. of her. 'No such problems for all you holy fellows who lived over there all those years ago either,' she muttered to herself as she struggled to steer back on to the road with difficulty. 'Or did you find yourselves falling for the local farmer's wife too?'

The ruined abbey was quite close to her when she reached an exceedingly narrow lane to make a call on an old man who lived in a cottage there. It was breathtakingly beautiful, the silvery stones of the broken arches glistening as the sunlight poured over them. No wonder her friend Andrea loved this place so much. There was something here that seemed to reach out to you – something that made you pause, and feel you wanted to pray. If Andrea had been facing her situation, she would have prayed about it, Julie knew; but then Andrea was *not* facing her situation, with a husband who did not trust her and a man who was waiting to wreck her marriage. Andrea would have found it easy to pray, which Julie did not – not outside church anyway. Though she did at times offer silent, private prayers for some of her patients who had much suffering to bear.

'Dear God, please tell me what to do about Matt,' she breathed as she drew slowly to a halt outside a cottage built of the same huge blocks of stone as the abbey.

Inside the cottage there was a welcome waiting for her from Mr Butterfield, who was going on for ninety years old, frail but amazingly contented. She was concerned about him living here alone since the death of his wife some years earlier.

'Don't you find it lonely here, Mr Butterfield, at this time of the year?' she asked when she had finished dressing his leg and was preparing to move on to the next patient.

He chuckled as he got to his feet to escort her to the door. 'Oh no, lass. Not me! I like a bit of solitude, now I've got used to it. I've always got the birds for company, and a few wild creatures who come to my garden for food. I have old friends who come to see me sometimes too: the farmer's wife from where I used to work, the nice young lady minister from Nyddbeck, and old Joe who was with me in the army a long time ago. Then I've got my friends the monks from the abbey. I've read so much about them and the way they lived that they seem to be very close to me at times. Yes, I've everything I need here – even a nice young nurse to keep an eye on me when I need her.'

Julie felt her spirits lift when she heard that. It made all her own problems seem small. 'I'll see you again on Friday, Mr Butterfield,' she promised before driving away.

'What's happened to your knee, darling?' Bill wanted to know when Andrea began to slip off her slacks to go to bed.

'Nothing much. I just fell,' she answered tersely as she slipped into her dressing robe and made for the en-suite shower. She was far too tired to go into explanations with him. All she wanted was to shut out all the worries and frustrations and weariness of her too-long day in a deep sleep.

Besides, Bill would not like to hear that she had been so angry with him after the phone call from his agent that she had been careless in going over the wall with Lucky and had only herself to blame for her injury.

'Where did you fall? How did it happen?' Bill was frowning now and too persistent with his questions, which he sometimes could be if he thought she was being devious with him.

'When I was going over the wall with Lucky I landed awkwardly on a bit of icy stone, that's all.' Perhaps he'd let the subject drop now. Her hand was on the door of the shower, but before she was on the other side of it Bill was speaking to her again. This time his voice was softer.

'That's not all, is it, my love? You were a bit careless, I suppose, because you are overtired.'

Usually his concern for her was one of the things Andrea loved about Bill. Tonight, because she knew he was speaking the truth, a truth she did not want to hear, she reacted angrily. 'I was *not* careless because I was tired. It was too early in the day for that. I was careless because I was angry about Miriam's phone call and having to hear from *her* about your American tour when you hadn't even told me about it. Now I *am* tired and I'd like to get to bed.'

With that she closed the door on him.

When that happened, Bill knew that he really had got it wrong this time. Worse still, he simply could not think of how to put it right. Not in the mood Andrea was in tonight. He could not remember ever having seen her so coldly angry with him. Even when he had gone on his tour last year she had not been so outspoken in her condemnation of him, though they had got seriously at odds with each other over it. Of course, her extreme tiredness would be partly to blame, he conceded. What was he going to do about that, when she would not slow down?

He had begun to undress, but now his need for sleep after his long hours of painting out in the fresh air had deserted him and he felt wide awake – far too wide awake to even want to go to bed. Andrea would not welcome his love-making tonight, he knew. She would not appreciate him tossing and turning beside her while he tried to sleep either. With a shrug of frustration he slipped on his bathrobe again and went downstairs in his bare feet to seek solace in a hefty dram of whisky.

The sound of the phone ringing broke into Paula's despair. She would let it go on ringing, she decided, because it would not be anything important. Certainly not anything that would matter to her now that everything had changed and all her plans for the future would have to be abandoned. If it was someone responding to her advertising and wanting to make a booking for meals or accommodation, there would be no point in going ahead with that, since the Mill House would probably have to be sold again quite soon, now that she knew someone else would have to share her inheritance.

There would be phone calls *she* would have to make later cancelling work she had arranged to have done, but she did not feel able to cope with doing that yet. Her throat hurt and her eyes were sore after all the weeping she had indulged in. Let the damn thing go on ringing! She got to her feet and rushed out into the garden to get away from the sound of it. The air was still and icy out there; the bare branches of the trees on the perimeter bore frosted snow. She could still hear the phone, but the sound was distant now and could be ignored. In her early days here, just after she and her father had moved in, she had hurried to answer every call, hoping each time that it would be Gareth telling her he was sorry about the row and that he could not do without her. Hope had died after many disappointments. She knew now that Gareth would not ring. He had told her that he was not willing to come second to her father, and he had obviously meant it.

So she must accept that and stop grieving about it. There was enough grief for her to bear from the loss of her dear dad.

Because this last thought brought the threat of more tears to her, she turned away from the house she had already come to feel so much at home in and began to run along the drive until she reached the open gates that gave access to the long, winding lane that would in turn bring her to the village. There, since she was breathless now with her exertions, and her emotions, her footsteps slowed and she began to breathe deeply and evenly. It would do her good to have a walk, to get away for a while from the confines of the Mill House, where everything reminded her of her father. The fact that she was not dressed for outdoors on a freezing late March day was forgotten as she walked on, leaving behind the bigger houses on the outskirts of the village and finding herself now close to the beck from where she could see the village green and Nyddbeck Church.

She came to a stop then as the memory entered her mind of her father's coffin, laden with her own floral tribute and those of the family members not known to her, being carried into the little church. As she hesitated, wondering whether to go on or not, a vehicle drove slowly past her, then came to a halt a little ahead of her. It was a Range Rover, elderly and obviously well used. The driver was jumping down from his seat as she turned to walk back to the Mill House. His voice came from behind her to startle her with his use of her first name.

'Paula!'

She swung round to face him, a question in her eyes. He

was only a little taller than she was, and of burly, broad-shouldered build. There was something vaguely familiar about him but she could not at first place him.

'Do I know you?'

'No, not really. We've only met once. It was over there, a few days ago.' He pointed to the church with a square, toil-scarred hand. 'I don't suppose you remember me. There were so many of Harry's friends there that you had to speak to before they went back south, and we knew we'd be able to talk to you later when you were not so upset.'

She swallowed, then guessed who he was likely to be. 'Of course, you'll be one of my dad's relations!'

Now it was his turn to hesitate before he answered her.

'Yes. You could say that. I'm Daniel. Daniel Price.'

He reached a hand out to her and she put her own cold fingers into it to be held firmly, warmly, for a long, long moment while the truth sank in. If this man was Daniel Price, and she had no reason to doubt it, he was the man who was to share her inheritance.

Julie had lain awake for much of the night while Dave snatched a couple of hours of exhausted sleep before going back downstairs to check on the lambing ewes. She ought to have been exhausted too after all her hazardous driving on the icy roads, interrupted at intervals by changing dressings for her patients, giving them reassurance, trying to impress them with the importance of keeping really warm when they were not able to move about much and hearing their latest news of close family members living far away. Of course she loved her work, but it was hard going when snow came so late in the winter to cause extra problems. If she had slept as well as she usually did she would have been looking forward to what awaited her at Nyddford Health Centre this morning. Instead, all she longed for now was to stay here beneath the duvet and catch up on her rest. Even as the thought crossed her mind her alarm sounded. Maybe she would feel better when she'd had a large mug of tea and some toast and honey . . .

She was towelling herself down vigorously when she

91

remembered something she ought to have done yesterday but had forgotten about because her mind had been so full of Matt's card and what to do about it. Wandering Joe! She had promised Jack that she would make the poor old chap a lemon and honey mixture to soothe his cough, and had also decided that she would try to persuade him to go to the health centre and see a doctor there. Would there be time to do that before she started work? There would if she made do with toast and honey instead of her more usual cereal and eggs. Hurriedly, she dressed and brushed her hair then ran down to the kitchen.

What she found there was the breakfast table she had set the night before bearing empty mugs and cereal bowls to indicate that Jack had gone out with his dad to give a hand with the lambing. A pathetic whimper from the vicinity of the Aga rewarded her with the sight of a tiny lamb tucked into a box close to the warmth that would keep the little creature alive.

Julie smiled and bent to touch the raggy fleece. 'Hello, and welcome!' she murmured before straightening her back and going to lift the steaming kettle. As she did so, a sobering thought hit her: an orphan lamb in the house could mean a lost ewe. The price paid, perhaps, for late snow when spring should be here. She sighed as she made her coffee, then began to put together the old country remedy that could ease the cough of an old countryman who would probably not take her advice about seeing a doctor.

Jack came dashing in as she was finishing mixing this.

'How are you doing out there, Jack? Ready for a hot drink and something to eat?' she asked, smiling at his spiky hair and rosy cheeks.

'Not bad,' he replied, bending over to inspect the pet lamb. 'We lost a ewe, though. That upset Dad. He wants a hot drink taking out to him.'

'I've made up the cough mixture for old Joe. If you tell me where I'll find him, I'll take it to him when I take out the flask for your dad.'

'He's in the back of the old tractor shed. He says it's warm enough for him in there. You won't tell Dad, will you, Julie?'

She sighed. 'The poor old chap won't do any harm there, though he'd be better indoors in such weather. He ought to be by the fire in his own cottage.'

'Joe said he had to come now because his friend is poorly. He said his friend was at a place called Dunkirk with him when they were both in the army, and they had to wait a long time to be rescued from there in the same little boat. Survivors, they were called. You have to stick by your old army mates when they need you, Joe says.'

'I'm sure he's right about that. I'll make sure he gets his lemon and honey, and a lift into Nyddford with me if he'll come,' Julie promised as she slipped the bacon she had grilled into two big baps and handed them to Jack. 'Take these out for you and your dad. I'll follow with the coffee in a minute.'

'Thanks, Julie. You're ace!' the boy said as he dashed out with the bacon butties and left her feeling warm with love for him.

He wouldn't want to go to school this morning, she guessed. He would want to stay and help Dave with the lambing. Would Dave let him do that? She'd better slip the bottle of cough mixture into her pocket if she didn't want it to be seen by Dave, though for the life of her she could not understand why her husband was making such a fuss about the poor fellow staying in one of their farm buildings for the night. She would ask him about that, but not until she came back tonight. Time was running away with her this morning!

In spite of that she could not tear herself away immediately from what was happening in the hayshed, where the miracle of birth was happening again. Sometimes, especially when she witnessed it at close hand, she wished that she had specialized in midwifery. She could perhaps still do that, but not while the longing was still inside her for a child of her own. It would be the wrong time. Would it ever be the right time for her and Dave to have a child? So far, Dave had thought it was not . . .

She pushed the thought, and the feeling of resentment it aroused, aside and left father and son to get on with their vital work while she went to find Wandering Joe. He was where Jack had told her he would be – in the old tractor shed, which was only used now for the storing of farm implements that were rarely used. As she approached the tarpaulin he had rigged up to provide shelter from the draughts which sneaked in through gaps in the roof, she heard a warning growl from his dog, followed by a soft reprimand from his master.

'Quiet, Archie! Behave yourself,' Joe began when he saw who his visitor was. The rest of what he might have been going to say was lost in a spasm of coughing.

'Good morning, Joe. I brought you something for that cough.' Julie held out the bottle, and a spoon that would be just right to drink it from.

Joe was recovering now, taking the bottle and the spoon from her and starting to voice his thanks. The violence of his coughing fit had brought tears to the faded blue eyes, she noticed, and his hands were shaking.

'Young Jack has a good mother in you. You're a grand lass. The sort of daughter I would have liked if I'd been as fortunate as Dave Bramley,' he told her.

'Don't you have any family, Joe?' He needed someone to care about him, though he was clean about his person and spoke well.

He waited too long before he replied. So long that she guessed the answering was not going to be easy for him. 'No, my wife was killed during the war.'

'You really ought to see a doctor about that cough. He'll give you something that will ease it for you,' she began, even though she could already guess at what his answer would be.

His reply came quickly, and firmly. 'I can't do that in case he sends me to hospital. You see there'd be no one to look after Archie for me if he did.'

Julie did not argue with him. She knew better than that. Besides, if she didn't get a move on right away, she would be late reporting for duty. What she would do, she decided, was keep an eye on the old soldier and see that he had some hot food. If Dave didn't like it, he would just have to put up with it, as she had to put up with his uncertain moods!

'I'll come and see how you are after I finish work, Joe. Take care now. Keep out of that cold wind if you can.'

Wandering Joe smiled as he raised a hand to his ancient khaki beret bearing a brightly polished regimental badge and gave her a military salute.

'Thank you, ma'am!' were his final words as Julie left him to walk through a flurry of snowflakes to where her car waited.

Ten

Paula stared speechlessly at the man who did not show much resemblance to her father and waited for him to tell her what it was all about. He still held her hand, and seemed reluctant to let go of it even when she tried to withdraw it from his firm grasp.

'I think all this must have been a terrible shock to you, Paula,' he said quietly. 'I'm very sorry about that.'

She withdrew her fingers with difficulty. Looking down at them instead of into his face, she noticed that they were trembling visibly. 'I just don't understand,' she began.

'It's something we need to talk about,' he broke in when her voice came to a halt. 'But not here. This is the wrong place, and maybe the wrong time for you.'

Paula pulled herself together rapidly. 'I was taken aback at meeting you like this,' she said. 'I was expecting you to phone me, or write to me, once I'd heard from Dad's solicitor what was to happen.'

'I intended to phone you, once you'd had time to recover from the shock of losing him. I had not expected to meet you here today.'

'Why are you here?' Maybe she ought not to have asked him that?

'I came to—' He hesitated, then went on. 'I came to put flowers on my mother's grave. She died a year ago today.'

'Oh, I'm sorry,' she began, wondering then what relationship his mother had shared with her father.

'It was a merciful release. She had been ill for a long time,' he cut in abruptly. 'I mustn't keep you standing out here in the cold. You look frozen already.'

She shivered. 'Yes. I'll soon get warm walking back home though.'

'So the Mill House is home to you already?'

'Yes, I love it, and this village.' She bit her lip, then went on, 'I'll find it hard to leave, now.'

'Surely you're not thinking of doing that, after all the work you've put into the place?' As he spoke, his thick brows lifted to indicate his amazement.

Paula frowned. 'I could be compelled to leave. I mean when all Dad's affairs are finally sorted out.' She stared hard at him as she told him that, and saw that he was embarrassed.

'It might not be necessary. We need to talk, but not now. Can I call in and see you later? On my way home perhaps?' He spoke very quickly, as though anxious now to get on with what he had come to do.

'Yes. The sooner the better' – before she went on doing any more work on the house, or allowed herself to become too fond of it, she meant.

'I'll see you soon then, Paula.'

With that he got back into his vehicle and drove the short distance to the church while she strode back along Beck Lane. She looked back once, after the sound of the engine and the slam of the door had died away, and saw him jump down from the driving seat and reach for a bunch of flowers. He must have been very fond of his mother to do that, she thought. As she walked on she found herself wondering yet again just how closely *she* was related to Daniel Price. Well, she would soon know, because when he arrived at the Mill House she would want to know what it was all about – why she looked like having to share everything her father had possessed with him.

In Nyddbeck Manse, Andrea awoke and reached out across the bed for Bill. All she found was the chilly, empty space which was usually occupied by her husband. Her eyes flew open and moved straight to her bedside alarm clock. Almost nine, and she was still up here! She ought to have been downstairs over an hour ago; why hadn't her alarm wakened her before now? There could be calls on her answerphone, urgent letters lying behind the door and Bill waiting to share breakfast with her. This last thought brought her to her feet too quickly and she was forced to sit down on the bed again as dizziness caught her unawares. Oh, she felt quite ghastly!

Where was Bill? Why had he allowed her to oversleep when he knew she liked to make an early start to her day? She stared about her and saw the unfamiliar sight of Bill's clothes abandoned untidily instead of being piled on the dressing stool. Next she discovered his dressing robe was not, as she expected it to be, hanging beside her own. Bill must already be downstairs, so why had he let her oversleep for so long?

It all came back to her then: the way they had got so badly at odds with one another over his proposed American lecture tour that she had poured out her anger against him non-stop when he had expressed his concern about her injured knee, then fastened herself in the shower room after banging the door on him. When she had flopped into bed soon afterwards, feeling sorry for herself because her knee hurt and she was too tired to think straight, she had fallen into exhausted sleep at once. In a moment of shocked disbelief, she faced the fact that for the first time she had ended her day full of bitterness and fury against the man she loved. How could she have treated Bill like that?

Such a wave of shame washed over her that she knew she must go to Bill at once and put things right – even though he had been partly to blame for what had happened, she thought wryly.

'Dear Lord, please forgive me, and help Bill to forgive me,' she prayed silently before making for the door, grabbing her robe on the way but not stopping to put on her slippers.

As she went down the stairs, slowly because her head felt so muzzy, she was puzzled by the silence all about her. Where was Lucky? Why wasn't he coming to greet her with a pleased bark and a wagging tail? Had Bill taken him out already? Surely not? Even as the thought came into her mind she heard the sound of the dog's metallic identity disc moving against his collar as he shook himself. The sound came from the other side of the sitting-room door, which was closed. As she opened it, she saw the lanky red retriever stretching himself upright from his position on the big sofa where he had been sprawling across the feet of his master. A moment later he was at her feet giving her his usual warm morning welcome of wagging tail.

Bill was still out for the count, she saw then, with his arms outstretched, his thick auburn hair wildly tousled as though he had passed a rough night on the sofa, and his eyes firmly closed. A flash of alarm hit Andrea as she stared at him. His face looked haggard. Was he ill? If he was, why hadn't he told her? She was across the room in a few hasty strides and bending over him to make sure he was still breathing. It was then she discovered why Bill looked so haggard – why he was still so deeply asleep in spite of the noise Lucky was making as he demanded to be let out into the back garden to water the grass. Bill had been drinking. Seriously drinking. He still reeked of whisky and there was an almost empty bottle on the carpet beside him.

'Bill! Wake up!' Her hands were on his shoulders, grasping him firmly enough to bring him back to wincing consciousness.

'Oh!' he moaned as he clapped a hand to his brow. 'What the hell is the matter? Leave me alone! Leave me alone!' Turning his back on her, he buried his head into the cushions and promptly went to sleep again.

Impatience with him was building up in Andrea, fuelled by the fact that a glance at the clock on the mantelpiece warned her that in less than half an hour one of her church secretaries would be arriving to help her with the correspondence.

'Bill! Get moving, damn you!' She encouraged him to do this by giving his shoulders another fierce shake.

This time he grunted as he opened his eyes and stared at her. 'What's the matter? Why can't you leave me alone?'

'Because I don't want Oliver Oldfield to see you in the state you are in this morning. That's why! This is a manse, not a nightclub. There's urgent work waiting to be done here.

I can't do my sort of work as and when I feel like it, as you seem to be able to do, Bill Wyndham!'

All of a sudden the full horror of his situation hit Bill. He dragged himself to his feet, with some difficulty, and reached out to her. 'Oh Andrea, darling, I'm sorry! So sorry!'

'So you should be! First keeping me in the dark about what's happening in your life, then this!'

Bill rubbed one of his rusty eyebrows in the way he did when he was at a loss for words, then gave her a hug so passionate that his unshaven chin made her wince. 'I've said I'm sorry, love. I can't do any more than that, can I?'

He looked so comical with his hair sticking out in random clumps, as currently favoured by some of the lads from Nyddford High School, that her lips began to twitch. 'Yes, you can, Bill Wyndham! You can go and wash the reek of whisky away and let me get this room put to rights before Oliver arrives. Or Jane comes to help and finds what sort of husband *I've* got.'

Already Bill's sense of humour was coming to his aid. 'At least I've only been sleeping with my dog,' he reminded her. 'It could have been worse, you know.'

'Speaking of dogs, there's one here waiting to go out. He must be desperate by now.'

'He's not the only one!' Bill said with a laugh. 'But I'll let him have priority.'

With that he made for the door, until Andrea's voice halted him. 'I should put some clothes on first, but do hurry.'

'There's just one thing I have to do before that.' Before she could guess what he meant he was sweeping her into his arms and kissing her soundly. 'Good morning, darling,' he said then.

Andrea fought against the laughter that was bubbling up inside her. 'It was obviously a good night for you. Too good, I'd say!'

Bill sighed, sobering suddenly. 'I'd rather have spent it with you. I wouldn't have needed the whisky then to put me to sleep.'

With that he was making a dash for the back door to let Lucky out. When he came back through the hall, Andrea had

100

already made her way back upstairs to dress. There was no time to shower this morning. It was not the best start to her day, but she couldn't waste time thinking about that now, because Oliver Oldfield was always punctual. He would probably be on his way from Nyddford already . . .

While she waited for Daniel Price to come, Paula filled the kettle and set out mugs for the coffee she guessed Daniel would need when he arrived. What would he have to say to her when he did? He appeared to have been surprised when she had told him she would probably have to leave Nyddbeck when her father's will took effect. Didn't he realize that the bequest to *him* of so much money was going to change all *her* plans for the future? If not, she would soon make him aware of the fact.

She sighed as she looked around her at the spacious kitchen, which had been created by taking in one of the old pantries; at the shining stainless-steel range, which she had chosen as being ideal for cooking dinners for the locals as well as for tourists; at the primrose-yellow walls, which brought light in to supplement that pouring in from the enlarged picture windows. Oh, she had been so looking forward to working in the super-kitchen she had designed! – to trying out some recipes made with local produce as well as using the most popular ones from the London restaurant. Now it was not going to happen, was it?

Impatiently she moved over to the window, from where she could see the curve of the drive as it swept in from the far end of Beck Lane. Why didn't the wretched man get himself here and put her out of her misery? The weather was not right for hanging about in churchyards! When she left here, she would not come back to visit her father's grave. It would be far too painful. She would try to remember her dad as he had been before the chest infection put him into hospital.

A smile touched her lips as she recalled how much her dad had loved the garden that surrounded the Mill House, the plans he had had for improving it, the work he had already put in clearing overgrown shrubs and planting spring bulbs. Some of the crocus bulbs were already bringing bright splashes of purple and gold to the snow-touched earth on either side of the drive to remind her of him kneeling on a warm late-autumn day to plant them. Strong green daffodil leaves were spiking through behind them. By the time they were in flower she could be preparing to leave Nyddbeck. There was a vehicle turning in now from the end of the lane. Daniel Price was here. She hurried to open the door for him.

'Come in, Daniel. You must be frozen. Would you like some coffee? I've already got some brewing in the kitchen,' she said hurriedly.

'Yes, please. It smells good.'

Paula opened the door into the sitting room, where a log fire sent out leaping flames and warmth. 'I'll be with you in a minute,' she told him.

When she came back into the room, Daniel was not warming himself beside the fire as she had expected. He was close to one of the built-in bookcases, staring at a framed photograph of her father. It was the most recent one she had, and it showed him as he had been before his accident, a fit, handsome man in his early fifties, casually dressed and laughing.

'Was this a good photograph of him?' he asked her without turning round.

'Yes. It's as he was just before the accident.'

'What happened? Was he badly hurt?' Daniel was facing her now, his thick eyebrows arched and a faint frown on his high forehead as he asked the questions.

'Yes. It happened at the garden centre he owned, during a gale. An unstable tree fell where Dad was working and came down on his head. His sight was seriously affected.' Paula began to pour the coffee as she spoke.

'Did you live with him then?'

She hesitated. 'No, not then. I had my own place. I moved out of it when Dad came out of hospital. Then I decided to come here with him.'

'So his accident affected your own life?' Daniel said thoughtfully.

'Yes, very much so.' It had been the beginning of the end between her and Gareth, but she was not going to reveal that to this stranger.

'What about your mother?'

'She had already left him a few years earlier.'

'Perhaps I shouldn't have asked that?'

She sighed. 'These things happen, don't they?' She handed him sugar.

He nodded. 'Yes, they do. My wife walked out on me.'

'I'm sorry.'

He shrugged. 'You have to get on with your life. I suppose that's what Harry did?'

'Yes, but he took it badly at first. I don't think he ever got over it. At least, he didn't meet anyone else.'

Daniel sat down in a big chair opposite her own and took a couple of long gulps from his mug before he spoke to her again. It was the chair her father used to sit in, the one he had moved from his old home next to the garden centre. Paula found it painful to see someone else occupying that sturdy oak chair with the faded tapestry cushions. She had avoided using it herself, and tried not to even look at it. Her mouth began to tremble. Then Daniel set down his empty mug and spoke.

'I suppose you're wondering what it's all about, Paula?'

She nodded, then stared down at her hands folded tightly in her lap. 'I knew Dad had some family around here, that he grew up on a farm here until he went to work at a stately home in the south; but I don't know why he didn't keep in touch with anyone here. I don't even know what relationship we have with one another – why he should feel the need to leave so much of his money to you.' She looked up at him as she finished speaking, and then fell silent as she waited for his answer.

Daniel got to his feet and began to pace about the room. He knew what he would have to say would probably shock her, but it would have to be said. When he was at the furthest point in the room from her, he told her. The words came from him slowly, reluctantly, and his eyes were full of his compassion for her.

'When he was very young, before he went away to work, Harry was expected to marry my mother. Now do you understand, Paula?'

'Yes,' she said, on a long sigh.

'This is not something that I wished to happen,' he said then. 'In fact it was almost as big a shock for me as it must have been for you.'

After a silence that went on for too long Paula spoke again. 'Do you mean you were never in touch with him? That he never gave you any support, either financially or otherwise?'

He shrugged that off. 'There was no need for him to do so. Because his brother married my mother before I was born I was never told about my true parentage until I was about to marry, then they told me that they adopted me after my mother had suffered a miscarriage and been unable to have any more children. That's why I refer to your dad as Harry, because Tom was always Dad to me.'

Tom, which one of the Price clan was Tom? Was he the one who had been very abrupt with her at the funeral? Or was it the kinder, gentler brother called Ted? Not that it mattered to her, what mattered was that even though he was not a blood relation Daniel had inherited half of all her dad had possessed. 'So you're not my half-brother? You are a sort of cousin?'

'Yes. I'm sorry if you find that distressing, Paula. I only wish I had not been forced to tell you at such a time,' he said gently.

She sighed again. 'At least it helps me to understand why Dad arranged things as he did.'

Daniel moved towards the door as though about to leave. 'The only other thing I have to say is that I don't want you to have to leave here since you obviously like the place so much, and as you've put so much work into doing it up,' he added.

'But what else can I do? I don't have enough capital of my own to be able to pay you what you would inherit without selling the Mill House.'

'There could be another way of sorting things out. I could become a partner here, as your father was.' He waited, with his hand on the door, for her answer.

104

'Do you mean you would work here with me? I don't think that would . . .'

'No! Oh no! I don't mean that,' Daniel broke in. 'I have a perfectly good business of my own. I meant I was willing to wait for most of my inheritance until you built your business up.'

Surprise kept her silent for a long moment. Then, 'I don't think that would be fair to you.'

'Surely that's up to me to decide? You ought at least to consider it. I'll leave now and give you time to do that. I'll be in touch with you again in a few days. In the meantime don't change any of your plans; the ones you and Harry made. I'm sure he would not have wanted you to suffer.'

With that Daniel was making his way into the hall. She followed him and opened the front door for him, then held out her hand. 'Thanks for trying to help. For being so kind, Daniel.'

He smiled at her. For some reason tears pricked behind her eyes. She blinked them away as he spoke again.

'Surely that's what families are for. At least, my sort of family.'

He left her then and strode out to his car. She watched him drive away with questions crowding into her mind. Was she disappointed that Daniel was not her half-brother? Or was she for some reason glad he was not?

Eleven

It was going to be one of those days, Andrea knew by the time she had spent a couple of hours in her study with Oliver Oldfield. They were interrupted several times by phone calls, which had to be answered rather than left till later. There had been a muddle somewhere along the line in the planning of services at her two churches, which needed to be sorted in a way that would not cause any hurt feelings at either of them. Worst of all was a letter from the builders who were carrying out repairs to Nyddford Church roof, which informed her of some extra work that needed doing – work they had not estimated for.

'Are you not feeling very well today, Andrea?' Oliver asked when she seemed to lose the thread of what she meant him to say in reply to this last letter.

She sighed. 'I'm just so tired that I'm having trouble thinking straight,' she admitted.

'Perhaps it would be better if we left the rest of the letters then and I came back tomorrow?' he suggested.

Her frown deepened as she answered him. 'I've got a school assembly to do in Nyddford tomorrow morning, followed by a meeting with some councillors that could go on too long. Then it's hospital visiting in Harrogate; but thanks for offering, Oliver. The trouble is that I overslept this morning and didn't have time to get a breath of fresh air to help put my brain into top gear.'

Oliver hesitated for a moment, then decided to voice his concern again. 'You haven't been looking well recently. Some of your friends have noticed it and are worried about you. We know there's a heavy workload for you, with your two churches and so many elderly people to visit at home or in

106

hospital, but we don't want you to wreck your health by working too hard. Perhaps you and Bill could get away for a few days' rest at your cottage?'

Andrea sighed again. 'There's no chance of that at the moment; not until Bill . . .' She broke off then because she did not want to mention Bill's planned US lecture tour yet. Not until they had sorted things out between them. It could mean that Bill would not be available to stand in for Brendon May as organist, for one thing.

'Bill must be worried about you too, I'm sure.'

Oliver's face was full of his concern for her as he said that. So much so that the irritation which had been stirring inside her at what she considered was nothing to do with either Oliver or any other members of her churches died a swift death. She was so lucky to have Oliver, and others like him, to help her. Oliver had told her once how much he wished he had had a daughter of his own to worry about. So: 'Yes, he is at times, but I think he understands that it's always going to be a trying time of year for me when so many people are ill or needing help coping with bereavement.'

'You're very fortunate to have such a husband. Bill's a real blessing for us all, the way he helps out with so many things,' Oliver said then.

He spoke with such sincerity that all of a sudden it came home to Andrea how much *she* was going to miss Bill's help when he was away in America. They hadn't even got to discussing the date for that yet, though. She could only hope it would not be in the very near future; not while she was still feeling so unwell. Determinedly she pushed the thought away from her and suggested to Oliver that they stop for some coffee to help her concentration.

Julie was also having a difficult morning. One of the other nurses had slipped on the ice and broken her wrist, so her duties had to be fitted in somehow until a bank nurse could be found to replace her. So busy was she that for a time the problem of what to do about Matt's pursuit of her retreated into the back of her mind. It did not resurface until she answered a call on her mobile phone and found herself speaking to him.

'Hi! Julie! Are you staying in Nyddford for lunch today?' Matt spoke cheerfully, confidently.

She hesitated, and while she waited for the right words to come, words that would discourage him, he spoke again.

'I thought you probably would be, with the weather being so bloody awful.'

'I haven't decided yet. I might not have time for lunch at all because we're short-staffed today so I've got several extra calls to do.' That should put him off, she thought.

She was wrong about that. 'Which means you could be driving in bad conditions without any food inside you. Not very sensible, Julie,' he reminded her. 'If you tell me what time you'll be able to take a break, I'll buy something at the take-away place and bring it to your cottage for you. How does that sound?'

A take-away meal, sizzling hot and spicy, sounded wonderful to her after her hours of tricky driving from one patient to another. Her stomach churned at the thought of it. After all, she hadn't had time for a proper breakfast and since then nothing more than a cup of lukewarm coffee had passed her lips. She was famished!

'It sounds good, but—' She broke off thinking of the vow she had made so recently to keep her distance from Matt unless there were other people present.

'No buts!' Matt broke in. 'I'm sure my dear step-ma would be pleased to know I'm looking after her precious daughter-in-law.'

That might be so, but Dorothy's son would certainly not be! Did Dave have to know, though? Did he deserve to know, after the way he had spoken to her last night? Besides, she was absolutely starving. She would have to eat something or she might flake out on her round and frighten the life out of one of her nice old dears. That last thought made her mind up for her.

'I won't have long, Matt,' she warned him. 'I'm just leaving Nyddley now so I should be at my cottage in ten or fifteen minutes.'

'What would you like, darling?'

'Anything, as long as it's hot. Bye!' She slipped her phone back on the passenger seat and set her car in gear, ready to tackle the treacherous stretch of road between the hamlet and the market town. All her concentration was needed to negotiate the tight bends; there was no time for second thoughts about the wisdom of sharing another lunch with Matt Harper.

The rugged landscape all about her was breathtakingly beautiful, dressed with a light covering of frozen snow, but Julie dare not take her eyes off the few yards of road immediately in front of her. It was an immense relief to her when she found herself bumping slowly over the ancient cobbled surface of Nyddford High Street and coming to a halt outside her own cottage. Matt's long, racy car was already parked on her drive. Dave would not be pleased if he saw that, she knew, but then Dave would be far too busy with the lambing to come to Nyddford market today . . .

Matt had made himself at home during the short time he had been waiting for her to arrive. He had put plates to warm in the oven and set trays, put the electric kettle to boil and switched on the fire in the living room. As she commented on this, while at the same time slipping off her coat, he laughed and moved towards her.

'Maybe I deserve a kiss, then?'

Instantly she regretted having been talked into this. Before he could get any nearer she backed out towards the hall. 'I need something out of the car,' she muttered, and was out of the house even as the words were leaving her mouth.

'Don't be long. I'll be serving up,' he called after her.

Her heart was racing as she squeezed past his vehicle and opened the door of her own. Then she slammed it again and went back into the house, thrusting her hand into her pocket and bringing out her car keys.

'I'd left these in the lock,' she said breathlessly. 'Very careless of me!' Then: 'How did you get in, Matt? You don't have a key, so . . .'

'I didn't need one. I was prepared to wait in my car until

you arrived. Then I noticed you'd left your keys in the front door, so I let myself in.'

'Oh, God! I don't know what I'm doing today.'

'Probably because you're trying to do far too much. Sit down and eat! I've brought some wine too. You'll feel better when you've had some of that.'

Julie shook her head. 'Not for me, thanks. The roads are tricky enough today without me adding to the danger.'

'Go and sit somewhere comfortable and I'll bring your tray,' he ordered.

So Julie went into her living room and dropped into an armchair close to the warmth sent out by the heat from the electric fire. Matt followed with her lunch.

'It smells gorgeous. Thanks a lot,' she murmured as she raised her fork in a hurry to eat.

'You can thank me properly later,' he teased.

'*Don't* go any further, Matt,' she warned.

Matt grinned when he heard that, his square handsome face lighting up with his mirth. 'There won't be time for me to go any further today, darling, because I've got an appointment with one of our best clients at two, and you're back on duty before then. But there'll be another time, I hope before long,' he ended.

Julie swallowed a forkful of food hastily. 'There'd better not be,' she told him. 'If Dave finds out what you're up to, there'll be hell to pay.'

Matt smiled again. 'He won't find out, will he? Not from you, anyway.'

Julie gulped down more food, then spoke again, this time with anger in her voice. 'If your car is seen on my drive he could hear about it from someone else. Then he'll think I've been deceiving him. I don't want that, Matt, and neither should you!'

'It wouldn't bother me at all. Other people's opinions never do.'

She swallowed again before she hit back. 'It would certainly bother your father, and Dave's mother. Doesn't that worry you, Matt? It should . . .'

'I'll worry about that when it happens; if it happens,' he

told her. 'Now enjoy your meal and stop thinking about anything else.'

That was easier said than done, Julie discovered, because as she ate she was aware all the time of Matt's gaze resting on her. Without taking more than a few swift glances into his face she knew that he was enjoying having persuaded her to spend this time alone with him in spite of her better judgement, and that he was probably already planning when he could next meet her on her own. There would be no next time, though. She would make certain of that. Although she had not quite finished her meal, she got to her feet in one swift movement and headed for the door into the hall, carrying her tray.

'I'll have to go, Matt,' she told him.

'But you haven't finished—'

'I've run out of time.'

'Or are you afraid to stay here with me?'

'Don't be ridiculous!'

'Would you feel less guilty if we met somewhere else; somewhere away from where neither Dave or his mother would be likely to find out?'

Julie did not answer. Already she was dropping her plate into the sink and reaching for the coat she had tossed on to a kitchen stool.

'I'll ask you that question again one day soon,' he called after her as she went to open the door, holding it open so he could leave before her, since she had no intention of allowing him to stay on in her home after she had gone.

'You'll be wasting your time,' she said. 'But thanks a lot for the lunch.'

Before she could move out of his reach he bent his mouth to hers and kissed her long and hard in a way that told her quite plainly what he had not put into words. He smiled as he moved away from her to open the door of his car.

'I'll be seeing you, Julie darling,' he promised.

'Not if I can help it,' Julie vowed silently as she slammed her front door and hurried to where she had left her own car.

* * *

111

'It's time we did some serious talking, Bill.' Andrea's voice warned him that there was to be no escape for him from explaining away the events of yesterday – the events which had put distance between them in a way that he had found alarming.

'Yes, I agree, my love, but are you prepared to listen to me? Or are you going to fob me off with excuses again?'

Andrea frowned. 'Excuses about what?'

'About the fact that you're simply working yourself to a standstill these days.'

'You knew what my workload was like when you married me . . .'

'You seemed well able to cope with it then. Now you are not,' he told her, so decisively that she knew there were arguments ahead of them.

'Just because I'm a bit under the weather, as so many people are at the end of winter . . .' She could not meet his eyes as she said that, adding, 'It wasn't what I wanted to talk about, anyway. You know perfectly well what I want to talk to you about, so don't try to fob me off.'

Bill sighed, and rubbed a hand across one rusty eyebrow. 'Do sit down, while you have the chance, Andrea, and let's talk calmly about this.' He patted the empty space on the sofa where she usually liked to sit curled up beside him, but Andrea remained where she was, standing just inside the big bay window of the living room. He knew then that it was going to be far more difficult than he had imagined.

'Why didn't you tell me what you were planning? What you and Miriam were planning.' Her voice was cool, her eyes were accusing.

'I *was* going to tell you, just as soon as a definite date was set. I hoped that by then you'd be looking, and feeling, much better.'

'What difference would that have made?' she challenged.

He hesitated. 'I thought it might be easier then for you to accept that I needed to go, even though I still wasn't keen to leave you alone here. I'd so much rather have been taking you with me, but I knew you wouldn't even consider it.'

'I didn't get the chance to do that. The way your agent

112

spoke about it on the phone the pair of you had been discussing it for some time, and yet you hadn't breathed a word about it to me. That's why I feel so hurt, Bill, and so angry.'

'Oh, Andrea darling, I'm so sorry!' Bill was on his feet now and crossing the room swiftly to put his arms about her. 'The last thing I wanted was to hurt you. Like I said, I just wanted to wait until you were feeling better before I shared the news with you. Only you haven't got there yet, have you?'

Andrea bit her lip and fought against the tears that were threatening. When she felt she had won the battle, she spoke again, though her voice was unsteady. 'There's nothing wrong with me, it's only . . .' Was this the time to tell Bill what she suspected? He would be so disappointed if she was wrong, and it really was too early for her to be quite sure. Before she could make her mind up he was speaking again.

'That you're feeling a bit run down! So you keep telling me, but you're still working far too hard for someone who's not fully fit. Why don't you make an appointment with the doctor for a check-up, to set *my* mind at rest? Promise you will, darling, please.'

He was drawing her into his arms as he spoke and her head was coming to rest on his shoulder so that he would not see the tears of weakness, although he did just catch the mumble of words that he took to mean she would do as he asked.

'What I'd really like is to take you with me to America so I could share that part of my working life with you,' he murmured. 'I hated leaving you behind last year, even though we were not married then.'

Andrea sighed. 'I hated it too, but I couldn't have gone with you then and I can't go with you this year.'

'Isn't there any way you can manage to come out for part of the time?'

She shook her head. 'There's not enough time now to arrange about people to replace me while I'm away. Those who might have helped will have already planned their work schedules by now. If I had known earlier . . .'

'I didn't know myself until a couple of weeks ago. Miriam hasn't given me much notice,' he told her.

'Surely that wasn't fair of her?'

Andrea had taken an unreasonable dislike to Miriam, Bill guessed, even though they had never met. 'She was a bit concerned that sales of Howard's book were not going quite as well as we hoped, and as you know, that would affect me financially as well as Howard.'

'It would affect Miriam too, wouldn't it, since she's on a percentage of your earnings? That's why she wants you over there again . . .' Andrea pulled away from him as she spoke.

Bill sighed. His problems were not sorted yet. Was it just tiredness that was making Andrea so hard to reason with? She usually found it easy to see both sides of a situation, but that certainly was not the case today. He found himself at a loss now as to how to reason with her. When she found out how soon he was starting this tour it would be so much worse. He ought to tell her right now, yet even as he sought to find the words to do that the phone was interrupting them.

Already Andrea was on her way into the hall to answer what Bill guessed was likely to be more work for her to do. With his spirits fast sinking to zero he turned his attention to his dog, who was reminding him that it was time for fresh air and exercise. After picking up Lucky's lead he made for the back door, stopping on his way to place a hand on Andrea's shoulder as she bent over the phone. He reached to kiss her cheek in the way he always did when he was leaving her, but she did not even seem to be aware of him. All her attention was on the person who was calling her. As he moved away, he caught the concern in her voice.

'I'm so sorry. I'll be with you as soon as I can.'

Bill sighed, and went out into the dusk with his dog. As Lucky stopped to water the grass on the village green, he was able to hear Andrea backing her car down the drive. A moment or so later it passed them and he was left wondering who was needing her time now. Obviously someone whose needs were greater than his. This was something he sometimes found hard to accept – part of the price to be paid for marriage to a woman like Andrea. Yet as he walked on along

Church Lane to where the dark shape of Nyddbeck Church came ever closer, he knew that without her his life would be immeasurably poorer.

Andrea had not only brought a great love into his life, she had also helped him to regain the deep, quiet faith that had been so strong during his happy childhood. She had given him so much; now he must have patience with her as she carried on with her work while so tired and unwell. That was what he had promised here in this building less than a year ago: to support her in sickness and in health so long as they both lived.

'Time for home, Lucky,' he said as a few snowflakes drifted down on them. As they headed back over the bridge towards the manse, he decided to phone the florist in Nyddford and order some flowers for Andrea before the shop closed.

Twelve

Carla debated whether it would be worthwhile leaving the school bus down in Nyddbeck and dropping in to see Paula Price on her way home, just in case Paula had come to a decision yet about giving her the part-time job she was hoping would start during the Easter holiday. Then, as she looked out of the grimy window, the sight of another squally snow shower changed her mind for her and she stayed in her seat until the Nyddford Groaner was chugging towards the bus stop at the top of Abbot's Hill. Because if Paula had gone shopping she would be wasting her time, and she would be left to tackle the long uphill walk from Nyddbeck to her home in bad weather. That could make her very late getting there, which would not matter much if her dad was still busy with the lambing but would bring awkward questions if he happened to be in the house, as she was supposed to be helping out with the ironing tonight. She was barging her way forward from the back of the bus ready to hop off the minute it stopped when it began to slide sideways on one of the hairpin bends.

Alarm surged sickeningly through her as memories rushed back to her of the time she and Josh had been on the same school bus when it had swerved to avoid some sheep on the road and hit a wall. Josh had been injured then and she had been badly shocked. This time the driver managed to avoid disaster, and was rewarded with a cheer from the students of Nyddford High School who were still on board. There was no cheering from Carla, who discovered to her deep embarrassment that, as she had struggled to keep her balance, her overloaded backpack had come to rest on the shoulder of one of the sixth-formers.

116

'Sorry!' she gasped.

'Are you OK?' he asked. 'Not hurt or anything, I mean?'

Carla gulped down the remains of her fright and tried to answer him coolly. 'I think so. It was just that I thought we were going to hit the wall.'

'So did I!' There was relief in his voice. 'The driver was real cool to miss it.' He was frowning now as he remembered something. 'You were on the bus when it came to grief last year, weren't you?'

Carla nodded. She recognized him now. He was Simon Price, the brainbox. Fancy him remembering her. Of course, she had been almost hysterical with fear when she had realized that Josh had been injured. Simon Price was probably thinking how stupid she had been.

'Take care then.' He was hoisting her bag back into place and steadying her as she tried to hurry to the front of the vehicle, where she was now the only person left to get off.

'Thanks!' she said. 'Thanks a lot!'

Then the driver was smiling at her, also remembering her, she guessed. 'Take your time as you jump down, love; there's a lot of ice about,' he warned.

So she made her way down the steps with more care than she normally used, then waited to give him a wave as he moved carefully on to his next stop. To her surprise, she saw that Simon Price was also giving her a farewell wave. This sight brought a wave of guilty colour to her cheeks, because she knew now that she had misjudged Simon Price; he was not a stuck-up brainbox at all. He was a nice guy, wasn't he? A really nice guy. She was glad now that she had changed her plan to visit Paula that day, because if she hadn't, she would not have met Simon. Not *really* met him. Seeing him around on the school bus or in the school corridors was not the same as him actually speaking to her, or showing concern for her, was it?

This thought stayed with her as she trudged along the lane to Abbot's Fold, and kept coming back to her when she was standing with her back to the Aga, ironing school shirts for herself and Jack. So entranced with it was she that she went on to do some of Julie's stuff as well.

*   *   *

117

After Daniel Price's visit Paula found herself unable to make up her mind which of the changes and improvements that had already been started at the Mill House ought to be carried on and which postponed. Her mind was in a whirl now that Daniel had voiced his idea that, rather than the place be sold so he could claim his inheritance, she should carry on and open it at Easter, as she and her father had planned. How would it work if she did that? It would *have* to work if she decided to accept his offer. The only alternative would be for her to turn down his suggestion and put the Mill House up for sale at once. If she did that, what would she do with the rest of her life? Coming here with her father in the first place had wrecked her plans to share her future with Gareth. All she had left now was her work. Ought that work to be here, where she had already expended so much time and energy and hope? Or would it be better to cut her losses and sell the place? If she did that, she would probably be able to buy a home for herself, but she would have to go back to working for someone else, which would be the death of her ambition. One thing was certain: she would need to make her mind up quickly, because already her first advertisements placed in the local paper and the tourist centre at Nyddford were bringing enquiries from would-be customers. If the weather continued to improve, there would probably be more still.

Suddenly the thought of improving weather made her long for fresh air and exercise. She might as well take advantage of the weak sunshine to walk into the heart of the village and post some of the letters she had written in answer to the ones that had arrived from friends of hers or her dad who had not been able to come to the funeral. Before she could change her mind she was grabbing her fleece from behind the back door, slipping it on and changing into her boots. She could not wait to get out there.

Checking that the windows were closed and the back door locked, she was hurrying through the hall when the sound of a vehicle turning into the drive brought her to a standstill. Annoyance stirred inside her. Now that she had made her mind up to go she wanted to be out there before the sun changed its mind again. It couldn't be one of the workmen, because none of them were due to come today. Could it be Daniel Price come to talk to her again? That thought set her heart hammering. If it was, this could well be make-your-mind-up time for her, and she had not yet done that. At least she was dressed for outdoors, so if the caller was someone she didn't want to talk to, she could make an excuse about having to catch the late-afternoon post in the village. Yes, that's what she would do.

Someone was slamming a car door close to the house. Footsteps were crunching on the gravel. She waited for the doorbell to send out its chime, at the same time zipping up her fleece. Then she took a deep breath and made herself walk very slowly down the length of the hall. It was foolish of her to be apprehensive just because she knew herself to be alone here in this big house, which was set well back from the road and surrounded by a wooded garden. If she was going to stay, she would have to get used to this. Or get a big dog to protect her! The bell pealed again as this last thought brought a smile to her face. Then she heard him say her name.

'Paula! Open up!'

Her heart gave a great leap as she recognized the voice. It was a voice she had not expected to hear again. Especially not here. At first when she and her dad had moved into the Mill House she had been constantly hoping to hear that voice; constantly longing to hear that voice on the phone every time she went to answer it. Until eventually hope had died and resignation had taken its place. Now amazement held her feet rooted to the black-and-white-tiled floor of the hall. Was it *really* Gareth, or was her imagination playing tricks on her?

'Come on, Paula! It's cold out here.'

Yes, it was Gareth. There was no mistaking the slight trace of Welsh accent. Or the impatience in his voice. She moved quickly and held open the door.

'What are you doing here?' The words tumbled out of her mouth so fast that she knew they would not sound like words of welcome. Though surely Gareth would not be expecting her to welcome him warmly after the way they had parted? Their words then had been full of bitterness on his part and disbelieving sadness on hers.

'I came to see you, of course. Why else would I come?' His voice was equally brisk. 'Aren't you going to ask me in? It's been a long drive and it's freezing out here.'

He shivered as she stepped aside so he could enter the house, closing the door behind him with some force.

'I'll soon have some hot coffee ready for you,' she said over her shoulder as she moved away towards the kitchen.

Before she reached the place on the worktop where the electric kettle stood he was close behind her. Too close, so that her hands were clumsy as she lifted the kettle to take to the tap. When she had half-filled it and activated the switch, she kept her back to him while she reached into one of the cupboards to find ground coffee and a cafetière. From there she moved to the fridge to get milk and set it on a tray with two mugs and a spoon. All the time as she did these things she was aware of a strange sensation. It was not one of joy, as she might have expected. It was something quite different. Something she could not define. Something that kept her silent while she waited for him to speak.

'How are you then, Paula?' he said very quietly.

'Oh, not too bad, thanks.' Her own voice was low. Her attention was given to the coffee-making rather than to him.

'I was sorry to hear about your dad. It must have been a shock for you.'

'Yes. Very much so.' The aroma of the coffee was filling the kitchen now.

'Sorry I couldn't get here in time for the funeral.'

She spun round when she heard that. 'I didn't expect you to come. I didn't even know you'd heard about it.'

'The man who bought the garden centre from your father came into the restaurant for a meal a couple of days ago. He remembered meeting me with you there once. He told me he'd been up here for the funeral service that day.'

'He was a friend of Dad's. That's how he came to buy the place.' It seemed quite difficult, this conversation with Gareth. More like talking to a stranger. Yet once, not that long ago, it had been so easy to talk to him. It had been easy to share everything with him then: her working life and her home life in the flat they had moved into above the restaurant.

'So, what are you going to do now, Paula?'

There was a moment of silence before she spoke. Then: 'I'm going to pour some coffee for you. We'll take it into the sitting room; there's an open fire in there.'

It wasn't what he had meant, Paula knew, but for some reason she found herself playing for time, unwilling to step across the gulf Gareth had created when he had told her that, if she stayed on with her father instead of moving back in with him, there would be no shared future for them. So she picked up the tray and carried it into the hall, and from there into the sitting room, where she placed it on a low table close to the fire before going to sit in one of the armchairs. She saw him hesitate on the point of taking a seat on the sofa, then drop into a big chair opposite her own. A moment later she handed him a mug of coffee, sweetened but without milk. Then she added milk but no sugar to her own, clasping her hands round the mug as though feeling the cold herself.

'How are you managing here on your own? It's quite a big place, isn't it?'

'Yes, but we're not open for business yet, as you've probably already noticed.'

'How *will* you manage when you do open? It won't be easy, will it?'

'It wouldn't have been easy if Dad had still been here, because there were still things he could not have done. But he *did* love it here. That's the only comfort I can find, just knowing how happy he was to be back, even though it didn't last very long before he became ill.'

Gareth had stopped drinking his coffee and was frowning. 'What do you mean by back? Had he lived here before?'

'Yes. Though not in this village. He grew up in a hamlet quite near – before he left to work in the garden at a stately home in the south.' It was as if she told this to someone she had just met: a stranger rather than the man she had loved. Perhaps the man she *still* loved. It was hard to know with this distance between them. Was he still the same Gareth, the same fiery-tempered, quick-witted, handsome man she had been sharing a kitchen with a little over a year ago? The same tender lover she had shared a bed with until her dad's accident had brought such drastic changes into her life?

'What will you do now?' he asked as he set down his empty mug after a silence that had lasted for too long.

'I don't know. I'm not sure,' she answered honestly.

'Don't you think it might be best to sell this place now? Before you have to spend any more money on it.'

'I don't know. I just don't know,' she said again.

'It's so out-of-the-way here. Almost out of the village, and not a very big village at that.'

She took a deep breath and spoke calmly, watching his face as she did so. 'We did quite a lot of research into the area before we made our mind up which property to buy. Then we decided that this one was the best bet because of it being on the way to the abbey, where there are no places providing refreshments. Also because it was large enough for us to provide guest accommodation, with several en-suite rooms. The area is very popular with tourists from Europe and America as well as from other parts of Britain. I've already had some enquiries in reply to my first adverts, which only appeared last week in the tourist centre and the *Yorkshire Post*.'

'You'll need help to cope with the cleaning and serving, won't you? Where will that come from in such a small village?'

'I've already had an offer of help from a local farmer's daughter. I'm sure I'll get more when I advertise for staff.'

'What will you do for a social life? I don't suppose you know anyone here yet. You haven't been here long enough, have you?'

He was taking too much for granted, Paula thought. Surely he hadn't come all this way just to point out to her that her life here was not going to be easy? She had already discovered that for herself, even before her father had died.

'There are some relatives of Dad's living quite near. Some of them came to the funeral service and back here afterwards. One of them has been to see me since then,' she told him. She paused, wondering whether to tell him why Daniel Price had been to see her. Then she dismissed the idea as being nothing to do with him. Because if she told him that Daniel Price had inherited half of her father's property and money, he would feel sorry for her. He would be more than likely to think she had thrown away a much better life with him than she was now going to have on her own here. Her pride revolted at the thought of that.

'You must miss what you had in London,' he insisted. 'Friends of your own age, and places to go for nights out. The buzz of the restaurant on busy nights . . .'

'My life had changed before I came here,' she reminded him.

'It could change again, for the better, if you come back to me.' He was on his feet now, full of urgency as words poured out of him without pause. 'You could put this place into an agency; let them deal with all the hassle while you settle in again at the flat until we find that place of our own that we planned on having. So, how about it, Paula?'

She was unable to believe what she was hearing – didn't want to believe that he could just abandon her at a time when she had needed his support and help and then just turn up here, certain that she would be willing to forget, or forgive him for not being willing to wait a few months longer for her. Just long enough for her dad to be able to manage on his own. Of course he would not know the anguish he had caused her, the nights she had spent longing for him to understand. She got to her feet and gave him a long, searching stare.

'Is that why you came, Gareth? To try and put the clock back to where we were a couple of years ago?' she found herself asking him quietly.

'Why not? You're free now to do as you like, and with the means at your disposal to help you without being overloaded with loans or mortgage repayments.'

As he spoke he crossed the room to take her shoulders in his hands. Her body tensed then, warning him of her resistance. Anger was beginning to stir inside her at his assumption that he only had to ask and she would do as he wished.

123

'Aren't you taking too much for granted, Gareth?'

'What do you mean?'

'Assuming that I still feel the same about you as I once did?'

He shrugged that off. 'There's no one else, or you'd have told me by now, wouldn't you?'

Now it was her turn to shrug *him* off by twisting her shoulders out of his hold and putting distance between them. 'That doesn't have to mean that I feel the same about you as I did a year or so ago. A lot has happened since then.'

He smiled. 'Of course, darling. You've had a traumatic time, and I haven't really given you the chance to come to terms with it yet as I ought to have done. It must have been quite a shock for you when I just turned up without any warning.'

'Not as much of a shock as I got when you told me our engagement was off if I stayed on any longer with Dad!'

He shrugged again. 'Oh, I admit I lost my rag with you a bit,' he began. 'But I thought by now you'd have seen things from my point of view. That's why I came. I've got three days off, so I don't have to go back tonight,' he told her before she could think of what to say next. 'How do you feel about me staying with you while we talk things over?'

That was something she had not expected him to ask. Though maybe she ought to have done. What would he be expecting if he did stay over? Did she want him to do that? Suddenly, and quite definitely, she knew that she did not.

'I'd rather you didn't.'

'Why on earth not?' His dark eyes and frowning black brows showed his displeasure.

'Because it's not convenient for me to have you here.'

'Why not? You've got plenty of room.'

That was as far as he got before the phone broke in. Paula left him and moved into the hall to answer it. The caller, she discovered, was Daniel Price.

'I was wondering whether you'd come to a decision yet about what I suggested we might do. Or if you'd rather I came to talk to you about it again?' he said.

Relief engulfed her. Here was a reason for her to put

Gareth off staying the night at the Mill House. 'Yes, I'd like you to do that,' she told Daniel hurriedly. 'Could you come tonight, please?'

There was more relief when he said he could. 'It would have to be fairly late, when I've had time to finish here and have a meal.'

'You could always have your meal here – I mean, if it would help,' she found herself suggesting, and being glad when he accepted.

'I'll see you about seven thirty then, Daniel,' she said.

She was smiling when she faced Gareth again. 'I'll have to ask you to go now,' she said crisply. 'Someone – a friend – is coming for a meal. You'll find a good pub if you drive to Nyddford, four miles away. The Golden Fleece in the market place. You can't miss it. They do accommodation too.'

As she finished speaking she was already on her way to the front door to show him out.

Thirteen

Andrea could feel the now familiar burden of exhaustion descending on her again as she left the District Hospital in Harrogate and walked to where she had left her car in the overcrowded hospital park. While she had been visiting the two patients who were members of her flock, listening to their concerns and sharing a prayer with them, she had been able to forget her tiredness; but now she was all too aware of it again. Yet it was so good to feel sunshine touching her face and dry ground beneath her feet after the icy winds and late snow showers that had recently made her job even more difficult than usual.

Today there was good news to take back with her to Nyddbeck because the people she had been to see were both recovering so well from surgery that they hoped to be back in their homes soon. As she dropped into the driving seat, she found herself wondering whether she would have her baby in this hospital towards the end of the year, or whether her extreme weariness and other symptoms were being caused by something more worrying. There seemed to be no hiding the way she was feeling from Bill, however hard she tried, and the concern he had expressed for her so often recently had somehow managed to put them seriously at odds with one another. She must not risk having this second chance of happiness go wrong, as her first marriage had done. Suddenly she could not wait to get home to Nyddbeck to put things right with Bill.

Yet even as she prepared to move off from the car park she knew putting things right with him was not going to be easy, that she would need to ask for help from where her help always came. So she bent her head over the steering

126

wheel and offered up a silent prayer asking for forgiveness for her angry words to Bill, and the courage to cope with life on her own while he was away in America. Then she began to thread her way with some impatience through the heavy traffic surrounding the hospital.

There was a bonus for her today on that stop-and-start journey because it was crocus time in Harrogate, which meant that every time she came to a stop and looked out of her window she was able to glimpse the green acres of The Stray alive with the colour brought by the thousands of purple and gold flowers spreading out beneath the trees. It really *was* spring at last. There were more of these to be seen on the roadside verges as she left the town behind and drove through a few sunlit villages home to Nyddbeck.

When she reached the manse she found more flowers awaiting her. Jonquils and freesia blooms in a basket trimmed with satin ribbons were spilling their fragrance about the warmth of the hall. She bent over them and inhaled their fragrance, at the same time reading the words on the small card tucked into the heart of them: '*Sorry, darling, please forgive me. I love you.*'

Bill was already there, waiting to draw her into his arms. There were tears in her eyes as she gave herself up to his long embrace. He wiped them away gently with one paint-smeared hand.

'I'm sorry too. I don't know what got into me . . .' she began.

He sighed. 'Of course I ought to have told you at once when I knew I'd have to go on this trip. I realize that now, but you were so tired that I thought it best to leave it till you were feeling better. Only you are not, are you?'

The words hovered inside her, waiting to be shared with him – words that might have reassured him, and herself; but before she could voice them Lucky was hurling himself at her with such an enthusiastic welcome that she was forced to steady herself against the hall table while she recovered sufficiently to be able to stroke his silky auburn head. It was then that she noticed the red signal coming from the answer-phone. It might be urgent, and she had been out for hours, so she must give it priority. She pushed Lucky firmly away so she could do so.

'Come here, my lad,' Bill said ruefully. 'We'll have to wait our turn. We might as well make some tea.'

So once again an opportunity was lost as he went to do that while Andrea involved herself in someone else's problems.

At Abbot's Fold Farm Julie also came home from her work to find a phone message awaiting her. Carla, clearing away a pile of freshly ironed garments, turned from placing them in the airing cupboard to tell her about it. 'Gran rang and asked if you'd get in touch with her when you had time.'

'Right, I'll do it later when I've had something to eat. Did you remember to take the shepherd's pie out of the freezer like I asked, Carla?'

'Oh no! I forgot, but I did do the ironing,' Carla answered guiltily.

'So I see! Thanks. It'll have to be fish and chips then.'

'Good!' That was Jack, supposedly starting his homework but in reality watching the portable TV set. Until he remembered something. 'Will there be enough for Wandering Joe, Julie?'

Julie frowned. 'I didn't know he was still here. I thought he'd gone back to his home since the weather improved.'

'He was going to, but his leg was so bad he couldn't walk properly,' Jack told her. 'I had to walk Archie for him.'

'You'd better not tell Dad, our Jack,' Carla warned. She was feeling really cool because when she had got on the school bus today Simon Price had made room for her to sit beside him. In the upbeat mood she was in she didn't want to see Jack get a ticking-off.

'He doesn't do any harm,' Jack defended his old friend.

'Archie might if he gets among our new lambs.'

Carla's words brought a problem to Julie that she didn't want to be bothered with just now, but while Dave was so tired after all the work involved with the lambing, even though that was over now, his temper would be on a short fuse, so she must do what she could to avoid provoking him. It was not that he meant to be unkind to the old soldier who had taken shelter in their disused barn, it was simply concern for the safety of his flock that was always uppermost in Dave's mind. A dog on the loose could do so much damage. He had told her what had happened a few years ago when people renting Jacob's Cottage at this time of the year had allowed their dog out alone. A couple of lambs had been killed before the dog was recaptured. So she must go and have a word with Joe right now before Dave came in for his meal.

'I'll go and see how Joe is before I start cooking,' she told Jack.

'I'll come with you.' Jack was already on his feet.

'I thought you had homework to do?' Julie asked on her way to the back door.

'I'll finish it later, I promise!' He hadn't even started it yet, but Julie didn't have to know that.

When they reached the old barn, after first being warned off by Archie, who was very protective of his master, Julie knew that Jack had been right to be worried about his old friend. Joe's knee was alarmingly swollen and discoloured and he was breathing with obvious difficulty. He was hardly able to answer the questions Julie put to him. It did not take her long to decide that if he was not admitted to hospital very soon, he probably would not survive. Jack, now making a fuss of the cross-breed black dog called Archie, would be upset, she knew.

'Why don't you take Archie out for a few minutes while you're here, Jack love?' she said.

The old man nodded when he heard that but did not speak. Julie waited till the boy and the dog were out of the way before she spoke again.

'You need to go to hospital, Joe, or you won't be able to go out walking with Archie any more. You do you realize that, don't you?'

He nodded again, then tried to speak. 'What about . . .?'

'We'll look after Archie for you,' she promised. 'I must go and ring the doctor now.'

By the time Jack had finished his homework, and his fish and chips, Wandering Joe was in Nyddford Cottage Hospital and Archie was fastened up in the barn, fretting for his master. Dave had accepted this, after some straight talking from Julie, but had done some plain speaking of his own to his son.

'That dog is your responsibility while the old chap's in hospital, Jack. He is to be kept fastened up. You know what can happen to dogs that attack sheep, so make sure he doesn't get loose!'

'Yes, Dad. I'll look after him. Can I take him some food now?'

'Yes. We can't have him going hungry, can we?'

Julie gave her husband a smile of thanks, but Dave failed to see it as he gave a sigh of weariness and dropped his lean frame on to the old sofa, where the *Yorkshire Post* he had lacked the time to read earlier in the day awaited him.

In Nyddford another boy, a much younger boy, was also worrying about a dog – a large black dog who had dashed hopefully to the front door when Tim Lindsay prepared to return to his flat so he could mark books ready for his work tomorrow at Nyddford High School after spending a couple of hours with Jane and his children.

'Sorry, Darcy. You can't go with me this time,' Tim had said as he reached down to stroke the floppy ears. 'You must stay here and look after Elliot and Kerry, and Jane, for me.'

His dad had closed the door then and left him and his mum, and Darcy, behind while he went back to where he lived on his own. Kerry was already in bed upstairs and Elliot knew it would be his turn to be sent up there next. Darcy had gone to lie across the mat behind the door with his head on his paws and a sad look in his enormous brown eyes.

'Darcy's unhappy, Mum, isn't he?' Elliot said.

'No, of course not. He's just a bit cross because he can't go for another walk,' Jane told him.

'He's not!' Elliot argued. 'He misses Dad when he's not here because he used to be with him all the time. Except when Dad was at school.'

What could Jane say in answer to that? She could not tell

Elliot that Darcy might be missing his owner, the woman teacher who had died a few months ago. The woman who had stolen Tim's love while she had not been there to fight for it . . .

'I'll make your bedtime drink, and you can have a biscuit if you like,' she said.

Elliot did not answer but went to lie down beside his dog. She left him to it while she made his drink. He was still there when she came back.

'Come and get your drink now, Elliot. You're already late for bed,' she reminded him.

'I'm five now, so . . .' His voice broke on that and Jane saw then that he had been crying. She set down the mug with the spaceman on it and gathered him into her arms.

Elliot wasn't one for crying. 'Where does it hurt?' she asked urgently.

'Here!' As the word came out on a sob he pointed to his throat.

'A sore throat?' she guessed.

He shook his head and pointed to his chest.

'A sore chest?'

He struggled to find words but shook his head. Then: 'I hurt there when Daddy goes away.'

'Oh, Elliot darling, I'm so sorry.' Her own eyes burned as she fought back tears. What damage had they done to their children, she and Tim, since their marriage had fallen apart? Guilt racked her.

'You're not sorry! Not really sorry, are you?' Elliot's angry words were interspersed with suppressed sobs, which made Jane feel even worse.

'Oh, I am, Elliot. I really am,' she hastened to assure him.

'If you were really sorry you'd let Daddy live here all the time like Darcy does now he's come back from the vet hospital.'

What could she say in answer to that? She could not tell such a small child of her fear that if she let Tim come back to live with them, he might get involved again with someone else and she would have to go through all the pain and humiliation once more.

Instead she spoke words that were meaningless to him. 'It's not as easy as that, Elliot darling. One day you'll understand. When you're a bit older.'

'I'm older now, I'm five!' he declared.

His words stayed with her for long after she had tucked him into bed. He had been five last week. So she and Tim had made a birthday party for him with a few of his school friends coming to tea. It had been a hectic affair that had gone on rather longer than planned. Then, after Elliot and Kerry had gone to bed tired out with excitement, she and Tim had set about the clearing up before Tim gave Darcy his final walk of the day. He and the dog had come back wet through, having been caught in a sudden downpour. She had felt her heart lurch with love for Tim when he had insisted on drying the dog first before saying he'd better be leaving now.

'I'll make you some coffee while you dry yourself off a bit. Give me your fleece and I'll put it into the tumble-dryer,' she had found herself saying.

The hot coffee had long been drunk, the tumble-dryer had switched itself off, and still they were there on the sofa side by side. Somehow the distance between them had disappeared and her head was on Tim's shoulder. Somehow his arms were easing her gently closer and closer. Then all at once the tiredness was gone and there was only the hunger left; hunger for something they had not shared for so long. She was unable to resist that feeling – did not even try to resist it. Neither of them attempted to, and it had been wonderful. So much so that she had not wanted it to end. When it was over, when he had stopped telling her how much he loved her and how much he had missed her, he had given her one long, final kiss and got to his feet to look down at her. There was an expression on his face then that had bewildered her.

'I'm going now,' he had said. 'Then you can get some rest. You must be tired.'

She was, but it was the sort of tired feeling she had missed so much during the last year. 'Why?' she had asked. 'Don't you want to stay?'

He'd shaken his head before he answered. 'Not like this, when we've both allowed ourselves to do something we were not prepared for.'

'Why not? I thought it was something you wanted, to come back for good?' she had whispered.

'I do, but only when you can trust me again. Not because we've just made love and you might already be regretting it.'

'Oh, I never thought about that!' She had thought of nothing except the joy of being with him.

He had kissed her again, tenderly, before starting to get dressed. 'You've told me several times that you can't trust me now. Ask me to come back when you can,' had been his final words.

All the time Tim had been with them this evening she had been thinking of what she would say when Elliot was in bed. Then it turned out that Tim had to go back to his flat early and do his preparation for tomorrow at Nyddford High. So Elliot had gone to bed unhappy, and she had realized that she had been longing for Tim to ask if he could stay. Not just for long enough to make love to her again but for good. Only he hadn't done that, had he? She did not regret what had happened on the night of Elliot's birthday, but perhaps by now Tim did . . .

Fourteen

Paula felt a mixture of emotions struggling inside her as she heard Gareth's car moving away from the Mill House at a speed which probably reflected his anger with her. He must have arrived on her doorstep expecting her to shower him with gratitude because he had come to tell her what she ought to do now that she did not have her father to talk things over with. His whole attitude had expressed his certainty that she would be only too pleased to take up again with him where they had left off in London. Only she was not the same woman now as she had been then. Too much had happened to her since then.

The change had begun with the accident to her father. At first Gareth had been sympathetic and supportive when she had needed to spend much of the time she had been used to spending with *him* with her dad. Then gradually, as the problem with Harry Price's sight had worsened and she had become too worried about him to feel able to go back to living in the flat above the restaurant with Gareth, his resentment had led to so much tension between them that she had known it would explode one day into an almighty row.

When it had erupted, that row and the ultimatum Gareth had delivered at the end of it – that she must choose between going back to live with him or staying with her dad – had left her devastated. By then the sale of her father's garden centre and the house that went with it had gone through, so she had asked her father to move right away from where things had gone so wrong for them both. Harry had been feeling so guilty about the breaking-off of her engagement that he felt it only fair to her to do that. Their plans to develop the Mill House into a new home and a business which would support them both had given them something challenging to do with their lives: something for her dad that would help him come to terms with his sight impairment; something for her that would help her to build a life that did not include Gareth.

She had not known then that only half of the home and business which had brought them to North Yorkshire in search of a new life would belong to her after her father's death; that the rest of his estate would be going to this man called Daniel Price. Why had he not told her that? This was something that had troubled her mind often during the last few days and haunted her troubled nights. The only way she had been able to come to terms with it was by deciding that, since he was only fifty-five and apparently in good health apart from the problem with his sight, her dad would not have been expecting to die so soon.

A new thought entered her mind as the sound of Gareth's car zooming away faded and the only sound left was that of the rustling branches out in the garden. Why hadn't she told Gareth that she was no longer in a position to do exactly as she liked with the Mill House? There was something vaguely troubling about having to ask herself that question. Because it was such an unwelcome thought she pushed it away and gave all her attention to considering what she would give Daniel Price to eat when he arrived. Since she had no idea of his likes or dislikes in the food line, this was challenging enough to occupy her as she made her way to the utility room, where there were freezers to help her choose.

Inside these were many prepared meals to choose from which she had made when the worst of the winter weather had kept her indoors. Also frozen fruit from the garden, which would make easy desserts. She had been looking forward to catering for the first paying guests in the days when she was spending those hours in the kitchen. Would they ever be used for that purpose? she found herself wondering as she made crumble topping for the Bramley apples.

By the time Daniel Price was pushing the front-door bell there was soup simmering on the hob, chicken and potatoes roasting in the oven along with a medley of colourful vegetables, and the kitchen table was set for two. She had considered using the dining room but come to the conclusion that it might appear too formal for someone who, after all, was a family member. It still seemed strange to her that there were other members of the Price family left besides herself. After her mother had left, Paula had believed that she had no one else except her father. It had taken her a long time to come to terms with the fact that her mother had simply walked away from her home, her husband and her child ten years ago and, apart from birthday or Christmas cards posted from Australia, had never had any other contact with her. A new thought came to startle her as she went to open the door to her guest. Had her mother known about Daniel Price? Was that why she had left them?

'How are you, Paula?' Daniel's smile was warm as he stepped over the threshold into the hall. The hand he held out to her was firm and strong as he gripped her own slender fingers for a long moment..

'I'm fine, thanks,' Paula told him as she waited for him to slip off his leather jacket and place it on the hall chair.

'I'm glad to hear that. You've had a bad time since you came here: first losing your dad, then finding about his will. It must have been a shock to you.'

'Yes. I certainly wasn't expecting it.' She turned away from him as she spoke. His next words caused her to turn around quickly.

'Neither was I, I can assure you.'

Her eyes widened. 'You're telling me you had no idea of what was to happen?'

'No. Absolutely not.'

'But I don't understand . . .'

'Neither do I. Until the letter came from your father's solicitor, Harry was, as far as I was concerned, just an older member of the Price family who had left Yorkshire long before I was born to go and work somewhere down in the south. He was not often spoken of in our house. I was staggered when I heard about the will.'

'So you didn't know him?'

136

He shook his head. 'No. I never even met him.'

Paula felt bewilderment stir again. 'But you said it was because my dad should have married your mother. So I thought . . .' She did not go on to say what she had imagined: that Daniel Price might be her half-brother.

'I can guess what you thought,' Daniel broke in. 'That can't be the explanation though, because my mother told me I was adopted when she and Dad found they couldn't have any children in the usual way.'

'So why . . .'

'I don't know. When I asked Dad – the dad who had adopted me – what it was all about – why this money was to come to me – he said the only reason he could think of was because before he left Yorkshire to go to his new job your father was engaged to my mother, but then she had changed her mind and married him instead. That was not very much to go on, as far as I was concerned. So I feel badly about the way my good fortune must have affected you, Paula. I can only say I'm very sorry and I'll do my best to make things up to you if I can.'

Paula shrugged her shoulders. 'At least it's good news for you and your family. It has to be. I mean, the way things have been going in recent years for farmers, you must have been going through tough times?'

Daniel looked uncomfortable as he answered. 'We probably would have been if we were still farming in the traditional way. But we're not. When we saw the way things were going a few years ago in the farming industry, we decided to diversify by opening a farm shop. It went so well, especially during the tourist season, that we then went into the business of ice cream – the luxury versions – and iced desserts. My mother handled that side of it and was very good at it.'

At the mention of desserts Paula remembered what was still in the oven: a large apple crumble. It was time she rescued it. 'You must be ready for some food by now if you've been working all day. Everything will be ready to eat now, so come and sit down. It's in the kitchen; I hope you don't mind?'

'Of course not. Everyone eats in their kitchen round here, you'll find.'

Paula managed a laugh. 'I haven't been here long enough yet to discover that. I'm still a stranger here.'

Now Daniel laughed. 'We don't call them that. They're tourists if they're here on holiday or incomers if they've come to stay. So you'll be an incomer, Paula.'

She had been indicating where he should sit at the big pine table, in the centre of which stood a pot of blue hyacinths that her father had planted last autumn. For a long moment she was silent, considering what he had said. Then: 'I think that will depend on you, Daniel. Whether or not I can stay, I mean.'

'We'll discuss it later, if you don't mind. I'm absolutely ravenous.'

His appetite and his so obvious enjoyment of the food she served were proof of that, but Paula found herself struggling to eat anything because she was too wound up about what she was likely to hear from him when the eating time was over and the talking time began. It was fine for Daniel to talk about wanting to help her stay on in the Mill House, and he seemed to mean it; but how was it going to be possible?

Spring really had come to North Yorkshire now that wintry March had blown itself out in gales that brought work on the roof of Nyddford Church to a standstill and lifted many loose slates or tiles from farmhouses and cottages. April had arrived with sunshine and a few scattered showers to shimmer on the thousands of daffodils blooming in golden splendour on the grass verges either side of the lanes which led from one Dales village to another. Flowering cherry trees cast pink and white petals over gardens scented with wall-flowers in the light breezes that spoke now of the warmer summer days not too far away.

Abbot's Moor, in winter so bleak and forbidding, was beginning to show a faint green haze on the sturdy tufts of heather, which would later in the year become a carpet of deep purple. Young lambs frolicked alongside their mothers and pheasants strutted across the moorland roads as though aware that for the time being they were safe from the guns of those who would later come to Yorkshire for the shooting. Andrea, strolling beside Bill, who held Lucky safely on his lead, remarked on this.

'Aren't the pheasants handsome, Bill? They seem to know they're safe at this time of the year from the shooting parties. I don't think I could bear to eat them.'

Right now, especially in the early mornings, she was having difficulty in eating anything. It was hard to conceal this from Bill, but she was determined to do so until he was back from America. Time enough then to give him her wonderful news, or he would be worrying about her all the while he was away. He wouldn't *be* away for long this time – only for a couple of weeks. There was just one more day left for her to keep her precious secret, because at this time tomorrow he would be on his way to America.

'You're not eating much of anything at the moment, are you, my love?' Bill's voice broke into her thoughts.

'Only because I've not quite recovered from that horrible bug I picked up the week before last. By the time you get back I'll be eating like a horse and putting on weight,' she told him with a laugh.

'I hope I can trust you to do that.' Bill put an arm about her as he spoke. 'You know I don't like leaving you when you're not well.'

'We've been through all that before,' she said with a touch of impatience in her voice, 'and it didn't get us anywhere. We both have our work to do, and you having to go on this lecture tour is part of yours.'

'I wish it wasn't, right now. I don't want to leave you. I never want to leave you ever again. Remember that when I'm away, won't you, darling?'

'Of course. You're only going for two weeks, not for good.' As she said it, a shiver of apprehension shook her.

Bill, feeling the tremor, held her tightly and bent to kiss her lips long and hard. 'I'm not going for any longer than that this time, whatever Miriam may have in mind. I can promise you that. The tour will be hard work, with a lot of travelling involved. So I want us to have a few days up in

Andrea's Cottage as soon as possible after I get back. I hope you'll be able to arrange that while I'm away. Now, let's get back home, because the wind is freshening. I think the weather could be on the turn again.'

'There's some paperwork waiting to be done when we get back, and hymns to choose for next Sunday,' she reminded him. There would be no Bill to keep her company on her way to church next Sunday. No Bill to stand beside her at the door when the people were leaving at the end of the service. No Bill to share the bits of local news with over coffee. Andrea felt desolate, and also vulnerable in her present condition, but she was determined not to let him become aware of that. Her duty was to be here where she was needed while Bill was away. She knew she must endure their separation with courage, and face up to it with faith.

When Julie consulted her diary to check on what was due to happen in the next few days, she knew she must fit in time to see Andrea as soon as possible, because Andrea would be missing Bill terribly now that he was away on his lecture tour. Especially as she still seemed to be so unwell. Julie had promised Bill that she'd keep an eye on Andrea for him while he was away. He had been so worried about her and there had been little Julie could say to him to re-assure him. There was, however, a suspicion in Julie's mind about what the reason for Andrea's continuing extreme fatigue could be – though she had not felt that she could share her suspicion with Bill.

If Andrea had known for certain that she was pregnant, she would surely have told Bill, Julie reasoned. Yet he did not seem to be aware of this. So was she wrong in her assumption? There was no doubt in her mind that *if* her friend was indeed expecting a baby, she would be overjoyed. The loss of her little boy, the child of her first marriage, at only three years old was something that still brought pain to Andrea, Julie knew. So she was certain to be thrilled by the prospect of another child. How would Bill feel about it, though? Would he be equally pleased? Julie was not so sure about that.

Since he and Andrea had only been married for a few months, Bill might well have different feelings on the subject. He might not be ready yet to share Andrea with a child who would be sure to need a huge proportion of her time – that precious time which he was already compelled to share with her demanding work. He might not even *want* to be a father, since he had almost reached the age of forty when he had married Andrea. It was different when people married young, as Dave and Jill had done. Sometimes then the children came too early, as Carla had to them.

Dave was also almost forty, and plainly *he* did not even want to contemplate fatherhood again, which was something Julie was becoming increasingly unhappy about, because her own biological clock would soon be winding down. The longing for a child of her own had not yet subsided, as she had imagined it might well do once she married Dave Bramley and became step-mum to his children. Of course she loved his children. She had loved them both from the time they had been born to her friend Jill, but they were growing up fast. Jack at twelve was still an affectionate lad. Carla at sixteen was a problem at times but was beginning to grow out of that and would all too soon be leaving home to go to nursing college.

Julie knew she would miss Carla when she went to college, but she had been hoping that by then there would be another child at Abbot's Fold Farm – a baby born to *her*. Only every time she began to broach the subject with Dave he came up with yet another excuse about why they ought to wait a while longer. But less than a year ago, when he had believed she was about to marry Matt Harper, he had given her the impression that he understood her wish for a child and would agree to it. Of course she could cheat and make certain she became pregnant, but it was not in her nature to be any less than honest with either family members or strangers.

If Andrea *was* in early pregnancy, it was going to be so hard watching her putting on weight and blooming with happiness. Julie was honest enough to know that she would be envious and resentful that the same thing was not happening to *her*. She might even begin to wonder whether she had made a mistake in marrying Dave Bramley when, as Matt Harper's wife, there would have been no obstacle to her having a couple of babies before it was too late. This was a dangerous thought to be dwelling on, she realized even as it lingered in her mind. The thing to do was to forget it and ring Andrea at once to see if they could arrange a meeting soon. Matt Harper, and what might have been, were best kept as far away from her mind as possible. A moment or so later she was talking to Andrea and promising to call in at the manse on her way home from the health centre that evening.

Jack Bramley was taking his responsibilities as custodian of Wandering Joe's dog while the old man was in hospital very seriously. Every morning before he went to school he would take food to the old hayshed and when Archie had gobbled it up at speed he'd clip on the lead and give the cross-bred collie a good fast walk. When he came home late in the afternoon, he went through the same routine. He knew that the rough-coated black-and-white dog was pining for Joe because all the time they were walking Archie was looking about him as though for a sight of his master. At the end of each walk, when he was tied up again with a long strong rope until Jack's next visit, he would let go an enormous sigh of disappointment and flop down with his head on his paws and his eyes fixed on the door, watching for his master's return. Jack hated leaving him like that, but he knew there was nothing else he could do. His own marvellous dog Brack and his dad's collie Tyke were used to one another and would tolerate each other, but neither of them would have accepted this stranger, so they must be kept apart at all costs.

'Sorry, Archie! Got to go now. See you in the morning!' Jack bent to give Archie a final pat on the head before leaving him, then unclipped the lead before fastening the rope on to the dog's sturdy leather collar.

Of course, he'd got it wrong! He knew that as soon as Archie made a dash for freedom. He was supposed to attach the rope *first* before unclipping the lead. A swift glance over his shoulder told him that he really was in trouble, because he hadn't quite closed the door and Archie had only needed to give it one hard shove with his powerful nose to open it wide enough for him to squeeze his way through and gain his freedom. Panic gripped Jack when he realized what the outcome of this could be. He must catch Archie before Archie reached any of the sheep. He simply *must* do that.

'Archie! Archie! Come back!' His words were muffled by the thick mist that had begun to rise as an unexpectedly warm day brought moisture out of the ground. The mist was making it impossible for him to catch sight of the escaping collie, so he had to make a guess at which way Archie had gone. The barking of Brack and Tyke seemed to indicate that he might have raced past where they were fastened up close to the house and gone beyond there to the moor. Jack knew he needed to get there fast and recapture Archie, because there were young lambs up on the moor.

His heart pounded uncomfortably as he ran on, upwards and upwards to where no lights were visible, no sounds were to be heard, and the only thing to be seen was fog. Ghostly, menacing fog. Archie would soon be lost in it, and so might he. But he *must* get Wandering Joe's dog back. He simply *must*. There would be an almighty row if he didn't, because the lambs could be hurt. He felt sick at the thought of what a rogue dog might do to them. It gave him the extra energy he needed to dash on to where the huge oddly shaped rocks loomed close to him. He knew some of these could be dangerously slippery when damp with fog, but all he cared about was his dad's lambs. In the distance he heard a faint bark. He turned too quickly, and felt himself falling . . .

Fifteen

Paula returned to her preparations for the opening of the Mill House for business the morning after Daniel had shared a meal with her, even though she still felt unsure how things would work out for her. After listening to everything Daniel had said to her during the couple of hours he had stayed on after they had finished eating, she had been left with the feeling that if she went along with what he was suggesting, there might still be a worthwhile future here for her. Daniel had pointed out to her that if she turned down his offer and put the place up for sale at once, she would have wasted all the time and hard work she, and her father, had put into it. He also reminded her that when she got a buyer she would have to start looking for a job and for somewhere else to live.

It was the thought of having to do that, instead of taking the risk of staying on and finding out whether Daniel's idea would work, that she found so difficult to contemplate. Because after the months she had already spent living in Nyddbeck she knew that she certainly would hate having to leave it. So, with her mind made up to give it a go, she was busy applying emulsion in a delicate apricot shade to one of the top-floor bedrooms. A local plumber was installing an en-suite shower, basin and loo in another spacious room on the same landing which she intended to keep for her own use. When he had finished, she would move in there with her paint and start work on the walls, she decided.

While she was working with her paint roller, her portable radio was belting out spells of frenetic pop music in between local news items, keeping her informed that there was plenty happening in this peaceful area of North Yorkshire – plenty

144

of things she could get involved with if she chose, and if she had enough spare time. Because of the combined sounds of the radio in this room and the plumber using power tools in the one next to it the ringing of the doorbell from two floors below did not at first break into her consciousness. In fact it took two hearty shouts from the electrician working in the large ground-floor room that her dad had used to alert her to this.

'Front-door bell's ringing, miss! Can't you here it? Or do you want me to send him away?'

The bell sounded out again as she switched off the radio. 'Damn!' she muttered. 'Just when I want to get this finished before I go into Nyddford this afternoon.' She would have to answer the door in case it was anything important, but she would make sure that whoever it was did not linger too long. Wiping her paint-smeared hands down the sides of her oldest pair of jeans, she ran down the stairs and flung open the door without even stopping to take a look at herself in the hall mirror to see whether or not she was presentable.

'Hi, Paula!' Gareth greeted her with a grin. 'I suppose it *is* you underneath the paint? That colour does quite suit you, darling.'

His casual dropping of the endearment, plus the reference to the state of her face, brought a swift flush to her cheeks – followed by words she knew were not guaranteed to make him feel welcome. 'What are you doing here? I thought you'd have been back in London by now.'

Her words left him unruffled, she guessed as she stared resentfully at this man who had once been the centre of her world. His reply was cool and his eyes were amused. 'I told you I'd come to see *you*, Paula, not this out-in-the-sticks village. Or this monstrous old property you've saddled yourself with. Or even the Golden Fleece at Nyddford, excellent as it is.'

Paula deliberately misunderstood him. 'So you decided to stay there and go back this morning? I suppose you just called to say goodbye to me on your way?'

Now he was frowning, and at the same time moving closer to her. 'No, you're wrong about that. I didn't have time to

145

talk to you properly last night before you were chasing me off to the Golden Fleece. So I've come to talk to you now. Aren't you going to ask me in?'

Paula stood her ground, just inside the front porch. 'As you can see, Gareth, I'm busy.'

The frown disappeared and he was laughing at her again. 'I can see you're not very skilled with a paint brush, darling. Certainly not anything like as good as you are with cake-icing tools. If you were to ask me in, I could give you a hand with the painting, if you're absolutely determined to go on with it instead of getting yourself cleaned up and coming out to lunch somewhere with me.'

For a long moment as she stared at him Paula was strongly tempted to do just that: to pack up the painting and take a shower, put on some decent clothes and let Gareth take her to a place where someone else would cook for her and someone else would clear away the dishes afterwards and wash them. It was some time since she had enjoyed such a luxury. Even longer since she had shared the treat with a young and handsome man. Gareth was certainly in that category, but Gareth had come here to tell her she had made a mistake and ought to sell the Mill House and go back to *him*.

What a nerve he had to do that after the way he had refused to listen to her when she had pleaded with him to be patient and wait until her dad could cope on his own before she went back to live with him. She had felt badly let down when Gareth had ended their engagement. So much so that she had been glad to put distance between them by coming here to make a new life with her dad. Now, even though the sight of him standing before her with his dark eyes sparkling and his long, thin face alight with self-confidence was already stirring into life the physical attraction he held for her, she was determined to keep him at a distance. Pride would not allow her to do otherwise.

'I need to finish my painting before I go anywhere,' she replied crisply. 'Because I'm determined to open this place by the end of April, in time for the May bank holiday. There are a lot of special events arranged for that weekend around here to bring tourists in, and I want to get my share of the business then.'

'So you're not even considering what I wanted you to do?' The scowl was marring his face again as he spoke.

Paula raised her eyebrows. 'What was that, Gareth?' She was smiling faintly as she waited for his answer, enjoying keeping him guessing.

He was wearing the soft suede jacket she had bought him for his birthday last year, she noticed then, and his hair gleamed blue-black in the slightly shorter style she had persuaded him to try. He was certainly pulling out all the stops in his attempt to get her back. Except that he had not so far attempted to embrace her . . .

'I thought I made myself plain last night, but maybe I didn't.' He took a deep breath before going on. 'I told you I thought you were wasting your time and money on this place and would do better to sell it, now that you don't have to do as your father wanted.'

'It wasn't just what Dad wanted. It was what *I* wanted too. What I *still* want to do.' She was not going to be talked out of her decision, now that it was made. It would be interesting to see what Gareth's reaction was to that. She did not have long to wait.

'I can't believe what I'm hearing! That you're actually prepared to go on wasting your time on this outdated dump when you could be back in London with me in the sort of life you are used to. The money you could raise on this property while prices in the area are so high is all you'd need to put down as deposit on the sort of really decent place that we always planned on having one day. You ought to think again about that, Paula. Think fast while I'm still up here. I've already put my own flat up for sale.'

As she listened to him, Paula felt the physical longings his presence had ignited inside her fade, to be replaced by a slow wave of disillusionment. Was this why Gareth had really come to see her last night, because having heard of her father's death and knowing that she was an only child, he had been certain she would come into a good inheritance? – the sort of inheritance that would be shared with him if

147

she went back to him? It was not comfortable having that thought about Gareth sliding into her mind. Not fair to him, perhaps, to harbour such a suspicion. But once there it would not seem to go away.

One part of her wanted to believe that it was not true – that Gareth had come here because he still loved her and wanted to share his life with her. The other part, the more worldly part, had to know the truth. Maybe the way to find the truth was to invite him in and give him more time to talk? – give *her* more time to discover for herself whether all that was left between them now was what had drawn her to him when they had first met, a powerful physical attraction? Acting on impulse, she opened the door wider and invited him in.

Once inside he stared about him, noting the spaciousness of the hall and the beauty of the broad oak staircase, the handsome carved doors, which led into high-ceilinged reception rooms.

'I can see why your father was tempted by the place. All this space and light, and of course the huge garden he could make use of to extend the building if he needed to,' he admitted as he followed her into the kitchen, where she went to switch on the kettle to make coffee for the workmen.

'It wasn't just Dad's idea,' she corrected him. 'I fell for the place too. That's why I want to stay here.'

'You can't be serious! Not now you don't *have* to stay here.'

'I am,' she insisted as she reached into a wall cupboard for mugs.

He sighed. 'Why can't I make you see sense, Paula? There's no point in you staying on here now. You know there isn't!'

She was busy spooning coffee into the mugs. 'I think there is.' She did not turn round until the coffee was made.

'Only because you haven't had enough time yet since your father died to realize that you've got no one here who cares about you.'

'You're quite wrong about that. There is someone here who cares enough to want me to make a success of the Mill House.' He didn't have to know that the 'someone' was the

148

man who was to share her inheritance, did he? Or that she had to make a success of her business venture so that there *was* something to share.

'You've met someone else, already! It didn't take you long, did it?'

Now she was angry. 'It didn't take *you* long to end our engagement when I needed you most, did it, Gareth?'

With that she carried away the two steaming mugs to the grateful workmen. One of them, the middle-aged electrician, expressed his concern for her. 'Is everything all right, Miss Price? I mean, he's not being a nuisance to you, is he? Because if he is I'll soon see him off for you.'

Paula was touched by his thoughtfulness. 'Thanks, but I don't think you'll need to do that, Mr Middleton. I can deal with Gareth! We used to be engaged, and he's convinced that I've made a mistake in coming here to live. I'm making it clear to him that I haven't – that I love it here and will make a success of this place.'

The huge man who towered above her gave her a grin that transformed his massive face into a very pleasing sight before he answered her. 'Then that's what you'll do if you work hard. I had some folk telling me I was making a mistake to set up on my own a few years ago, but they were wrong. Your dad was another one that believed in working for himself, wasn't he? He was telling me about his garden centre not long before he became ill. I'm sure he wouldn't want you to pack in because he's not here to help you. He would want you to go on and give it a go, wouldn't he?'

Paula blinked away a couple of tears, then nodded. 'Yes, of course. I'll make sure I do that.'

Gareth was getting impatient, she found when she went back into the kitchen. Pacing about on the tiled floor, he had been picking out areas where he thought she ought to have planned things differently. Plainly he was not in the best of moods at being kept waiting.

'If we are going out to lunch, isn't it time you were getting ready, Paula? We can talk while we are eating instead of hanging about here.'

Paula made up her mind. 'There's really nothing more to

be said, Gareth. If my selling this place is a condition of my coming back to you – being engaged to you again – then I won't be doing it.'

In two strides he was reaching to pull her into his arms, holding her tightly – so tightly that she was left in no doubt of what his feelings were for her. 'You know how I feel about you, darling,' he said when the first long kiss had ended and another was about to begin. 'How I've always felt about you since the day we met. So don't send me away again. Let's go out and eat then come back here. I only booked in at the Golden Fleece for last night, and I'm not due back at work until tomorrow night. So let's get back together and start enjoying life again.' As he finished speaking, he was already kissing her with the sort of urgency that she found hard to resist. What he was offering her was so tempting. It would be so easy to allow herself to give way to it after the long months spent existing without his love. Only now there was a condition attached to Gareth's love; a condition she was not willing to accept. Ought she to tell him that if she did as he asked and put the Mill House up for sale only half of the proceeds would belong to her? Would he still want her when he was made aware of that? Suddenly she had to know.

'It's not quite as straightforward as you might be thinking,' she said as she pulled herself out of his arms and moved a yard or so away from him. 'You see there is someone else involved.'

'Not now,' he broke in impatiently. 'Whatever you promised your dad won't apply now that he's dead, will it?'

Paula took a deep breath. 'What I'm trying to tell you is that someone else owns half of this place; that it was left to him in Dad's will.'

'Someone else?' Gareth broke in. 'Do you mean what I think you mean? I thought you didn't have any other relatives?'

Paula hesitated. 'Dad didn't keep in touch with any of them, but the person who is to share everything with me is also called Price. He has suggested that I go ahead with everything Dad and I planned to do rather than putting the place up for sale. I've decided to do that, because I want to go on living here.'

Gareth's frown deepened. 'I don't like the sound of it. How do you know you can trust him?'

'Because we'll be having a proper legal agreement and I'll be running the Mill House while he continues to run his own successful business a few miles away.'

'Can't you contest the will? There could be a mistake, if you've never heard of this man until now . . .'

'There's no mistake. I contacted the solicitor as soon as I read his copy of the will. He assured me it was quite genuine, and told me that Daniel Price is part of my father's brother's family. I knew that he had some family here even though he never kept in touch with them.'

There was a silence so long that a faint hope rose in her that Gareth was going to offer to come and join her here. Or at least offer to come up and spend time with her whenever he was free. No such offer was made. Instead he shrugged his shoulders and prepared to depart.

'Then I'm wasting my time, because London's the place for me. I thought it would be the place for you too once you didn't have your dad to consider. Obviously I was wrong. So I'll be on my way. If you change your mind, you know where I am.'

With that he turned away from her and strode swiftly through the hall and out to his car. Paula stayed where she was, feeling an ache in her throat and a smarting behind her eyes. A moment later she heard the engine roar into life and take him speeding away from her.

It had been later than she had intended before Julie was able to leave the farmhouse and drive down to Nyddbeck to see Andrea. Dave hadn't wanted her to go – he'd wanted them to have an early night; but the promise she had made to Bill was heavy on her mind, so as soon as she had washed up after the evening meal shared with the family she had left Carla doing homework in her room while Jack went to give old Joe's dog his supper and a short walk. Since the fog was still lying thick over the moor she had been about to warn the boy not to go too far, but then had second thoughts because Jack had lived here all his life and he would not welcome her fussing over him now he was twelve and at high school.

It was not the best of nights to be leaving Abbot's Fold behind and driving down Abbot's Hill to Nyddbeck. Even in low gear the hairpin bends seemed to bring the drystone walls alarmingly close at times. When she reached the foot of the long incline and came to the outskirts of the village, the fog was so dense over the fields on either side of the beck that the lights from the larger properties set back on the slope behind Beck Lane were scarcely discernible. She drove carefully over the bridge that spanned the beck and came to a halt on the road outside the manse with a feeling of relief at having got there safely. Even though the gates were open she would not park on the drive in case Andrea needed to go out in a hurry. There were times, she knew, when Andrea's presence could be as much needed in a family emergency as her own was during a medical crisis. Though she hoped that wouldn't be the case tonight. An hour or so of girl talk over coffee would be good for them both.

'Oh Julie, I'm so glad you're here,' Andrea greeted her. 'We've both been so busy that I can't remember the last time we got together for a good natter.'

'I think it was probably at the drama group a couple of weeks ago, and we didn't have that much time then,' Julie remembered.

'I've got some coffee in the machine,' Andrea told her as she led the way into the kitchen, with Lucky getting in the way as he came to give Julie a boisterous welcome.

'Mm! It smells gorgeous,' Julie told her as she dropped into a chair beside the table.

'There are some gorgeous biscuits to go with it too, made by Miss Poppleton, who thinks I'm not eating properly and looking a bit peaky.' Andrea ended that sentence with a chuckle, but she had left the opening Julie needed to voice her own worry about her friend.

'Miss Poppleton's right. You *are* looking quite unwell. I'm not surprised that Bill is so worried about you. Is it *really*

152

just end-of-winter tiredness? Or are you hiding some more serious symptoms from us, Andrea?' Would Andrea's answer be a truthful one, or would she continue to insist that there was nothing wrong with her?

Andrea set a mug of coffee in front of Julie and one at her own place. She waited till she was seated, with Lucky's head on her lap, before she spoke. 'There *are* no serious symptoms, Julie. Only the tiredness, and I think a lot of other people will be feeling the same after coping with the worst months of the year. I thought, when Jane came to help me today, that she was not so well, but she insisted she was fine.'

'Is she still on her own? Or is her husband back with her now?' Julie sipped her coffee while she waited for what she hoped was going to be good news.

Andrea smiled, glad to find the conversation moving away from the subject of her own health. 'If Tim *isn't* back with her, I think he soon will be. She's unable, I think, to trust him yet, but she's certainly still very much in love with him.'

'It must be so hard to regain that sort of trust once it's been destroyed. So difficult to behave as if it hadn't happened. I don't know whether I could forgive and forget if it happened to me.'

Andrea put down her mug slowly and carefully, then put a question Julie had not been ready for. 'Do you think your Dave could, Julie?'

Surprise kept Julie silent for a moment. Then words came in a rush. 'Not Dave. He's very jealous where I'm concerned. Too much so.'

'Then you'll need to watch your step with Matt Harper,' Andrea said quietly.

Julie frowned. 'What do you mean, Andrea?' She waited uneasily.

'I know you love Dave, but I don't think Matt has given up on you yet. When you were both at Dorothy and Ben's party the other week his eyes were hardly ever away from you, and then I saw him leaving your cottage one lunch time. It was market day. If Dave had seen him . . .'

'Dave was busy with the lambing . . .'

'Sorry, Julie, I shouldn't have spoken about it.'

Julie sighed. 'I've told him he's wasting his time and that Dave won't like it, but he won't seem to take any notice.'

Now Andrea sighed. 'I see so many troubled marriages, and my own first one went wrong; but I don't want to see yours joining all the rest.'

Julie smiled as she replied. 'I'll make sure it doesn't.'

They went on then to talk of other things: that Bill would be back from America in less than a week; that the work on Nyddford Church roof was almost finished; that Andrea had been to visit the girl who was going to open a restaurant soon at the Mill House, and that Carla was hoping to do part-time work there during the summer. At nine thirty Julie said she must be leaving, as Dave had said he wanted to have an early night.

'I think I'll have an early night too because I've a school assembly to do in the morning at Nyddford High so it means an early start tomorrow,' Andrea told her as she put on her fleece and headed for the door. 'Thanks for coming. Give my love to Dave and the children.'

'I will! Goodnight and God bless!'

With these words Julie headed back for Abbot's Fold, but when she got there she found there was to be no early bedtime for her and Dave that night.

Sixteen

Dave came slowly out of the sleep he had drifted into while reading his *Yorkshire Post* and found himself with a crick in his neck. Reluctantly he straightened his body into an upright position and began to rub the painful place on his neck while at the same time starting to yawn. The crumpled newspaper lay on the floor where it had landed when it had slid off his chest a couple of hours ago. As he bent to pick it up, he gave an involuntary groan. His lower back was still protesting painfully, as it had been doing all day.

Of course, he ought to have been in bed long before now. He would have been if Julie had been at home instead of down in Nyddbeck with Andrea. He hadn't wanted her to go tonight. What he had wanted was to enjoy taking her to bed and making love to her. He had been looking forward to doing that once the long haul of the lambing season was behind him and the last of the orphaned lambs, which had needed frequent bottle-feeding, were out with the rest of the sheep. Only Julie seemed to have other ideas.

She said she had promised Bill that she would keep an eye on Andrea for him while he was away in America. Though why Bill should have thought that necessary Dave could not imagine, when Andrea was such a confident and busy woman. Even when Julie had explained that Bill was worried because Andrea was looking so tired and ill, Dave still did not understand. At this time of the year everyone was feeling the strain of coping with all the perils of a North Yorkshire winter, he had hastened to point out.

'Everyone doesn't have Andrea's workload to cope with!' Julie had said sharply, which had warned him that she was

155

not in the mood to see his point of view, and probably not in the mood to want an early night with him.

So he had opened his paper again and gone back to reading the latest farming news while Julie had driven off in the worsening fog leaving *him* to worry about her. She had not remembered to come to the sofa and kiss him before going, he recalled with simmering resentment. His thoughts moved on, to consider the increasing tension that never seemed far away from their relationship these days.

Was it just the stress being put on the Nyddford Health Centre staff by the flu and other winter bugs, plus the driving through snow, ice and fog that were making Julie so snappy these days? Or was it something else, something she was not telling him about? Certainly she was often on a short fuse as far as he was concerned. So much so that he was having to be careful what he said to her. Or forgot to say!

Where was Julie? Surely she should be back by now? What sort of mood would she be in when she did come back? He'd better have the kettle on the boil ready for bedtime drinks before he went out to check on the farm buildings; then they could go straight to bed when she arrived. Obviously both Jack and Carla had already gone upstairs while he had been asleep, because he could hear the sound of Carla's radio coming from her room. Jack was probably asleep by now, as there was nothing to be heard from his room next door to hers.

Moments later the kettle was checked, his old working jacket was slipped on over his pullover and he was opening the back door. God, what a foul night it was out there! Fog so dense that he was unable to see any more than a few feet in front of him, and the temperature so low that there could be patches of black ice on the roads. He felt a stirring of anxiety about Julie having to drive home from Nyddbeck, then banished it by telling himself that she was an experienced and competent driver. All the same, he found himself staring in the direction of the farm lane, hoping that he would catch sight of her headlights piercing the fog.

Closing the back door behind him, he felt for the heavy torch that he kept in the pocket of this old jacket and switched it on as soon as he was outside the range of the carriage lamp that gave illumination to the back porch. As he did so, a metallic rustle came from where Tyke occupied the kennel nearest the house, then a welcoming murmur as his dog recognized the familiar sound of his master approaching. He bent to unhook the chain so that Tyke could keep him company on this last task of the day, knowing that the collie would stay close to him without being restrained. A melancholy whine came from the next-door kennel, where Jack's dog Brack was housed – at least when she was not being sneaked into the house by Jack, as she frequently was in spite of Dave's disapproval.

Dave bent to give the young dog a pat and a word or two. 'Settle down then, lass. Jack's in bed now, where I ought to be,' he added wryly. Brack gave his hand a loving lick in return.

Brack was a grand little bitch, he thought as he moved on to start checking the buildings, even though when Jack had chosen her he had thought the choice to be a wrong one. He wouldn't be at all surprised if she helped Jack to win the Young Shepherd award at Nyddford Show this year. The lad would be so proud, and so would he. He was right about the black ice, he soon discovered when he moved across the ancient cobbles of the yard towards the building furthest away from the house. Twice before he reached the old hayshed he felt his feet losing their grip and only managed to right himself with difficulty.

As he drew nearer to the place, his thoughts turned to Wandering Joe, who had spent several nights there before being taken into the cottage hospital at Nyddford after Julie had found him very ill with a chest infection. Dave knew he had been a bloody fool to make a fuss about having the old soldier and his dog taking shelter in one of his buildings while on their way to visit one of Joe's old comrades who lived in Nyddford. This had seriously upset Julie and made life uncomfortable for him because she had not been able to understand that it was not Joe's presence that worried him but that of Joe's dog. In the end Jack had promised to look after the dog until his master was fit to return to his home

157

on the other side of Nyddford Abbey. Which had made both Julie and Jack happy.

On that last thought uneasiness hit him. By now Joe's dog ought to have become aware of his approach with Tyke, and be noisily warning the other dog off. Yet no such thing was happening. Dave came to a stop, ordered Tyke to 'Sit down!' and waited. Not for long, though, because now he was just able to see through the swirling clouds of mist that the door of the building was wide open. His frown deepened; he swung the torch beam about as he strode inside and knew then that there was no noise coming from the dog because there *was* no dog to cause it.

A huge gust of anger swept through him as he stared down at the length of rope that had kept Joe's dog at a distance from the Abbot's Fold sheep. Jack must have been careless enough to allow the dog to escape, in spite of the warnings Dave had issued. He would have something to say to Jack about that in the morning – something Jack would not like! In the meantime he would need to check on the sheep now to make certain that Joe's dog had not harmed them. He could not afford to pay extra vet's bills for the treatment of damaged animals. Nor could he afford to have any more dead sheep. The two he had lost at lambing were bad news enough!

So he made his way back over the slippery cobbles, past the farmhouse and the barn and the old implement shed that housed the tractor. Again, before he reached the gate that led into the field nearest the house, he almost lost his balance and cursed so loudly that Tyke whimpered in sympathy. Then on through the gate with Tyke staying close to his heel, sweeping the beam of the powerful torch this way and that as the animals moved uneasily away to huddle out of reach of the dog. All the time as he moved the ache in his back intensified, at times bringing a film of sweat to his brow in spite of the frosty air, but no amount of pain would ever allow Dave to put his animals at risk. They were not just his living, and that of his family; they were his reason for living – something passed on to him from his father and his grand-father and from generations of Dales farmers before them.

No matter how low the profits, however foul the weather, or the degree of discomfort to be endured, the animals came first.

Gradually, after far too long spent enduring the increasing ache in his back and the perilous conditions underfoot, he was at last satisfied that there were no injured or dead animals in this field or the next. There were sheep up on part of the moor that could also have been at risk, but common sense persuaded him that with visibility as low as it was right now it would be a waste of time to continue his search there. Particularly as there was neither sight nor sound of Joe's dog. So he would leave the searching of Abbot's Moor until morning brought daylight, and hope that by then the fog and ice would be gone.

When the gates were closed behind him again and he was back to negotiating the icy yard, a feeling of total exhaustion overcame him. He felt bloody awful, he admitted to himself as the faint beam of murky light from the back-porch lantern pierced the gloom ahead. It was agony now to place one solid-booted foot in front of the other, but at least Julie's car was back in place close to the house. She would probably be in bed now, and soon he would be too. He led Tyke back to his kennel, gave his head a brief stroke and told Brack to be quiet, then dragged himself wearily the last few yards to his home. It was after midnight when he locked the back door and there was silence all about him. Moisture clung to his face and his garments where the fog had settled on him. Exhaustion conquered him when he reached the warmth of the farmhouse kitchen. All he could do then was unfasten the buttons on his worn leather jacket and let it drop to the floor as he collapsed on to the saggy old sofa with a groan and closed his eyes.

Paula closed her book, switched off her lamp and prepared to go to bed. It was after midnight and she ought to have been upstairs long before now, but she had been unable to concentrate on reading or watching television because her mind had been too occupied with the unexpected visit of Gareth. She had not been prepared for the physical reaction which had swept over her when they were standing close to each other in the kitchen, and she was honest enough to admit to herself that if she had invited him into the house when he arrived the evening before, she might not have sent him away to spend the night at the Golden Fleece – because she had loved Gareth so much, for so long, and had been filled with an aching longing for him so often during some of her lonely, sleepless nights spent in this house.

Why had she sent him away then when she found him waiting on her doorstep yesterday? Her first reaction at the sight of him had not been one of gladness. Rather it had been one of deep shock, followed by resentment, because he had been the last person she had expected to find there. In the early days after she and her father had first moved into the Mill House she had constantly been on the watch for a letter from him. Each time the phone had rung she had hoped it would be Gareth calling, until gradually, imperceptibly, she had come to accept that this was not going to happen. It had been impossible, then, to ever believe that she might one day get used to living without him, but she had managed to do that.

It had been quite easy to send him away last night, when anger and pride had been fuelling her feeling for him. So much so that the phone call from Daniel had been just what she needed in the way of an excuse to send him away. Yet sending him away this morning had really hurt. What else could she have done, though, when he had made it so plain to her that London was where he intended to stay? If he had loved her still, he would surely have been willing to give life here in Yorkshire a try. Or was she at fault for not being ready to sell up here and join him in doing what they had planned to do before her father's accident – buy a restaurant in or close to London?

Suddenly Paula was impatient with herself for dwelling on that possibility. If she had not liked living in this house, which Gareth had poured such scorn on, or come to love the scenery that surrounded it, she would have been eager to do what *he* wanted rather than what she herself wanted. Did that mean that she no longer loved Gareth as much as she

160

once had done? Maybe it did. So she would push Gareth out of her mind, make herself a milky drink and head for bed.

While she was waiting for the mug of hot chocolate to heat up in the microwave she crossed to the window and moved the curtain aside so she could stare out to see whether the fog that had crept over the garden earlier in the day had cleared. It had not; it was much worse now. She shivered at the sight of it, and at the same time caught the sound of something moving against the back door, which was only a yard or so away from where she was standing. Dropping the curtain again quickly, her heartbeats quickening, she listened intently. There it was again, that faint noise which she could not yet identify. Was it someone trying to get in? The thought brought a small frisson of fear to her.

There it was again, a soft thud this time. Was it the sound of a foot moving out there in the shelter of the back porch? If so, who was it? Surely not Gareth; he would have been back in London for hours. Was it a tramp seeking shelter from the icy dampness? Were there still tramps about these days? That was something she did not know. What she did know was that she was alone here and out of range of the other village dwellings, so she was not going to open the door. Could it be an animal out there? A stray sheep which had wandered down from the moor? She had to know before she took her hot drink and went up to bed.

'Who's there?' she called, feeling rather foolish, since an animal would not be able to answer.

She was wrong about that, she discovered when a further thud sounded, followed by a whine. So it was a dog! Whose dog, and what was it doing out there at this time of night? Even as she wondered, she heard another mournful-sounding whine. It was all she needed. Not stopping to wonder whether there would be anyone with the dog, she pulled back the bolt and opened the door, allowing light to flood out on to the dark shape of a bedraggled creature whose white-muzzled face wore an expression of misery that touched her heart.

'Oh, you poor thing!' she murmured as she bent to lay a hand on the moisture-laden curly black fur.

This brought another distressed sound in reply.

161

'You'd better come in and get dry,' she murmured as she stepped back so the animal could slink slowly out of the porch and into the kitchen, where it stood on the doormat and looked about the room as though in search of something, or someone.

'Perhaps you'd like a drink first?' Paula decided, moving to the sink, then to a cupboard to find a bowl, which she filled with water and laid before the dog, who obediently began to lap at the contents.

'What about a biscuit? I bet you like biscuits, don't you?' This brought a bark in response as Paula brought the biscuit box and took off the lid.

'Oh, you are hungry!' One biscuit rapidly consumed led to another, and another, and brought a small wag from the wet black tail.

'Where've you come from, I wonder?' was Paula's next question. 'I haven't seen you anywhere around here before.' Would the dog allow her to take a closer look at his collar now that she had shown she was a friend? was her next thought as she put out a tentative hand. The dog reached out to lick this, so she stroked its head while turning the leather collar round in search of an identity disc. Yes, there was one. It was worn smooth by age but the lettering was still readable: 'Archie. 3 Abbey Cottages. Nyddham was all the information it revealed.

'So that's where you've come from,' Paula said. 'You're a good few miles from home here, aren't you, Archie?'

At the sound of his name Archie wagged his tail again. Looking down at him now that he was relaxing and beginning to lick his paws clean, she decided that, though he appeared quite at home now, someone, somewhere, must be missing him because, bedraggled as he was, there was something very appealing about him. She must look in the phone book and see if she could make contact with his owner. As she moved across the room on her way to the hall and the nearest phone, the dog got up and followed her.

'It's all right, Archie. I'm not going to abandon you,' she told him gently as he flopped down on the carpet while she began to scan the directory. That was when it came home to

162

her that she did not have a name to look up, unless of course Archie was the surname of the dog's owner. She would try that.

It was, she found, a waste of time. No such name was listed. So now what?

'I suppose we'd better try the police station next, Archie,' she told him as she bent again to give his head a caress. 'See if anyone's reported you missing.'

This also proved to be a waste of time. No one had. 'What shall I do with him?' she asked the voice on the other end of the line, having already given her own name and address.

'You can either bring him to the station in the morning, or keep him with you until the owner contacts us. If they ever do,' came the answer.

Paula had not expected to hear that. 'Do you mean that they might not?'

'They don't always,' said the male voice. 'Sometimes they just take the animal they no longer want out in their car and dump it well away from home.'

'Oh no!' Paula could not hide her distress.

The police spokesman sighed. 'Sorry to disillusion you, miss, but that's the way it happens.'

'But he's such a nice dog,' she protested.

'A lot of them are. I'm afraid it's the owners who are not so nice. Does he have an identity disc on him?'

'Yes, but there's only *his* name on it. No owner's name or phone number for me to contact. Just an address in Nyddham, which I'd never be able to find in such foggy weather. So what should I do with him? I can't just turn him out into the fog again.'

A brief silence, then: 'You could get in touch with one of the animal-rescue organizations like the RSPCA or the Canine Defence people in the morning. Or you could keep him yourself.'

'What if the owner turns up?'

'We'll have your name and address so his owner can collect him from either you or the rescue kennels.'

Paula made her mind up. 'I'll keep him, for the time being anyway. Goodnight, and thanks for your help.'

It hadn't been any help, though, had it? Because here was this poor bewildered-looking dog still lying at her feet while someone, somewhere, might be fretting for him. Or maybe, just maybe, some heartless person had turned Archie loose in the fog, hoping never to see him again.

'So, where are you going to sleep tonight, Archie?' she said as tiredness began to overcome her. 'We'll see if we can find your master in the morning, if the fog has gone by then.'

Archie wagged his tail then got up to follow her back into the kitchen. Where could she put him to spend the night? It had to be somewhere safe, but somewhere he could not chew carpets or rugs or drape his damp body over upholstered furniture as her own schooldays pet dog had done until he grew out of it. Somewhere like the utility room. That would do until she found out how house-trained Archie was. A search in the linen cupboard brought a faded travel rug for him to lie on. She rubbed him dry with an old towel and folded the rug before placing it close to a radiator. Then she gave him his orders. 'Lie down and go to sleep, Archie,' she told him as she pointed to his makeshift bed.

Archie flopped down on it with a reproachful look and placed his head on his paws.

'Good boy! See you in the morning,' Paula said as she headed for the stairs and her own bed.

As she did so, she already knew that she would be sorry if his owner turned up to claim him. It would be good to share the Mill House with Archie . . .

Seventeen

Julie stirred in her sleep, waking from a dream in which she was running away from something that she could no longer tolerate. It was something which was stifling her, threatening her, yet which she was helpless to defeat. A cold sweat of fear dampened her brow and made her hands feel clammy. Her heart was racing as she came to half-consciousness and reached out to touch the bedside lamp, which sent out a glow as she made contact with it. She must have overslept! An uneasy glance at her alarm clock steadied her. No, she had certainly not slept in. It was only two forty and not eight ten as she had imagined. With a sigh of relief she turned on her side and prepared to resume her slumber.

That was not so easy to do, though, because the bed felt cold. She turned her body the other way, seeking the warmth of Dave's muscular back to curl round. Only Dave's back wasn't there. He must have gone to the bathroom next door, she decided. That was probably what had brought her so unpleasantly out of her deep sleep. She shivered as she recalled the nightmare she had been experiencing and moved across the bed to where the warmth of Dave's body would still be. But there was no warmth, no slight hollow that still carried the faint musky scent of him. No creases even on his pillow.

Slowly she rolled back the duvet and listened for the sound of water running. There was no such sound; nothing except the sonorous ticking of the clock close to her side of the big bed. A frisson of disquiet crept over her because of that silence. Where was Dave? Why was there no soft movement to be heard as he padded back to bed from the bathroom? Had he been taken ill in there? Was that what had woken

165

her – the sound of him flaking out on the tiled bathroom floor? As that thought hit her, she was already on her way out of bed and making for that room, pushing open the door, staring at the floor. Finding only emptiness.

Back in the bedroom again and reaching for her robe, she looked about her for the clothes that Dave would have tossed on to the linen chest at the foot of the bed last night. There were no clothes to be seen – not even a discarded sock. Had Dave dressed hurriedly and gone out to investigate something he had heard from the farm buildings? A fox on the prowl, perhaps? He did not usually wait to dress if any such sound disturbed him but dashed downstairs and out of the back door half-dressed, determined to stop any harm that might be done to his animals.

Had Dave even come to bed last night? Guilt engulfed her as she remembered how on finding the kitchen empty and the house silent on her return from Andrea's, and being by then exhausted by her long working day and the strain of driving home from Nyddbeck through the fog, she had assumed that Dave was out on his late-night inspection of the farm buildings and animals. She had not stayed downstairs to wait for him but gone straight up to bed, to crash out at once. What if he *had* gone out on his routine late-night safety inspection, and slipped on the ice that made the cobbled yard so treacherous and knocked himself out. Her heart gave a lurch when her thoughts reached that point. She must find out. Right now!

When she reached the foot of the stairs and opened the door into the kitchen, a huge surge of relief engulfed her at the sight of him sprawled out on the old sofa fast asleep. 'Oh, thank God,' she found herself murmuring. Then, puzzled again, she stared down at the worn leather jacket on which moisture was still plainly to be seen. Why hadn't Dave come up to bed when he had seen her car standing in the yard and knew she was back from visiting Andrea? She was still wondering about this when she bent to pick up the coat so that she could hang it in the back porch with Jack's bad-weather coat. Was Dave fast asleep down here in the kitchen because he was still annoyed with her for going to Andrea's last night?

166

The coat was still in her hands, and she was about to reach up to hang it on the hook next to the one where Jack's farm coat was kept, when a new thought came to perplex her. Where *was* Jack's coat? He would not have worn it to school; it was far too shabby for that, but he would have needed to wear it when he went to feed and walk old Joe's dog while she was visiting Andrea. Nor would Jack have taken the coat to his room, because it was a firm rule that such smelly garments reeking of mud and dung did not go beyond the back porch. She had been surprised to find that Dave's coat had found its way into the kitchen. There was something here that she did not like. Something vaguely alarming.

She walked back into the kitchen and stared down again at Dave, frowning as she tried to decide whether to wake him and ask him if there was anything wrong. But he looked so utterly lost in sleep, and she was probably worrying needlessly anyway, so she would go back to bed. At the head of the stairs she paused, still unable to shed her uneasiness completely. The house was so silent. It felt almost eerie, with the fog seeming to blot out even the usual country night sounds like the hooting of an owl or the cry of a vixen. She could not even hear the gentle rhythm of Jack's snores tonight. This was unusual, since the boy slept with his door slightly ajar so that when he sneaked Brack into the house while Dave was not looking, the dog was able to get out and go downstairs if it wished.

Julie was very close to that slightly open door now, and she could certainly not hear any snores. Slowly she pushed it wide enough ajar for her to be able to see with the aid of the light from the landing into the room. Then she knew why the snores were missing. Jack's bed was empty. It did not appear to have been slept in. The duvet and pillows were all undisturbed. There was no heap of school clothing on the carpet. No sign of the boy either. Fear hit her when she realized that, until she quelled it and started to wonder if Jack had decided to sleep in one of the other bedrooms. Though why he should do that she could not imagine. She moved quickly to the first spare room and found it deserted, then to the second to find the same.

167

That left only Carla's room. It took only a moment to turn the knob and look in. Carla was, as usual at this time, lost in sleep. So there were no more possibilities left. Except for the possibility that there was something very seriously wrong at Abbot's Fold tonight. Something she could not even begin to guess at. Something Dave was not aware of, or he would not be sleeping so soundly down there on the kitchen sofa. She must wake him at once!

'Dave! Dave, wake up!' As she shouted the words, she was already shaking him with some force. Though not with any success. He was still out for the count. Her hands were rough on his shoulders as she bent over to pour her fear into his ears in words that were on the edge of hysteria. 'Dave! Wake up! Wake up!'

'Go away,' he mumbled. 'Leave me alone.'

This time she grabbed his hair, that rough, blue-black thatch which carried now some silver threads, and tugged it hard enough to make him wince and curse at the same time. He was coming out of his sleep at last.

'Dave, where's Jack?' she shouted. 'Tell me where Jack is. Tell me!'

Now he was rubbing his eyes and groaning as he became more fully awake. His temper was at the ready too. 'What the hell's all the shouting about?' he wanted to know.

Julie wasted no more time. 'I can't find Jack. What's happened to him?' She was trembling as she waited for him to tell her where Jack was – that place she had been racking her brains to think of where Jack might have gone in his old farm coat and not yet come back from.

'He's in bed, of course! Where we ought to be.' As he said this, Dave was already letting his head slide back on to the cushion and his eyes close.

Julie's hands gripped his shoulders so fiercely that the pain brought another curse from him.

'He's not in bed, Dave! He's not! Get up and look for yourself if you don't believe me. He hasn't been to bed yet. So where is he?'

All of a sudden she was through to him. He was on his feet and halfway across the room on his way to the door.

Julie heard his feet thudding on the stairs before she ran up after him. His face was ashen when she met up with him in the doorway of Jack's bedroom.

'Where is he? Where the hell has he gone?'

'I don't know, Dave,' she whispered.

'Was he here when you came back last night?' He was staring at her intently as he asked.

Julie bit her lip. 'I don't know, Dave. I just assumed that he was. I didn't look into his room to make sure.'

'Why not?'

His voice was accusing. She brought out swift reasons why not to cover her own regrets, her own sense of guilt. 'Because he was fine when I went out. He was just going to feed Joe's dog and give it a walk. There was nothing then to indicate that he would go missing. He's not a toddler, Dave; he's twelve years old.'

Dave ignored her explanation, all his attention lingering on the words about Joe's dog. 'He didn't walk Joe's dog. He let it get loose, knowing it could be a danger to the sheep, and him a sheep farmer's son! I've spent hours since then looking in the home fields where the ewes and their lambs are, and making sure none of them has been damaged by that bloody dog. It was after midnight when I got back and crashed out in here.'

'How do you know Jack let the dog loose?'

'Who else could it have been?'

Julie sighed; she could not argue with that. Jack had taken on the responsibility for the old soldier's dog, but it looked as if he had been careless and allowed it to escape. Or was Jack with the dog? Had something happened to them both? She was quick to voice her fears. 'You don't think Jack has got so upset about letting the dog escape that he's afraid to come home and tell you, do you, Dave?'

Dave bit back a hasty denial. He *had* laid the law down too strongly with his son, and not for the first time. Why could he never seem to remember that Jack was only twelve, and had been forced to grow up without the mother who had been so good at explaining things to him, and having patience with him when he got it wrong?

169

'I just don't know what to think,' he said despairingly. 'I only know that if we hadn't kept that damned dog here, we wouldn't be worrying about Jack now. We don't even know where to start looking for him. He could be anywhere, and more than likely will have lost his way in the fog. Oh God, who in their right senses ever wants children!'

Now Julie's temper, already fully stretched, erupted in angry words hurled across the room at him. 'The people who really want them *don't* get them. Those who do don't appreciate them. You are one of the lucky ones, to have a lad like Jack who cares so much about a poor old man and his dog that when he finds the dog has escaped he'll go out in such bad weather to try and get it back for him. Because that's what could have happened here, Dave Bramley! Sometimes I think I know your son better than you know him, and love him more too.'

Which was just as well, Julie thought with tears pricking behind her eyes, because it was becoming more and more obvious to her that she would never have a child of her own to love and worry about. Unlike her friend Andrea who, she suspected, was in the very early stages of pregnancy. She pushed the thought away from her as Dave came up with a new possibility for Jack's disappearance.

'He could have gone to stay over with one of his mates.'

Julie disagreed. 'Not without telling us. That's not Jack's way of doing things.'

'He might have told Carla where he was going. I'll soon find out!' Already Dave was on his way to wake his daughter.

Julie stayed where she was, waiting for what might be a stormy scene if Carla *had* known where her brother was going and had forgotten to tell them. At least she could make a hot drink while she was waiting, because there would be no more sleep for her tonight. Raised voices were sounding from the room overhead now. Carla's was penetratingly clear.

'I told you, I don't *know* where our Jack's gone. So don't keep on at me about it. He might have run away if he thinks you're mad with him about something.'

That was what Carla herself had tried to do when Julie had been living over in Jacob's Cottage before she had married Dave. Carla had been subjected to a frightening experience that night by a van driver who had offered her a lift. A cold sweat of panic invaded Julie when she remembered that. If Jack had made his way to the main road to hitch a lift, his life might even now be in danger, because it was not only attractive young girls who could become the victims of evil men . . .

'I can't get anything out of Carla. She keeps saying she doesn't know where he's gone, but I don't know whether to believe her or not.'

So alarmed was Julie at the possibility of friendly, nice-looking young Jack being prey to a pervert that she had not been aware that Dave was back with her and pacing about the kitchen while trying to deal with his own sombre thoughts.

'You *have* to believe her, Dave. Carla wouldn't lie to you about anything as important as this. You know she wouldn't.'

'I don't know that she thinks it is important,' Dave said morosely. 'She couldn't get her head back under the duvet quickly enough. She'll be asleep already, while we're worrying our heads off about whether the lad is out there somewhere with his life in danger.'

Julie turned round from filling the kettle for the hot drinks to rebuke him. Carla beat her to it. She was there in the open door that led to the hall, shivering in the outsize T-shirt that did duty as nightwear, her long blonde hair tangled from sleep, and her eyes wide with distress. Her voice was fierce and tearful as she put her father in his place.

'I'm not asleep! How can I go to sleep when my stupid kid brother's gone out and got himself lost in the fog? What do you think I'm like, Dad, to be able to not care about anything like that? I want to know where our Jack is. I need to know he's safe; that no one's harmed him. Tell me he'll be safe somewhere, Julie, please!'

The tears had won now and the girl was sobbing unrestrainedly. Julie was crossing the room to gather her into her arms before Dave was able to think of what to say to her.

Julie swallowed her own panic and tried to speak calmly. 'I expect he will be, love, but we can't be sure. So we have to sit down and try to work out where he might have gone. It's just not like him to disappear, is it?'

Carla shook her head and brushed away a few more tears but said nothing. Dave also remained silent, afraid now of upsetting his daughter again. Julie led Carla to the sofa, then spoke sharply to him. 'Make some coffee, Dave, while we try to remember what Jack was talking about before he went out to feed the dog.'

Dave did not argue, because there was an air of authority about his wife now that was born of dealing with crisis situations in her work at the health centre or in the remote dwellings of the Dales hamlets and villages. Besides, he was too sick with worry to do anything except obey.

'He wasn't talking about anything much,' Carla began. 'He was watching the sports news on telly and moaning because we don't have Sky Sport like most of his mates do.'

A swift hope rose in Julie when she heard that, and was voiced at once. 'Do you know if there was a big football match on last night? If there was, he might have gone on his bike to watch it at one of his mates . . .'

Hope brought quick words from Carla too. 'I'll take a look at the programme in the paper.' She scooped up the *Yorkshire Post* from the floor and began a rapid scan of the pages.

Dave had another idea. 'I wonder if his bike is missing? I'll go and take a look.' He was already on his way to the tractor shed where Jack's bike was kept.

Carla's hopes were fading. 'I can't see anything listed, Julie.'

Julie finished making the coffee as she waited for Dave to reappear. It didn't take long. One look at his face dashed her hopes. 'His bike is still here, even if he isn't. So now what do we do?'

Julie took a deep breath. She must keep this situation low-key for as long as possible and make sure father and daughter did not lose their cool. 'We drink this,' she said as she handed steaming mugs to Dave and Carla and began to sip from her own.

'Perhaps we ought to ring the police,' Carla whispered.

'I think we ought to check every farm building first,' Dave answered. 'I'll make a start right now; then if we haven't found him, we'll go on from there. I'll start with the building where the old man and his dog were staying.'

172

'I'll take a torch and go through the buildings near the house in case he's been taken ill in one of them.' Julie put down her unfinished drink and went in search of a fleece and some slacks, plus a sturdy pair of shoes.

'I'll go with you, Julie. I can't stay here on my own. I just can't!' Carla insisted.

Julie hesitated for only a moment. Then: 'You'll need to put some warm clothes on because we could be out there for some time. Go and do it now!'

Upstairs, having hastily dragged on the slacks she had discarded last night, and the same roll-neck sweater, Julie was soon pulling on thick socks with hands that were shaking. She could not bear to contemplate what her life would be like at Abbot's Fold without Jack. Because Jack was so special to her. He had all his mother's best qualities: her sunny disposition and caring nature along with his father's dedication to the land and the animals. How would Jill have dealt with this crisis? Would she have known where to search for her son?

'Please God, let him be safe,' she found herself praying silently. 'Please don't let any harm have come to him. Please bring him back to us soon. I'll settle for not having a child of my own as long as Jack comes back to us. I promise!'

She knew it was wrong to try and strike bargains with the Almighty – that Andrea would not approve of it; but Andrea did not know how much this quiet, kind, sometimes funny, sometimes awkward twelve-year-old boy had come to mean to her.

'I'm ready, Julie,' Carla said from behind her as she raised her head from the silent prayers.

They went down the stairs and out into the fog together.

Eighteen

When Paula woke early and went downstairs to make tea, she was startled to hear from behind the door of the utility room sounds of movement followed by a canine whine. Of course, the dog was still in there! She had slept soundly and forgotten all about him being in here all night. He must be desperate to get out into the garden by now. As the thought came into her mind, Archie let go of a couple of sharp barks. Instantly she pushed the door open for him. He flung himself at her, remembering that she was the one who had taken him in and dried him off. Most of all, that she was the one who had fed him.

'All right, Archie, calm down now.' As she spoke to him, Paula bestowed an affectionate touch on his curly black head. After which she went to open the back door with the dog following close behind her.

'Ugh, what a horrid morning,' she told him as he dashed off into the shrubbery to relieve himself. The fog did not seem to have lifted at all. It was thick and clinging all about her, damp and icy too. She shivered and moved back into the house, leaving the door ajar so that Archie could get back in if he wished. Would he do that? she wondered as she dropped a tea bag into a mug and switched the kettle on. Or would he start making his way back to where he lived? At least he would have the chance to do that if she left him alone out there. She was not left to wonder for long before Archie was back with her, licking his lips and casting his soulful gaze at the empty dish where she had placed food for him last night.

Paula laughed. 'So you've decided to stay with me for breakfast, Archie? Let's see what I can find for you.'

Archie barked his agreement and wagged his tail while she opened the fridge and decided he would have to make do with the remains of the corned beef that she had opened for his last meal. While he was busy demolishing this at top speed, she began to make toast for her own breakfast. She was eating this, with the dog sprawled beneath the kitchen table waiting hopefully for a share of it, when the phone sounded out in the hall. Getting to her feet, she tossed a crisp crust to him, then went to answer it. It could be one of the workmen ringing to tell her that he would be late arriving because of the fog, she guessed.

'The Mill House,' she said as Archie came to join her, still crunching his toast.

'Daniel here, Paula. I hope you don't mind me ringing so early, but I wanted to let you know that I've made an appointment with a solicitor in Nyddford to discuss the details of our agreement and I wanted to find out if the time would suit you.' He went on to name a day at the beginning of the following week, which she was able to agree with.

'I'm glad I don't have to drive to Nyddford today in this fog,' she told him then. 'As I still don't know the area all that well, I'd probably get lost on the way.'

'Yes, it is a bit dodgy driving this morning. I didn't enjoy the short journey from home to the farm shop. Bad weather can keep some of our customers away too.'

'I thought your call might be from one of the workmen telling me he was going to be delayed.'

'They must be well on with the work now if you're planning to open just after Easter?'

'Yes. We had been hoping to open at Easter, until Dad became ill, but we had to suspend all the renovation work then for a time. At least I'll be able to get on with more of the painting in my own room today.' As she told him that, Archie, alerted by the sound of the postman's van on the drive, began to bark enthusiastically.

'Have you got a dog already? I didn't realize that. I was going to—' Daniel began.

'No, he's not mine! I just found him in my back porch last night, very wet, very hungry and apparently lost. So I

175

fed him and let him sleep in the utility room. He has a name on his collar, but no surname or phone number for his owner, just an address at a place called Nyddham. I rang the police, but they couldn't help because no one had reported him missing. So I suppose when the fog lifts I'll have to drive him to Nyddham, wherever that is, because someone might be missing him.'

'Maybe that's something I can help you with, Paula?' Daniel offered.

'Oh, would you? I'd be so grateful, Daniel, because Archie's quite a big dog and I might have problems getting him into my car.'

'I could do it tonight, as soon as I've closed the shop. If that time would be convenient for you?' he suggested.

'I'll have a meal ready for you then, unless – unless anyone else is cooking for you, that is.' She knew there was no wife waiting for him; he had already spoken briefly to her about his broken marriage, but had not mentioned having another partner.

'No one else will be cooking for me. These days I cook for myself. Or eat out,' he told her.

'We'll see you tonight then, Archie and me, and thanks for being so good to us,' she said as she prepared to end the call.

'It's the least I can do,' he said abruptly.

Paula was perplexed. 'What do you mean, Daniel?' she asked.

'I'll explain later. When we know each other better. For now I've got work to do.'

So Paula was left to go on wondering what he meant while she went to find out what the postman had delivered, and whether the van that was now approaching the house was the one belonging to the plumber or the electrician.

The atmosphere at Abbot's Fold Farm was taut with the anxiety they had all been forced to endure since they had discovered that Jack was missing, even though they had attempted to conceal it from one another. Breakfast cereals and milk had been placed on the table by Carla, at Julie's request, but the three who sat there gazing at them, because

176

it was not easy to look at one another, knew that they would remain untouched until Jack was safe in his home again. They had said everything there was to say as night turned into day and their worry deepened. It was Carla who broke the silence that had lasted too long.

'I'm not going to school today,' she told them. 'So don't ask me to go because I won't be able to concentrate.'

Dave and Julie exchanged troubled glances. It was Julie who made the decision. 'You'll be better here at home, I think. Someone will need to be in the house all the time while your dad goes out and searches the moor now there's a bit more light, and I'll have to go out soon to my more urgent cases until one of the other nurses can take over from me. You mustn't just sit around letting panic get at you, though. Find something to do. You must have some home-work or reading to do?'

'I don't think I can concentrate on anything like that,' Carla protested.

'Then do the ironing; there's plenty of that waiting to be done. Or prepare the dinner.'

'We won't want to eat, will we?'

Julie bit back the sharp words that her growing fear was pushing into the front of her mind. 'When Jack comes home he'll be starving, so we'll need to have a good meal ready for him,' she said instead.

'If he comes home! He could be—'

'Stop it, Carla!' her father broke in. 'Try to remember which lads Jack is friendly with at school, because I'm about to start phoning round to see if he's spent the night with one of them and forgotten to tell us. I don't want to ring the police at Nyddford until I've made sure he isn't sleeping soundly in someone else's home.'

'Why didn't you do it before now?' Carla said accusingly.

'Because at twelve years old, nearly thirteen, Jack would have been mortified if we'd woken his friends' parents in the middle of the night when he was safe all the time. You know he would. He hates a lot of fuss.' It was Julie who told her that. 'So let's have some names and addresses – the ones you know, anyway.'

177

Carla blinked away a fresh batch of tears and began. 'There's Rob Banks at Far Moor Farm.'

Dave frowned. 'Surely he wouldn't have gone there on foot, in the fog? His bike is in the shed, and he usually goes to Far Moor on that since it's three miles away from here. I'll ring them first, though, because they'll be getting up soon anyway to do the milking.'

He left the door open into the hall so that Julie and Carla could hear what was said. There seemed to be a long wait for the ringing to be answered at Far Moor Farm, but then it *was* only five forty. Dave's mouth was dry as he waited, and hoped, and even prayed silently that his boy was safe on the isolated moorland farm with his best mate.

Julie moved restlessly about the kitchen; Carla began to bite her nails. At last they could hear Dave speaking.

'Sorry to disturb you so early, Maurice, but have you got our Jack with you?'

Silence as the question was answered from another farm kitchen at the other end of the fogbound moor. Then came Dave's explanation, given hurriedly.

'We didn't know he was not in bed here as usual until very early this morning. Then Julie looked into his room and found his bed hadn't been slept in. It's not like Jack not to tell us if he's going to stay over with one of his mates. We just haven't a clue about where he is.'

Silence again as Dave listened to the father at the other end commiserating with him and saying that with their heads full of the latest football match their sons would forget all about anxious parents.

'Thanks, anyway, Maurice. I'd better try one or two other places before I do anything else. Yes, I expect he'll turn up safe for his breakfast in an hour or two.'

As Dave put the phone down, Carla went to stand close to him and spoke quickly. 'You could try Chris Brown now, Dad. He lives down in Nyddbeck. Jack goes there sometimes at weekends. Shall I look up the number?'

'Yes, though I don't suppose they'll think much to being woken up at this time.'

'They won't mind.' Even if they did, they'd have to put

178

up with it, because nothing mattered as long as their Jack was safe. Carla soon had the number and was dialling it, leaving her dad to speak to the other father, who might or might not be able to give them good news.

This time they had even longer to wait for an answer, and the news was not good. 'Sorry, he's not here, although we do see him sometimes. Hope he soon turns up safely. It must be a worry for you, but you know what they are at that age. Heads in the clouds half the time.'

'Thanks, anyway. Sorry I had to disturb you, but it just isn't like Jack not to tell us where he is if he's stopping over.'

'Oh, I know how you feel. We've been through it a time or two with Chris now he's feeling his feet a bit.'

Dave put the phone down. They hadn't been through it with Jack – not until now, anyway. It was time to look to Carla again for information.

'There's the lad who lives in Nyddford; the one who's mum and dad own the fish-and-chip shop. Jack likes to go there because he gets free fish and chips. Shall I look their number up?'

Dave nodded, and thought up another spur-of-the-moment silent prayer.

'I can't remember their name. He's called Andy something. Something to do with Scotland.'

Carla bit her nails again as she struggled to think of Andy's surname.

Julie began to clear the table, and to say her own silent prayer again.

'Galloway! That's his name: Andy Galloway. I'll find the number, Dad.'

It was easy to find the number in the local directory, but it didn't help them to find Jack. Once again there was sympathy, this time from a mum who was in a rush to tell them not to worry too much because Jack always seemed to her to be such a sensible lad. 'At least you know he won't have run away from home, as some do at his age. Jack's too fond of his collie dog to leave it, and of his step-mum too. Sorry I can't think of anywhere he might be,' the woman ended before going to take a look at her own two children, still safely asleep in their beds.

'Can you think of anyone else we might try?' Dave asked his daughter then.

Carla shook her head. 'What are we going to do now, Dad?' she whispered.

Dave sighed. 'I don't know. I know one thing, though: that woman from the fish-and-chip shop was right about Jack. He wouldn't ever leave Brack behind if he was going to run away, would he?'

Carla was puzzled by that statement. 'Jack wouldn't run away anyway. Not when you had said he had to look after Wandering Joe's dog while he was in hospital. I mean, last night he was watching something on TV when he remembered he hadn't fed Archie. So he didn't even bother to wait and see how it ended. He dashed off to walk Archie and feed him instead.'

'He let the dog get away,' Dave broke in then. 'Did he tell you that when he came back?'

Carla hesitated. She hadn't actually *seen* Jack come back because she'd been out in the hall having a long phone chat with one of her friends from Nyddford High while her dad was having a shower and Julie was out visiting Andrea.

'No, he didn't.'

Dave frowned. 'Did he seem upset when he came back in? Because he would have been, when he knew he'd let the dog escape after promising the old man he would look after him.'

Julie was recalling something – something that could be important. The shabby coat that had been missing from behind the back door. 'Did you *see* him come back, Carla?' she asked as she came to stand face to face with the girl.

Carla began to tremble. She wanted to lie, but she simply could not get that simple untruth out of her mouth. So it had to be the truth, or almost the truth, even if that got her into trouble with her dad.

'No. I was in the hall answering the phone; then I went up to my room to do my homework. So I didn't actually *see* him. I just thought he had come back,' she said, looking down at her feet.

180

'So he might not have done,' Julie whispered. 'If he had let the dog escape he probably went after it to try and get it back. Oh God, all those hours ago, and in such dense fog! He could be anywhere by now. If he went up on the moor he could be lost, or have fallen and been injured. In freezing fog that could mean . . .'

'Ring the police, Dad! Please,' Carla begged.

Dave's shoulders sagged with his despair. 'I'll do it now. I ought to have done it earlier . . .'

Jack opened his eyes with difficulty and wondered where he was. He certainly was not in his own bed at home; he was feeling far too uncomfortable for that. His whole body felt stiff and awkward. When he tried to move into a better position, a fierce pain shot through the top of his right leg. At least he thought it was his right leg. It might not be, because there was a strange muzzy feeling in his head that made him feel quite sick. He was very cold too. So cold that the fingers on one hand – he thought it was his right hand but he couldn't be sure – seemed to be welded to one of those pieces of limestone rock that were scattered all over Abbot's Moor.

What was he doing out here on the moor with the fog billowing all around him so that he was not even able to see the sheep he knew ought to be somewhere up here? Why wasn't he in his own warm bed at Abbot's Fold? Why did he feel so terrible? He couldn't stay out here all night or there would be trouble at home. Dad would be mad with him, and maybe Julie would be too. He didn't want Dad and Julie to be mad with him; he just wanted to be back with them and with their Carla, and Brack. Where was Brack? If he was out here on Abbot's Moor on his own, where was Brack, who should have been with him?

He couldn't stay out here any longer; he must get back to Abbot's Fold to make sure Brack was all right. If Brack was here he *would* be all right, because Brack would keep him warm, like he did at home when he managed to sneak him into the house while Dad wasn't looking. He must get home. He must! They wouldn't like him being out here instead of in his own room. Only he couldn't seem to move without

181

that awful pain shooting through his leg. The pain was so bad now that he felt very sick, and very frightened. He wanted to know why he was not at home instead of out here, but he couldn't remember, and he was so, so tired. It didn't matter any more that he was cold; he just wanted the pain to stop.

There were tears that felt warm on his cheeks until they froze. There was a numb feeling in his head that he didn't like. Inside him everything seemed muddle. There was Dad's voice and there was Julie's voice. There was the sound of Brack and Tyke barking, but it was getting fainter all the time until Jack couldn't be bothered to listen to it any more. He just wanted to close his eyes and go to sleep again, to sleep and sleep and shut out the pain that was getting worse all the time . . .

Nineteen

Andrea shivered as she hurried downstairs to switch on the kettle for early-morning tea. Lucky stirred in his bed in the kitchen when he heard her and bounced across the floor to bestow an exuberant greeting on her.

'Calm down, Lucky!' she ordered. 'I'm feeling far too fragile for anything like that. I'll take you for a walk when I've had some tea; for now you can go out into the back garden and water the grass there.'

She gave his silky auburn head a pat, and got a loving lick on her hand in return. Then the back door was open and out he dashed into a dense wall of fog. What a dreadful morning this was going to be for driving about from the manse to a school in Nyddford, then on to visit someone in the cottage hospital there. After that there was a meeting in a nearby hall to be chaired. She could only allow herself plenty of time to get from one place to another, and hope that by later in the day the fog would have gone.

Leaving the door slightly ajar so that the dog could barge his way back in when he'd had enough of the icy, foggy air, she dropped a tea bag into a mug and while it brewed switched on the radio to hear the early-morning news. Then she stirred the hot brew thoughtfully while she listened to the usual mix of local and national catastrophes, dour predictions and improbable forecasts that were really the wrong start to anyone's day. While she was still reflecting on the doom and gloom, Lucky was back with her and shaking drops of moisture off his luxurious rusty-coloured coat. Bill's dog had the same vibrant colouring as his master. Andrea thought with longing of how she would love to be curling up close to Bill right now, sinking her head into his short beard, lifting her lips for his long, warm, first kiss of the day.

It was not going to happen, though. Not today, anyway, because Bill would not be back from America for another few days. Those days would be busy days for her, as all her days were, but that would not stop her from missing Bill. She was missing him even more this time than she had done when he had been away on his US lecture tour last year. They had not been married when he had gone to the States last year, and the tour had been extended by Miriam, Bill's agent. Bill had promised her, before his departure, not to stay for more than the pre-arranged two weeks this time. In his phone call a couple of days ago he had told her he was sticking to that promise even though Miriam wanted to add another couple of lectures and demos to his schedule. 'I can't bear to be away from you now, darling,' he had told her. 'Do take care of yourself, and please try to arrange a few days off so that we can go to the cottage soon after I get back. Don't forget that I love you. I'll always love you!'

So now she was trying to reschedule some of her most important meetings so they could have a short midweek break at the cottage in the Scottish Border country that Bill had given her for a wedding present. That meant her fitting in more work while he was away, and it was hard going when she was feeling so tired all the time. Julie had remarked last night on how tired she was looking, but Andrea had managed to fob off her insistent advice that she should see one of the health-centre doctors. She would have to consult one soon, though, she knew, because she was becoming more and more certain that she was pregnant.

Pregnant! How wonderful it would be if she was right! She was *almost* sure now that she was, but she was not going to give the news to Bill via the transatlantic telephone; she wanted to give him it in person. Bill would be so thrilled when she told him. They both wanted so much to have a child of their own. Not a replacement for her wee Andrew, the child of her first marriage who had died so young, but a unique little person born of their love for each other. It was worth putting up with the early-morning nausea and the day-long weariness just to have that hope. Already she was feeling better after the hot tea and a plain biscuit.

She would have her shower now, then breakfast. After that she would take Lucky for his walk before Jane Lindsay arrived to do her ironing and dusting while she went to take a school assembly in Nyddford Primary. She would take Jake, her parrot puppet, with her to the school. The young children loved him, and would listen carefully when she used Jake to explain some of the Bible stories for them. Her parents had bought Jake for her on their last visit and they, along with Bill, had enjoyed a lot of laughs as they rehearsed with the bird puppet for his first appearance at a service of thanksgiving for the lives of three little brothers. Andrea was still smiling at this happy memory as she made her way up the stairs to have her shower when the sound of the phone broke into her thoughts and sent her back down to the hall.

'Andrea!' Julie did not wait to make sure she was speaking to the right person before she hurried to share her anxiety with her friend. 'We can't find Jack! He's not in his room, and his bed hasn't been slept in. Dave's just got in touch with the police. While he was doing that I wondered if you might have any idea of where he could have gone?'

The agitation so apparent in Julie's voice brought a lurch to Andrea's heart, because her friend was not the sort of person to get into a panic easily. Hers was the sort of personality that could deal calmly with a crisis situation, but of course Jack was her stepson, and the son of her long-time friend, a child she had known from his birth and probably loved since then too.

'Do you think he can have stayed over with a friend somewhere?' she asked. 'Is it the sort of thing he might do when the weather turned bad?'

'Not really. He has a few close friends, but if he *is* staying over to watch a match on Sky with any of them he always lets us know. Dave has already rung round all of them, but none of them saw him last night. He was still at home when I came down to see you, and when I got back I just assumed he was asleep in his room. Only he wasn't! Carla says he went out to feed the dog that he's looking after for an old

185

man who had to go into the cottage hospital a few days ago. The worrying thing is that when Dave went to check the buildings late last night, he discovered that the dog had escaped, so now we're wondering if Jack went to look for it and either got lost in the fog or hurt in some way.'

'Would he be likely to do that, do you think? To go off on his own without telling Dave, I mean?' Andrea was beginning to share Julie's concern.

'Yes, I think he might in this case. You see, Dave didn't want old Joe and his dog hanging about around the farm because of the danger to his lambs if the dog got loose. So he told Jack that the dog was his responsibility until the old man could take him home. Jack promised he would look after the dog, feed him and walk him. I suppose when he found Archie had escaped he was afraid to tell Dave, so he went looking for the dog on his own.'

Andrea was perplexed. 'Didn't Dave know that Jack wasn't in the house when you two went to bed last night?'

Julie sighed. 'No. You see when I got back from visiting you, Dave was out doing the late-night check of the buildings, as he does every night before we go to bed. So I went straight up to bed, thinking he would follow me very soon. I must have crashed out at once, because I didn't know Dave wasn't beside me till I woke in the early hours feeling very cold. When I went downstairs to see where he was I found him out for the count on the kitchen sofa with his farm coat, still wet with the fog, at his feet. I decided not to disturb him. Then when I went back upstairs I couldn't hear Jack snoring, as I usually can, because he leaves his bedroom door open. I took a quick peep round the door to make sure he hadn't kicked his duvet off and found his bed hadn't been slept in. That was when I began to get worried. So I woke Dave and asked him where the lad was. He didn't even know Jack wasn't in the house; he had just assumed he was in bed at the time he got back from checking the buildings. He did know that the dog had escaped, though, and we both can't help wondering if Jack went out to look for it and got lost in the fog, or fell and was hurt. Dave's already searched all our outbuildings. Now we just don't know where he can have gone and what has happened to him.'

Julie's voice died away on a note of despair. Andrea wondered what to say; how to comfort her. How to allay her fears. Dear Lord, please don't let there be another tragedy for Dave and Julie, Andrea found herself praying silently. Help me to help *her*. As prayer ended, for the time being, her thoughts moved from the missing boy to the missing dog, and from there to the owner of the missing dog. Could it be the same old chap she had spoken to yesterday in the cottage hospital? He had said something about missing his dog, she remembered.

'Did you say the dog's owner was in the cottage hospital just now?' she asked into the silence.

'Yes. The poor old bloke was walking with his dog to see one of his old army mates who is in sheltered housing at Nyddford, when he became ill with a chest infection. He was sleeping in one of our buildings overnight and I was so concerned about him that I asked one of the doctors to take a look at him. He needed to go into hospital at once, but he didn't want to leave his dog. Jack said he had met up with him and his dog before, so he would take care of the dog for him while he was in hospital, and he did. Until last night. Now we don't know where either of them are.' Again there was despair in Julie's voice.

'Was there an address on the dog's collar?' Andrea broke in as the idea hit her.

'I don't know.'

'If there was, that could be where the dog headed for, and Jack too.'

'I just don't know.'

'I'm going visiting at the hospital this morning, so I'll talk to Joe. It might help if I can find out just where he and his dog live.'

'Thanks, Andrea; I'll have to be going to work now.'

'Must you, when Dave needs you?' Andrea said too quickly.

'The patients need me too. I'll ask someone to take my place as soon as possible, and I'll be able to keep in touch with Dave on my mobile until I can get back. I need to go now, Andrea.'

'I'll be in touch with you after I've spoken to Joe,' Andrea promised.

Later, as she walked Lucky through the village, shivering as the fog seemed to seep through her sheepskin coat and woolly hat, her thoughts would not let go of the fact that somewhere in this wild moorland countryside a young boy could be lost, or injured. Or worse! That last thought made her feel sick again, so she swallowed hastily and hurried on to where her little church loomed up out of the gloom. As always when her mind was troubled, she would spend a short time there, seeking the help she knew would be waiting for her.

Inside the porch she fastened Lucky's lead to the heavy umbrella stand and indicated the mat where he was to wait quietly. Lucky grumbled softly deep in his throat but did as he was told while she opened the door and entered the building. Instead of walking right up to her usual place at the front of the church she stopped halfway down the centre aisle and dropped into a seat there. Before bowing her head in prayer she lifted her eyes to take a long look at the memorial window. Its colours were muted today by the poor light, but her gaze lingered on the figures of the children who stood at the feet of Jesus. She did not need to read what the letters beneath them said. The words were written in her heart: 'Suffer the little children to come to me.'

Jack had been christened in this church, where his grandfather had been a lay preacher and his grandmother a church elder. He had come here on Sundays with other members of the junior church. These days he did not come if there was work for him to do on the farm, but what he had learned here would be always there inside him to guide and comfort him in times of fear, pain or loss. Andrea was certain of that.

'Dear Lord, please look after Jack for us. Let him be safe. Help Dave and Carla and Julie to have courage while they wait for news, and help me to help them,' she prayed while a few tears ran slowly down her cheeks.

A few minutes later she was walking with Lucky beside the beck, catching glimpses of dead golden leaves floating on the ice-edged water while Lucky crunched happily through the frosted grass. Every now and then lights glinted mistily from some of the cottage windows where people were having breakfast or getting ready for work, but so far she had met no one else out walking. It was as she was about to head back to the manse that Lucky began to tug on the lead and let go a joyful bark because he had become aware of the approach of another dog in the distance. In no time at all the air resounded with a cacophony of canine sound. If anyone in the nearby cottages was hoping to have a lie-in, they would be unlucky, Andrea reflected ruefully. Her order to Bill's dog to 'lie down and be quiet' was ignored. Lucky was going to do things his way, and his way was to almost pull her off her feet as he struggled to meet up with this other dog, who was a stranger on *his* patch.

The 'incomer' dog was equally determined to face up to the opposition, as represented by the much younger retriever, and was making good speed, with his uncooperative owner trying hard to restrain him. They met up on the part of the lane where the dwellings were much larger and further apart, occupying the rising ground that led first to Abbot's Wood then on to Abbot's Moor. They met with an exchange of happy barking on the part of Lucky and a fierce snappy 'I'll soon show you cheeky young fellow who is boss' from the old dog, while the two women who held on to the restraining lead on one side and rope on the other wished they had been anywhere but here.

It was Lucky who got the worst of it, yelping pitifully when the other dog nicked his ear with a sharp set of teeth, before taking shelter behind Andrea. 'You should behave yourself, Lucky,' Andrea told him severely, 'instead of going looking for trouble.'

'I'm so sorry,' said Paula. 'The bloody dog almost had me off my feet! I must have got out of the habit of walking a big dog.'

Andrea laughed. 'Yes, they take a bit of getting used to.' She hesitated then, unsure of whether the other girl would wish to be reminded of when they had last met.

Paula was surprised to see her. 'Sorry about the language,' she said ruefully. 'You're Mrs Wyndham, aren't you?'

189

Andrea laughed again. 'Yes, but don't apologize, please. It was nothing I haven't heard before; in fact I've heard much more and survived it. I hope you are recovering now from all the stress and anxiety you've had since you came here. You'll probably find the company of the dog will help, once you get used to him. Is he a rescued dog?'

Now it was Paula who laughed. 'I suppose you could call him that, but he's certainly not *my* dog. I rescued him from spending a very cold night in my back porch last night, but I don't know who he belongs to. If I did, I'd take him back to them, because he's rather a handful, isn't he?'

Archie was proving that by whining and straining on his improvised lead as he struggled to make his way into Abbot's Wood.

'Is there a name and address on his collar?' Andrea asked, as hope began to stir inside her.

'There's a name. He's called Archie, but there's no owner's name or phone number – just an address at a place called Nyddham. Without a name I was unable to contact his owner, but I did ring the police to find out whether anyone had reported him missing. No one has yet, so he'll have to stay with me until a friend comes tonight to take him back to Abbey Cottage at Nyddham.'

Now Andrea was even more hopeful. 'I think his owner could be at present in the cottage hospital at Nyddford. Could you manage to hang on to him till I make certain? I'll be visiting at the hospital later this morning, after I've done a morning assembly at the primary school near there, so I'll give you a ring about lunch time, if that's convenient?'

'Yes, I'll be around then. I'll be busy painting.'

'I must dash now or I'll be late for the assembly. Bye now, and behave yourself, Archie!'

With that Andrea turned to hurry back to her manse with a subdued Lucky trotting at her side.

'Thanks a lot!' Paula called after her.

'You're welcome. I'll be in touch,' Andrea called back before she disappeared into the fog.

The school assembly was, as almost always, rewarding. The children remembered her from previous visits and were eager to know if she had brought Jake with her again. When she left, they were calling goodbye to her parrot puppet and asking her to bring him back another day. It would be wonderful when she was teaching her own children Bible stories in this way, she reflected as she made her way to her car and headed for the cottage hospital on the edge of the market town.

Once there, she had a quiet word with Staff Nurse Dawson, the daughter of one of her church members and, as they shared a quick coffee, enquired about the old man called Joe.

'Oh, Mr Robinson! He's making good progress, Andrea, so we won't be keeping him here for much longer, because he's fretting to be back with his old dog,' she was told.

'That's good news! But there's some not-so-good news too about his dog. It seems to have managed to escape from the farm where it was being cared for by the farmer's young son.'

'Oh, we mustn't let him know that. Not yet anyway.' The nurse's lovely face clouded with her concern for Mr Robinson.

Andrea hastened to reassure her. 'Oh, the dog's fine. Well enough to take a chunk out of our dog's ear this morning when we met out in the fog,' she said with a laugh. 'It's the boy who was looking after him who is causing concern. When the dog escaped, it seems that he must have gone to look for it and either got lost in the fog or been injured. Or something even worse,' she ended with a shudder.

'How old is the boy?' the nurse wanted to know.

'He's only twelve.'

'Where is the farm?'

'Up on Abbot's Moor.'

'Oh God! Imagine being out in that sort of weather all night. If he's lying injured somewhere, he could be in a bad way by now. The parents must be desperately worried?'

'They are. The stepmother is a close friend of mine. She's a community nurse at the health centre, and the boy seems to have been quite friendly with Mr Robinson.'

The nurse nodded. 'That'll be the boy Mr Robinson talked about. He said he knew he could trust young Jack to take care of his dog.'

Andrea hesitated. 'He mustn't know what has happened then. Not yet anyway. Not until Jack is back home again.'

The eyes of the two women met as the same terrible thought troubled them both. 'The problem could be if there's anything about it on local radio. A lot of patients like to listen to it. I suppose the police will have been informed, but they might not have released the news yet at this early stage. How long will he have been missing?' the nurse asked.

'For about fifteen hours now.'

'I'll try and keep the news from Mr Robinson. You can go and talk to him now if you like, Andrea. Do you know where to find him?'

'Yes. I spoke to him just after he was admitted. I'll be very careful what I say. Thanks for the coffee.'

'You're welcome. I hope there's good news about the boy soon.'

'So do I! It's hard to know what to say to people in these situations.' Andrea worried round this as she walked down the hospital corridor to where she knew she would find Mr Robinson.

She spent only a few minutes with him, just long enough to listen to him telling her again how good they had been to him here, and how much he was longing to be reunited with Archie in his own home.

'Where is your home, Mr Robinson?' she asked.

'I live in one of the cottages near the abbey,' he told her. 'Just me and Archie. I was walking with him to see my old mate who lives in Nyddford when my chest got bad.'

She expressed her surprise. 'That's a long walk for both of you.'

He chuckled. 'Not for us two! We walk everywhere. I got used to walking when I was in the army and I've kept it up ever since. That's how I met that nice young lad who's looking after Archie for me while I'm in here. He's good with dogs. That young dog of his will be a real champion one day. Jack's got his sights set on being Young Shepherd of the Year at Nyddford Show next September, and I think he'll do it.'

Andrea found it hard to smile as she agreed with him. 'I'd

like to be there when he does. His mum is a good friend of mine. She'll be so proud of him.' Andrea rose to her feet before he could ask any more questions about Jack.

'He's a grand young fellow; I enjoy talking to him. Thank you for coming to see me.' The old man hesitated, then went on. 'You'll tell Jack I'll soon be coming to collect Archie, won't you?'

There was a huge lump in Andrea's throat as she promised to do that. It was one of the most difficult areas of her work – having to make a promise to someone that she might not be able to keep. As she made her way back along the corridor and out of the hospital to where her car was parked, she reflected that all she could do now was to live in hope, and keep on praying that Jack was safe somewhere and would soon be back in his home.

Twenty

Jane was just finishing ironing the last of a dozen shirts and blouses, plus bed and table linen, when she heard the sound of Andrea's car door slamming on the drive outside, followed by the excited noise Lucky made as he prepared to welcome her home. It reminded her that when *she* arrived back at Nyddford Gardens, Darcy would be waiting to welcome her and Kerry, whom she would collect from nursery school on the way. She'd be glad to get home today, though she was not looking forward to the drive in such thick fog, because tonight Tim was coming to have tea with the children as soon as his school day ended. When she got home, she would make his favourite steak-and-mushroom pie.

'You're not going to enjoy your drive home much, Jane,' Andrea warned. 'The fog seems to be getting worse. I wish I didn't have to go out again this afternoon.'

'I've about finished ironing now. Is there anything else you'd like me to do before I go?'

Andrea shook her head. 'You'd better go early because it'll take you a bit longer to get to the nursery school in this weather. Have you had the radio on?' she added, wanting to know whether Jane had heard anything yet about the disappearance of Jack Bramley.

'Yes, there was something right at the end of the local news about a boy going missing from this area, but I didn't catch all of it. Is it someone we know, Andrea?'

Andrea sighed. 'Yes. It's Jack Bramley from Abbot's Fold Farm. His step-mum is a friend of mine. She's a nurse at Nyddford Health Centre.'

'Oh, how awful, and in such bad weather! How old is he?'
'He's twelve.'

'They must be worried out of their minds. How long has he been missing for?'

'About fifteen hours, they think. They're not quite sure when he went, and they've no idea where he might have gone – whether he's got lost or if he's been injured somewhere. I'm going to give them a ring now before I do anything else.'

'Perhaps he's stayed over with a friend and forgotten to tell them?' Jane suggested hopefully.

Andrea shook her head. 'They rang round all his friends as soon as they realized he'd been out all night, but none of them has seen him since they were at school yesterday.'

Jane shivered. 'It must be a nightmare, just having to wait for news and hope that nothing awful has happened to him. Was he at Nyddford High School?'

'Yes. He's in his first year there. I'll give Dave Bramley a ring right now.' Andrea went to use the phone in the hall.

Jane began to fold up the ironing board and empty the steam iron, listening all the time for the tone of the minister's voice that would indicate the safe return of Jack Bramley. It did not happen as she hoped. There was no gladness evident in Andrea's words for those who were waiting for news at the moorland farm, only the expression of her deep concern for them. So Jane slipped on her fleece, picked up her shoulder bag and left her to talk in private while she drove home.

'When I was at the cottage hospital this morning, I spoke to Mr Robinson, but I didn't tell him about his dog, or about Jack,' Andrea said after asking if there was any news yet of Dave's missing son.

'I'm not bothered about his bloody dog!' Dave broke in. 'All I'm bothered about is our Jack! I want to know where he is and whether he's all right. Nothing else matters to me except having him safe. I've been on to the police, and they've been to the school to talk to his friends there, but none of them were able to help. Now I don't know what to do next. I can't just stay here and do nothing. I can't!'

Dave was really stressed out. Andrea took a deep breath and spoke very slowly and calmly to him. 'I think I met Mr Robinson's dog this morning, Dave, when I was walking

Lucky in Beck Lane. He was with the girl who lives at the Mill House. She said he turned up on her back porch last night and wouldn't go away, so she rang the police about him. They were not able to help because no one had reported him missing, but of course Mr Robinson wouldn't know he had escaped, would he?'

'I'm not interested in the bloody dog!' Dave said again.

Andrea took another deep breath and hung on to her patience. 'The address on his collar was for one of the cottages up at the abbey. When I spoke to Mr Robinson he told me that he lived in one of the cottages there. So it might be worth your while to drive up there and find out if Jack went there last night to see if Archie had run to his home when he escaped.'

She heard Dave take a sharp intake of breath. Then: 'I'll go up there now. Carla's at home from school, so she'll be here when the police come to look round, as they said they would when they'd been to the school to talk to Jack's classmates. They still think he might just have taken himself off somewhere so he wouldn't get into trouble for letting the dog escape.'

'Will Carla be on her own, or is Julie there?'

An impatient exclamation came from Dave. 'Julie's gone to work, but she called me from her mobile and said she'd be back when her replacement arrived from Harrogate. I can't wait till then. I'm going to the abbey now.'

'I'll come and stay with Carla, Dave. I'll come right now,' Andrea said. She did not wait for him to argue with her but picked up her car keys and a few minutes later was driving in low gear through the fog up the long steep hill which she had been hoping not to have to cope with today.

Jane found herself unable to stop thinking, as she drove to the nursery school in Nyddford, about the young boy whose unexpected absence from his home was causing so much anxiety. Of course he was much older than Elliot, and might well be quite safe somewhere, but how would she and Tim be feeling if Elliot had been missing from *his* home? She remembered how on the day of Andrea and Bill's wedding he had vanished from her side while they were in the church hall waiting with Miss Poppleton for the pieces of wedding cake to be handed round. Her fear had soon been put to rest when Miss Poppleton had gone in search of him and found him on his way to the school where his daddy worked, walking alongside a busy road.

What would she have said to Tim if their little son had met with an accident there? What would Tim have said to her? Each of them would have blamed the other, because that was what happened once you got at odds with each other, as she and Tim had been at that time. They would never have been able to forgive one another for the fact that *their* son, their much loved little child, had been so desperate to spend time with his daddy that he had risked his life to see him. It must never happen again, Jane knew, because if there was a next time they might not be so lucky.

Once this thought hit her, when she was still a mile or so from Nyddford, she knew what she had to do and could not wait to do it. There was a small parking bay on the right-hand side of the road where she sometimes stopped on her way home when the children were with her so that they could say hello to the sturdy black horse called Dolly and the two soft-eyed donkeys who were her companions. As soon as she was safely off the road with the engine switched off she reached into her bag for her mobile phone and called Tim, who would be having his lunch break at Nyddford High School.

'Tim!' her voice was slightly breathless as she spoke. 'I won't keep you long.'

'What is it, Jane? What's the matter? Is it one of the children?'

'No. Not one of ours. It's the boy called Jack who's gone missing from home.'

'Has he turned up? We had the police in school this morning trying to find some information from his friends about where he might have gone.'

'No, he's still missing, but it made me think when I heard about him, Tim. Suppose it had been Elliot? What would we have done? How would we have coped with it? We would

197

have been blaming one another, I expect, and making things much worse.'

Tim could hear the distress in her voice, sense the anguish she was feeling for these other parents. 'Don't, darling! Please don't upset yourself imagining something that won't ever happen,' he begged.

'How do I know it won't?' There was a stifled sob now. 'Elliot *did* go missing once last year.'

'When? When did it happen?' Tim broke in. 'Why didn't I know at the time?' Now he was the one to be alarmed.

'It was when we were in the school hall on the day of Andrea's wedding, talking to Miss Poppleton. One minute Elliot was there, and the next he'd gone. I thought he had just gone to the toilet, but when Miss Poppleton went to look for him, she found him making his way along that busy road to your school.'

'Oh God! You must have been frantic. Why didn't you let me know at once?'

'Because Miss Poppleton brought him back before I needed to do that.'

'I'm sorry, Jane – so sorry for all you must have gone through at that time. I wish I could make it up to you . . .'

Suddenly Jane knew what she had to say; what she had been longing to say to Tim yet had been unable to because she had been afraid to trust him again even though the woman called Donna had been dead for months. 'You *can* make it up to me, Tim, if you'll come home for good,' she told him with a rush.

'Do you mean soon? Please say you do.'

'I mean today, Tim. Don't just come for tea. Please come to stay.'

'I've been longing to hear you say that! I will come today, after school, and thanks!'

Jane slipped the phone back into her bag and prepared to complete her journey home. 'Thanks, God,' she murmured as she did so. 'Thanks a lot!'

The fog was still thick, there were still patches of black ice to be negotiated, there was still a nice young boy missing somewhere out there, but inside her now was the feeling of a great burden of sadness moving away from her and her children. From today they would be a proper family again. As she moved the car carefully back on to the road again, she began to sing softly one of her favourite songs.

'Coming home, coming home . . .' she sang with great gladness filling her heart.

Matt heard the news about Jack on his car radio as he was driving to talk to one of the family firm's customers at Skellkirk. The late news item was slotted in between the bad weather warnings put out by the local radio station that covered the area between Nyddford and Skellkirk and requests for musical favourites from listeners. At first Matt wondered if he had been mistaken in what he thought he had heard. Because young Jack was certainly not the sort of lad to take himself off without warning and cause the wave of anxiety that would now be fanning out from his home, his school and his grandparents' home.

Oh God, what would the news do to them? To his own father, who was so fond of the lad, and to Jack's lovely gran, Dorothy. What if the anxiety triggered off another heart attack for his dad? If the news was correct, he must turn back right now and go to them, and to hell with the client he was supposed to be meeting. He felt sick at the thought of harm coming to Jack, who was just the sort of sparky, intelligent lad he would love to have had for a son. Jack would never act in an irresponsible way. There had to be a mistake. There must be! He needed to know what was happening at Abbot's Fold Farm; he had to find out right away. He could not drive on with his mind so full of anxiety that he would not be able to give enough concentration to negotiating this bendy, dangerous road in thick fog. As soon as he reached the place where a left fork led into a pub car park he would pull off the road and ring Julie on his mobile.

'It's Matt,' he began the moment he knew they were in contact. Her impatient exclamation in reply warned him that she was not pleased to hear from him.

'Not now, Matt. Dave could be trying to get in touch with

me. I've told you before: you're wasting your time,' she said sharply.

'Don't hang up on me yet!' he pleaded. 'I want to know what's happening about Jack. I just heard the news on my radio and I'm worried about him.'

'We're all worried about him. We've been worried about him for hours now. I must get back to Dave as soon as I can.'

'Do Dad and Dorothy know yet?'

'Yes. We had to tell them before they heard it on the radio.'

'I'm afraid for Dad – about what the worry will do to him. I was on my way to Skellkirk to see a client when I heard the news, but I'm about to turn back and go to see them instead. I just wanted to know if Jack was safe before I got there,' he ended.

'Sorry, Matt! I didn't mean to snap at you, but I'm so on edge because of what might have happened to Jack. It's not like him to go off without telling us where he's going, and with the fog being so bad too. He was looking after a dog for an old man who's in the cottage hospital. The dog managed to escape last night, so we're wondering if he went to look for it and got lost in the fog somewhere. I'm on my way home now, but I'll let you know as soon as we have any news. Look after Dorothy and Ben for me, won't you? Try to keep them calm if you can.'

'Yes, I'll do that.'

Driving on, at a speed much slower than he was accustomed to doing on this road in better weather conditions, Matt decided that if his parents were coping with the situation reasonably well, he would go to Abbot's Fold Farm as soon as possible and offer to join the search for the boy. He had to do *something*; he couldn't just sit around thinking about the sort of things that might have happened to young Jack. Or imagining how different Julie's life would have been if she had married *him* instead of Dave Bramley . . .

Jack moaned as he hovered on the edge of consciousness again and felt a sharp shaft of pain pierce his leg. He thought it must be morning now because everything around him was a strange murky white. Why wasn't he in his bed at Abbot's Fold? If it really was morning, why couldn't he hear any of the usual sounds coming from below as the dogs began to bark when his dad went about the buildings? The dogs! There was something about a dog in the dream he had just been having. Something about a dog running away from him. It couldn't be Brack, though, because Brack wouldn't ever run away from him. Brack would come to heel at once when told to. She was *his* special dog, the one Dad had not wanted him to choose but the one he had loved as soon as he saw her. If Brack was here now, he wouldn't be so cold, because she would be curled up close to him, keeping him warm, like she did when he managed to sneak her into his bedroom. He wanted Brack now; he wanted her so that he would know everything was all right. Everything *wasn't* all right! He knew it wasn't, because he shouldn't be out here feeling so awful and not being able to do anything about it. His leg hurt all the time except when he was asleep, but if he let himself fall asleep again he would never be able to find the dog that had run away from him. He had to find that dog, because he had promised he would look after it. Only he couldn't quite remember why he had to look after the dog called Archie. His head felt all funny again and he was so, so tired that he knew he was going to fall asleep again . . .

When Andrea steered her car into the lane that led to the farm, she could hardly see the farmhouse because of the fog that hung so thickly about it. She knew she ought not to leave the car out in the lane, because there wouldn't be enough room for another larger vehicle to get past without scraping the drystone wall. As she got closer to the farm gate, she saw that it had been left open for her. Dave must have been too worried to close it behind him when he drove off to Nyddham and Abbey Cottages. His dog must have gone with him because there was only the barking of Jack's dog to welcome her. Brack seemed to know that there was something wrong. Her barking stopped when she saw that it was not her young master who had come through the gate and she began to whine with a terrible melancholy sound that Andrea found hard to bear.

'Poor Brack,' she murmured as she stopped to give the young collie a swift caress on her way to the back door. 'He'll be home soon.'

'Dear God, please let Jack soon be safe at home,' she prayed silently again as she stepped into the porch and gave a tap on the door.

'It's Andrea, Carla,' she called as she opened the back door.

There was no answering sound from within the kitchen – no radio playing, no electrical equipment busily and noisily doing its job of cleaning floors or washing clothes. So Andrea hesitated before going any further. Then, as she waited just outside the kitchen door, she caught the faint sound of a stifled sob. Her heart gave a great lurch. Seconds later she was beside Carla on the old sofa that Dave had spent the night on, speaking softly but urgently to her.

'Has there been news, Carla, since I spoke to your dad?'

The answer was muttered into the girl's hands, covering her face as she tried to regain control of herself.

'No. No news. No Jack.'

Andrea let go of a long sigh. 'Then we can go on hoping he's going to be all right, wherever he is, can't we?' she murmured.

Carla's hands fell from her ravaged face as she began to speak. 'You don't understand. It's all my fault! If anything's happened to our Jack, it'll be because of me!'

There were more tears gushing down her face as Andrea waited for her to explain. 'What makes you think that, Carla?' she asked quietly, putting an arm about the shaking shoulders.

'I told Dad and Julie that he was watching TV, but I don't really know if he was, because I was talking to my friend on the phone out in the hall for quite a long time while Dad was out of the house checking the animals and the buildings. When I went back into the kitchen Jack wasn't there, so I thought he'd gone up to bed. Only he hadn't, had he?'

'That doesn't make it your fault that he's missing,' Andrea reasoned.

'But I lied about it, and it could have been important. Dad will never forgive me if Jack's dead. I know he won't.'

'Listen to me, Carla.' Andrea's voice was firm. 'You have to put that idea right out of your head, because your dad loves you, and always will. Also you have to show Julie, when she comes home, that you can cope in a crisis as you'll need to be able to do if you go into nursing.'

Carla pressed her lips tightly together to stop them trembling before she spoke. 'Julie knows I can cope in a crisis. She said so when I looked after her once when she fainted.'

'Show her you can cope in *this* crisis then and she'll know she wasn't wrong about you. She and your dad need you to behave in a grown-up way just now. They'll be proud of you then. It won't be long before she gets home now, so why don't you start preparing something for all of you to eat then? Something easy, like soup and cheese perhaps? I'm sure you'll have things like that in the pantry or the fridge.'

'Yes, we will.' Carla scrubbed at her eyes as she got to her feet. 'Will you stay please, Andrea? That's if you have time . . .'

'I'll stay till Julie gets back,' Andrea promised.

That would mean leaving her preparations for this evening's Lent meeting till later, but nothing mattered to her right now as much as being here for the family at Abbot's Fold when they needed her most.

'Thanks, Andrea. I'm glad you're here,' Carla said on her way to the pantry.

Twenty-One

When Dave finally made it to the hamlet of old stone cottages that were set about three-quarters of a mile from the ruined abbey, his shoulders and his face were wet with the moisture deposited on them by the fog that had drifted in through the open window of the Land Rover. He had kept the window open so he could keep peering out into the gloom, hoping for a glimpse of Jack, though why the boy should be out here in this foul weather at this time instead of being safe in Nyddford High School Dave simply could not imagine. Though, to be honest with himself, he could guess why Jack might have taken himself off last night after he had found that the dog called Archie had gone missing. It was something Dave *could* imagine all too well, because hadn't he specifically warned his son that *he* was responsible for keeping the animal fastened up so that it could not do any damage to the sheep?

Once he knew that old Joe's dog was on the loose Jack would have got himself into a panic and set out to search for it, in spite of the fact that it would be an impossible task in such bad weather. That was Jack: if you gave him a job to do, he would do it to the best of his ability. Only somehow, in spite of that, the bloody creature had given him the slip and he was obviously afraid of what his father would say when he found out. Shame stirred inside Dave when he faced that fact. What sort of father was he to have a son who was afraid of him? What would Jill have thought about this situation? Tears pricked behind his eyes as that thought came into his mind.

What was Julie thinking about it right now as she went about her work? She would be worrying about what might have happened to the boy she had known, and loved, since he was a baby. Maybe she was wishing she had not married *him* last year and taken on the responsibility for his children. He could not have blamed her if she did have such thoughts. All he could do now, as he came to the point in the narrow road where the centuries-old ruined abbey should have been in sight, was to hope that when he reached the few cottages beyond it, which made up the hamlet of Nyddham, there would be some clue there as to what had happened to Jack.

It was a bit late for him to start saying a prayer now about that – especially since his praying days had come to a swift end when Jill had been killed and his children had been left without a mother. Yet even as the thought hovered in his mind, he knew that several miles away at Ford House his mother would certainly be praying hard for the safety of her grandson. So would Ben, who had taken Jack on board as a grandson when he had married Dorothy Bramley. So would Andrea, who was not just a friend to Dorothy and Ben, and Julie, but was also their minister. If the handful of cottages now looming closer through the fog did not lead him to Jack, there would be nothing left for *him* to do except pray.

The silence all about him, after he switched off the car engine and came to a halt at the end of the row of ancient dwellings, was absolute. He got out of the driving seat and peered about him, but he could see no signs of life. No other vehicles except his own. No animals – not even a stray sheep. He shivered as he approached the nearest front door via a narrow track that could not really be described as a footpath. When he lifted a hand to knock on the door, he saw that the colour of the paint was indistinguishable. The sound he made echoed eerily. A glance through the window revealed that the place was empty of anything except a couple of wooden crates.

With a sigh he moved on to the next door. Again there was no response to his knock. The window was shrouded in tattered, grimy nets and there was a note pinned to the door giving the information that someone called Brown could now be found at an address in Nyddford. That left only two more cottages to go. Dave had a feeling they would also be deserted.

Surely the old man who was at present in the cottage hospital would not live in such an isolated place?

The footpath leading to the third dwelling was tidily maintained, the door boasted a brass knocker that had not been allowed to tarnish, and the lace curtains looked clean. With hope in his heart Dave used the knocker vigorously, but in vain, before turning away in despair. He was part-way down the path on his way to take a look at the remaining place when a voice hailed him from there.

'Not much use knocking there now Joe Robinson's away in yon 'ospital. If it's anything 'at can't wait, you'll 'ave to go there to see 'im.'

Dave covered the short distance between the two dwellings hastily. 'It's not him I'm looking for,' he began.

'There's nobody else lives there with Joe, 'cept that old dog of 'is, and I can't tell you where that's got to,' the voice broke in.

The voice belonged to a tall, thin man of advanced years who was inspecting him with a challenging stare that made Dave feel vaguely uncomfortable. So much so that he hurried to explain his visit. 'I'm looking for a boy,' he said. 'My son. He's twelve.'

'No good looking 'ere. There's nobody that age 'ere. Just me and Joe, and old Archie, nowadays,' he was told forthrightly.

'The boy was looking after Joe's dog, on my farm, and it got loose and ran away. I thought he might have come here to look for it, if it had made for home.'

'Dog's not 'ere either. Boy shouldn't be out in such weather on 'is own. You ought to know that, if you're 'is father,' the voice accused.

'I do know; that's why I'm here!' Dave hit back sharply, and prepared to get back to his car

'If you see Joe, tell 'im I miss 'im. We're old army mates, you see. Served together in France and 'Olland a long time ago, we did. '

'I'll tell him,' Dave called over his shoulder as he moved away.

'I 'ope you soon find your lad,' came the response.

'So do I!' Dave took the words and the hope with him as he got into the driving seat and tried to decide where to look next. Whether to continue on the narrow winding road to the next village or to go back to the main road. It was then that he began to wonder whether Jack had been picked up by someone who had offered him a lift – someone who had a liking for young boys . . . Fear engulfed him. He whispered his anguish into the fog that was creeping in through the open window.

'Dear God, not that!' Once uttered, he found his lips moving soundlessly as he prayed that Jack was still alive, still unharmed, still in a place where he could be found and taken home.

When Matt reached Ford House, he was relieved to find that Ben and Dorothy were coping with the anxiety better than he had dared to hope. As he let himself into the front hall, he caught the aroma of roasting chicken. After being enthusiastically welcomed by their golden retriever he followed the scent to the kitchen, where Dorothy was calmly making crumble topping for the apples Ben was peeling and slicing.

It was Dorothy who spoke first. 'I had a feeling you'd come, Matt. There's plenty of food for you, if you've got time to stay and share it.'

'I was on my way to Skellkirk to see Jim Watson when I heard the news on local radio, so I thought I ought to turn back and come here instead.'

'Have you let Jim Watson know you're not going to meet him?' Ben put in.

'Yes. He'd already heard the news, so he wasn't surprised.'

'I don't suppose *you* can think of anywhere Jack can have gone, Matt?' Dorothy rested her hands on the edge of the mixing bowl as she asked him this.

Matt shook his head. 'I only wish I could, Dorothy. It's a complete mystery why he should go off like this without telling anyone, isn't it?'

Dorothy bit her lip as she stared down into the bowl. Then she blinked away a tear as she gave him her answer. 'It seems he was looking after a dog for an old man who is at present in the cottage hospital with a chest infection, and he allowed it to escape. He must have gone to try and get it back. That was some time last night. So something must have happened to him, or he'd have been back long before now.'

Matt could guess why Jack was so desperate to recapture the dog. A wave of sympathy for Dorothy stirred inside him. She would know well enough what had motivated her grandson to leave the comfort of his home late at night to go in search of a stranger's dog. Fear of his father's wrath would be all he needed to push him into doing that.

'I know David wasn't keen on having old Joe spending the night in one of the farm buildings,' Dorothy said. 'But I think it was the dog he was uneasy about rather than Joe. Archie is a one-man dog who won't take orders from anyone except his own master. With so many young lambs about at this time of the year David was right to be worried.'

Matt scowled. 'Well, now he's got more than his animals to be worrying about, hasn't he? Who knows what can have happened to Jack . . .?'

'That's enough, Matt!' Ben warned.

'He's always been too hard on the lad, and on Carla as well. I don't know how Julie puts up with it.' Even as he uttered the words, Matt knew he had gone too far. His father's next words confirmed it.

'If that's the best you can do to help Dorothy's family at such a time, you would have been better going to Skellkirk to talk business with Jim Watson. Just watch what you say, lad!'

Matt took a deep breath. 'I'm not saying anything else. I'm on my way to Abbot's Fold right now to go out and look for the boy.'

As he finished speaking, he was already on his way to the door. When it closed behind him, the couple still in the warmth of the kitchen stared at one another in dismay for a long moment. Then, 'I told you he was still too fond of Julie,' Dorothy said with a sigh.

Ben shrugged. 'It could just be that he's very fond of the boy; very concerned about him.'

Dorothy stifled a sob. 'We're all concerned about him, aren't we?'

Ben put an arm about her. 'He'll turn up soon, safe and sound, I'm sure,' he murmured as he kissed her trembling lips.

Dorothy could not feel so sure, and now that Matt had rushed out of the house to go to Abbot's Fold there was another worry in her mind: in the mood Matt was in he might say things to David that were best left unsaid.

The sound of the phone broke into their conversation while Carla was preparing vegetables for dinner and Andrea was doing some ironing. Both women were startled by it. Both women were uneasy about it.

'Will you answer it, please, Andrea?' Carla begged as their glances met across the kitchen. Deep inside her fear stirred about what news this phone call might bring.

Andrea set down the iron and went into the hall to do so. 'It's for you, Carla. It's someone called Price,' she said as she went back to the ironing board.

'It'll be Paula, from the Mill House, I expect.' Carla put down the vegetable peeler and wiped her wet hands down the side of her jeans as she went out to take the call.

Paula was the girl whose father had died before they could open the Mill House to guests – the girl Andrea had felt so sorry for when she had gone to make arrangements for her father's funeral service. Paula was also the girl who was looking after Joe Robinson's dog since it had turned up on her doorstep after escaping from Abbot's Fold. Andrea carried on with the ironing, hoping that Julie would be back soon so she could go home to her manse and do some work at her desk. The phone call seemed to be quite a long one. She wondered if Paula Price was ringing to let them know that the dog had escaped again. At last, just before Jack's dog began to bark out in the yard to signal the arrival of Julie, Carla came back into the kitchen.

'I thought it was going to be Paula, about the job she's giving me at Easter, but it was one of her cousins. At least I *think* he must be a cousin or something because he's called

Price too. He's in the sixth at Nyddford High,' Carla added. Her expression was brighter as she spoke.

'Did he have some news of Jack?' Andrea asked.

Instantly Carla became serious again. 'No. He was just ringing during his lunch break to say how sorry he was. He asked if he could come here after school and help us to look for Jack.'

'That was kind of him.'

'Yes.' Carla bit her lip, then said, 'I always thought he was just a brainbox, because he's aiming to go to Oxford or Cambridge.'

That brought a chuckle from Andrea. 'Obviously he's a brainbox with a warm heart.'

'Yes, he must be,' Carla said dreamily as Julie hurried into the kitchen.

Julie's eyes went straight to Carla. 'I don't suppose there's any news yet or you'd have let me know on my mobile.'

The hurt was back on Carla's face as she answered. 'No. Dad's gone to Nyddham to see if there's any sign of him up there.'

Julie frowned. 'Surely he wouldn't be likely to walk all that way?'

'Could he have gone there on his bike?' Andrea suggested.

'He didn't have his bike. It's still in the shed. I suppose if he knew Mr Robinson lived there he might think Archie had made a dash for his home once he was free.' Julie was so tired now that she was having trouble reasoning what could have been in Jack's mind.

'And all the time Archie was just at the bottom of the hill in the Mill House, having a much more comfortable night than any of you,' Andrea commented.

'Is he still there?' Carla wanted to know.

'Yes. Paula's going to keep him with her until Mr Robinson is fit to leave hospital,' Andrea told them. 'I'd better be going home to my paperwork now, but I'll be in touch later.'

'Thanks a lot for coming, Andrea,' Julie's lips trembled as she gave Andrea a hug. 'Especially when you're not feeling too well.'

Andrea managed to smile as she replied. 'I'm not too bad

today, and I'll be better still when Bill gets back. Only four days to go.'

'By then all this will be behind us, I hope.' They were in the back porch as Julie said this. 'The fog makes things so much worse. I keep thinking that if Jack went up on the moor after the dog he could have got lost, or been injured, and there's nothing we can do about it.'

'There's always prayer,' Andrea murmured. 'Try to keep in your mind all the people who know Jack and love him, all those who will be praying for his safe return, and all those who only know about him as an item of local news but who will also be praying for him and his family. Take courage from that, Julie. Try to be strong for Carla and Dave.'

'I'll try,' Julie promised. 'And thanks again.'

She watched as Andrea slipped into her car and drove slowly through the farm gates on to the lane that led to Abbot's Hill then down to the village. As the fog swallowed up the vehicle and driver, she found words coming unbidden into her mind. 'Thanks, Lord, for giving me Andrea's friendship. Please help me, and Dave and Carla, and Jack, wherever he is.'

Jack was sure he could hear voices, but they seemed to be a long way away from him. He thought he heard a dog bark too, but that was also a long way off. If the voices and the barking came nearer, maybe he could shout and tell them that he was here and he was hurt, and that he wanted to be at home instead of lost and frightened and in pain. Words were waiting there in his mind to be shouted, but when he tried to take a deep breath, instead of sound coming out there was a nasty pain instead. The pain was so bad that it brought tears to his eyes even though he knew he was too big to cry now.

He heard the dog bark again, but it wasn't his Brack. If it had been Brack, she would have known his scent and been able to find him. It could be Archie, though! If it *was* Archie he ought to be on his feet running over the dead heather to catch him, because Wandering Joe would be disappointed in him for letting Archie escape as he had done. He had promised to look after Archie, hadn't he? Only he couldn't quite remember when.

'I know you'll look after him, mate,' old Joe had said when the ambulance came to take him to the hospital. Jack had liked that. He liked talking to Joe, who wore his regimental badge on his old army greatcoat. Jack wondered if they had let him keep his greatcoat and his regimental badge with him at the hospital. Then he wondered if they had told him yet that Archie had got away and was running free when there were young lambs about. His dad would be real mad with him about that. Why didn't his dad come and find him? Even if he was real mad and had lost his rag with him, Jack knew he wouldn't care as long as he was back home again. If he was home again, his leg might not hurt as much, and his head would not feel so funny. Everything would not seem to be so far away . . .

Matt's big estate car passed Andrea's vehicle part-way down Abbot's Hill, but he did not recognize her, nor she him, because both were too intent on keeping clear of the drystone walls on either side of them. It was not a place or a time to let your attention wander. Matt cursed as he missed the sign on the side of the road that indicated the entry to Abbot's Moor Lane and had to drive on for some distance before he was able to find a place where it was safe to turn round. As he did so, the thought came back into his mind of just how difficult a task it was going to be finding Jack Bramley if he had strayed from the moorland footpaths and was lying injured somewhere. By now the police would be looking for him, but there would at this stage be only a limited number of them available to do so. Probably not enough to properly cover such a vast and remote area in such appalling weather.

He was back on track now and making his way along the lane to the farm. As he came to a halt he heard Jack's dog giving warning to those in the house of his arrival. Why had Jack gone off without his dog, he wondered? The two were inseparable except for when Jack went to school. It was evident when he left his car and approached Brack that she was disappointed not to find her young master with him. Her melancholy whine expressed that plainly. 'We'll find him for you, lass,' Matt said as he bent to stroke her head, but she would not be comforted.

Julie met him at the back door. She was frowning. 'I thought you were going to stay with your mother and Ben?' she challenged him.

The light cast by the porch lantern clearly showed the lines of weariness and stress on her face. His heart lurched with pity for her – pity that he dared not put into words even though he longed to. Instead, 'I did go to them but they were coping, so I thought I might be of more use to you here,' he said.

'There's nothing you can do. Nothing anyone can do until we know where he is. I've got Carla with me,' Julie told him. Plainly, she was not pleased to see him.

'I can go out and search for Jack. I'll take his dog with me.'

Julie looked doubtful. 'You won't know where to look, and Brack might not go with you. She is Jack's dog,' she reminded him.

'I'd like to try.'

'You don't have to. You're not dressed for rough walking; you're in business gear.'

'I can soon change that. I keep a bad-weather coat in the car, and you must have spare wellies about the place that will fit me. So don't argue, just get me some gear, and a coat for Jack if I manage to find him.'

A moment or so later she was back with boots that were on the small side but would do, and with Jack's farmwork coat. 'Thanks for coming, Matt,' she said.

'I'd do more than that for you, and for him,' he said as he went to collect the dog.

Brack became very excited when he held out the muddy old coat that carried the scent of her master. 'Come on, lass,' Matt said. 'Let's see if we can find him.'

He unclipped her lead from the retaining chain and allowed her to lead the way across the farmyard, behind one of the

213

buildings and over a stile in the drystone wall to where a sheep track began to go upwards towards the moor. Soon, man and dog were enclosed by the fog.

Twenty-Two

Paula listened to the early-afternoon local news while she was painting. The missing boy, Carla's young brother, had still not turned up. She could imagine the anguish the family at Abbot's Fold Farm must be going through. This latest report said the police were asking people to search their garden sheds or garages in case the boy should be hiding anywhere like that. She had taken the dog called Archie all round the extensive garden of the Mill House three times since this morning in case Jack Bramley had taken refuge there, because she remembered being told by his sister that, in the days when the American Bolton family had been living there, he liked to come to their barbecues held in the garden.

'Please look round your garden again, Paula,' Carla had begged when Paula had telephoned to say she had the missing dog that the boy was supposed to be looking after. So Paula had taken Archie into every part of the garden, inspecting the summer house and the tool shed and the two garages; peering into the heart of bushes and underneath the hedges, all to no avail. She had done the same thing at lunch time and again in mid-afternoon, while all the time the fog seemed not to be lifting but to be getting worse.

It occurred to her now, as she heard one of the workmen speaking to Archie, who was fretting at being fastened up on his own in the utility room while she was painting, that there would be no point now in Daniel Price coming to take the dog back to his home when his master was still in hospital. Such a journey at the end of a day at work in his business several miles away would be something he would be pleased not to have to do. So she must phone him and tell him as soon as she had washed the paint off her hands.

215

It was time to take a break from painting anyway and make the plumber and the electrician mugs of tea.

As she waited for Daniel to answer, she reflected ruefully that she would have to eat supper alone tonight after all. Except, that was, for Archie. She had been looking forward to meeting Daniel again. Which was strange, she thought, when he was the reason why she was no longer the sole inheritor of her father's share in this house.

The voice that answered her call belonged to a woman, an older woman, who told her that Daniel was not available but would ring her back shortly. So Paula got on with making tea for the workmen. His call came while she was enjoying her own hot drink. 'Sorry to keep you waiting, Paula. I was involved with one of my wholesale customers when you rang and he was anxious to be on his way back.'

'I just thought I should let you know that there's no point in us taking Archie to his home tonight because there won't be anyone there. His master is in Nyddford Cottage Hospital,' she told him.

'Oh! So you don't want me to come after all?'

She thought he sounded disappointed. 'Well, as you were only coming to take the dog to his home, I thought you might be glad not to have to turn out in such bad weather at the end of your day's work.'

Daniel sighed audibly. 'So I won't be sampling your cooking again tonight, Paula? I was quite looking forward to it!'

Now she chuckled. 'Were you really? It wasn't going to be anything wildly exciting because I've been painting all day, apart from when I've been taking Archie for walks. It was only going to be pasta.'

'I like pasta, and I like walking dogs. So, if I can still have the pasta, I'll walk Archie for you afterwards; then you don't have to go out into the fog after dark,' he told her.

'I haven't enjoyed walking him in daylight very much because of the fog,' she confessed. 'In fact, since I took him out into the village this morning I've only been giving him walks round the garden here and at the same time looking round the bushes and hedges, hoping I might discover the missing boy somewhere out there.'

'Of course; there was something on the radio about him, wasn't there?'

'Yes. He's the young brother of a girl called Carla Bramley who's going to help me here during weekends and holidays.'

'His parents must be worried out of their minds.'

'Yes. So is his sister. She thinks the reason he's gone missing is because he was supposed to be looking after Archie while his master is in hospital and he let the dog get away from him. Carla thinks he ran after it, and then either got lost or has been injured and can't walk home.'

'Poor little devil!' There was a pause, then Daniel spoke again. 'Have you made your mind up yet, Paula?'

'Made my mind up?'

'About whether I can still come and eat pasta with you tonight, then do the dog-walking.'

She laughed. 'I have. I'll still be pleased to see you, Daniel.'

'Do you really mean that? In spite of . . .'

'In spite of what?'

'What my appearance in your life has cost you.'

Now she was silent for a long moment as she considered what he had just said. 'You were not aware of what was to happen, were you? It's not as if . . .'

'I certainly was not! It was almost as big a shock for me as it must have been to you.'

'So why should I feel badly towards you? I just wish . . .' She broke off there, unwilling to complete what she had been about to say.

'I can guess what you wish, Paula. When you know me better, perhaps you'll be able to understand the things I've not been able to explain to you yet. It might still be too soon for that.'

With that he ended the call and left her with yet more questions in her mind.

Andrea sat at the computer in her study, but she found it hard to concentrate on dealing with the more complicated documents that she had planned to get out of the way before Bill arrived home. This was the part of her work that she least enjoyed. What she liked most was her involvement with the people of her churches: the men and women who needed her assurance that with faith in their lives they would manage to cope with the problems, temptations, disasters and family tragedies which were all part of their lives. Today she found herself so acutely concerned with the troubled time her friends at Abbot's Fold Farm were experiencing that it was not possible for her to dismiss them from her mind for any more than a few minutes. How she wished that Bill were here with her to share, as he so often did, her search for ways to help those who needed the support of her faith, and sometimes her practical help.

She had been offering short prayers for the Bramley family throughout the day since hearing about Jack. As morning had given way to afternoon without news of him, and as afternoon was now moving towards early evening, her anxiety was deepening. It was pushing aside all the things the paper-work on her desk represented: the meetings, the plans for the festival to be held in celebration of the completion of the Nyddford Church repairs, and the remaining Lent courses. How would the Bramleys manage to cope if this day ended in tragedy for them? Would the marriage of Dave and Julie survive it? Or would it gradually destroy the relationship, which had been so precarious for a long time before they married? There were times when Andrea sensed that theirs was a fragile bond which might fail, as her own first marriage had done, when the life of a precious child was lost.

Then there were the two people at Ford House to be prayed for – the two who had both previously had to face the loss of partners, and in Dorothy's case the death of a beloved daughter-in-law. This latest worrying event could have the most serious effect on their health. Perhaps she ought to ring them and let them know that her thoughts were with them? Yes, she would do that. There was always the chance that Jack had been found now, in which case she might be able to give all of her mind to her notes for the Lent Group meeting tomorrow.

When she tapped out their number, the response was so swift that she guessed how close to the phone they must have been. 'It's Andrea, Ben,' she told him, and in the moment

218

immediately following heard his long sigh of disappointment.

'There's still no news of him. None at all!' Ben's voice
broke with his distress. 'I'm beginning to fear the worst,
Andrea. That's why I'm trying to answer all the phone calls
instead of Dorothy. This is so hard for her to bear! It's not
easy for me either, because I've become so fond of the little
lad.'

'Yes, Ben, I know, but Jack isn't really *such* a little lad,
is he? He's twelve, he's bright and fit and intelligent. So
there still *is* every hope that he's just got lost somewhere up
on the moor and will soon be found. That's what we have
to pray for.'

'Matt is out there now with Jack's dog, hoping that the
dog will pick up his scent and manage to find him. The
police are also keeping a lookout for him. Though they still
think he could just turn up and wonder what all the fuss is
about, because they have no real reason to suspect that
anything bad has happened to him. I hope to God that they
are right!'

'That's what we all have to do,' Andrea said quietly. 'Give
my love to Dorothy,' she added.

'I will. Can you believe it, Andrea; she's making a chocolate cake for when Jack comes home!'

'Yes,' Andrea said. 'I can believe it, and she's doing the
right thing.'

At number 14, Nyddford Gardens, Tim Lindsay was playing
with his children while Jane was cooking their evening meal.
Their big black dog, Darcy, seemed almost as excited as
Elliot and Kerry were.

'Darcy likes it when you are here for a long time, Daddy,'
Elliot said as he set up the carpet skittles again that the dog
had just knocked down.

'He doesn't like it when you go away again,' Kerry put
in. 'He sits behind the door and cries.'

Tim smiled. That was not going to happen tonight, because
tonight he would not be going away. He would be here until
it was time for him to go to school tomorrow morning. This

weekend he would be packing up at the flat he had been renting and moving back here for good, but the children were not aware of that yet. When they had all eaten, he and Jane would tell them. There was a huge surge of emotion inside him at the thought of doing that. Of course he should never have left Jane and his children, and now he could hardly believe that he had behaved in such an irresponsible way.

It was as if, during those long months when Jane was living in Devon with her parents while the builders were finishing off the house they had bought close to his new job at Nyddford High School, he had somehow lost his way and become a different person. It had been like going back to being a single man rather than a family man. There had been resentment at first with Jane for having decided to stay with the children instead of leaving them with her parents, or his own, rather than share the very basic rented flat in Nyddford with him. Loneliness at weekends had sent him to the walking group, and those weekend walks had resulted in him becoming friendly with his colleague Donna Dawson.

He had never intended it to go beyond friendship with her because his love for Jane was still there and always would be, but friendship had turned to pity when Donna had told him of her illness. Then, soon afterwards, comforting Donna had led to him making love to her. It had been so easy to do that after sharing a meal with her at her own flat, and he had vowed to himself that it would not happen again; but when she had told him that her illness was terminal and begged him to stay with her, he simply had not been able to bring himself to leave her – even though by then Jane and his children had been living here in this house.

The misery of those final weeks of Donna's life had been unlike anything he had ever experienced before, and had been made so much worse by the unhappiness he knew he was causing for his family. His visits here had been short then, and traumatic, with Elliot constantly asking when he was coming back to live with them and Kerry weeping herself into exhaustion every time he left. The burden of guilt he felt for what he had done to all of them was something he felt he would carry with him for the rest of his life.

220

He was still hardly able to believe that Jane was willing to take him back, even though he had been asking her to do that for so long.

'Please come back for good, Tim,' Jane had said in her phone call to his mobile while he had been with other teaching staff discussing the disappearance of Jack Bramley. 'Come back tonight!'

There was a lump beginning to swell in his throat as he remembered her words, and moisture in his eyes as he looked at his children and gave silent thanks for them.

'There's a car coming up the lane, Julie,' Carla Bramley said. 'Do you think . . .'

'I don't know, love,' Julie answered wearily. 'It might just be another policeman coming to see if he can help.'

Carla continued to stare out of the kitchen window, from which in good weather a clear view of the lane could be gained, and watched as the headlights of the vehicle became a little brighter before being switched off. Because of the swirling fog she was unable to recognize the person stepping away from it. It might be anyone, but it certainly could not be Jack. She blinked back tears. There were no warning barks to be heard from the dogs either, Tyke being out with her dad searching one area while Brack was out on Abbot's Moor with Matt Harper. Already Julie was on her way to the back door to find out who the caller was, and if they had any news of Jack. Carla heard the surprise in her voice as she spoke to him.

'You'd better come in, Simon. I'm sure she'll be pleased to see you. It's good of you to come.'

Shock kept Carla silent at first when she turned her head and saw who Julie had invited into the kitchen. It was Simon Price, still in his school gear and with his black hair standing up in spikes above his long, serious face.

'I thought I'd come and see if I can help with the search for Jack,' he told her as he stood there shuffling his feet awkwardly.

Carla bit her bottom lip to try to control the tears that were threatening to overflow again. All she could manage to do was look down at the floor and mutter, 'Thanks.'

It was Julie who broke into their shyness and eased it. 'If you've come straight from school, you must be ready for a hot drink, Simon. How about a coffee?'

Simon nodded. 'If it's not too much trouble, Mrs Bramley.'

'I'll make it!' Carla hastened to volunteer.

Julie let her get on with it. Turning to Simon, she put a question. 'Do your parents know you are here? They might be wondering why you are late home . . .'

'They won't be. They know where I am. Mum lent me her car,' he told her. 'She said it might be useful in the search.'

'That was nice of her. I think you'd better have a sandwich with your coffee before you go.'

'I'm going with him,' Carla said then. 'I know the sort of places Jack likes to go with Brack.'

'You ought to have a sandwich too because you could be out for some time, and you'd better take my mobile with you.' Julie was already buttering rolls and slicing cheese as she spoke.

'We won't need your mobile, Mrs Bramley, and you might need it yourself. I've brought my own with me.' Simon slid it out of his pocket to show them.

'If our Jack had one, we wouldn't all be so worried now,' Carla broke in, it being a sore point with her that Dave would not allow her to have a mobile phone, as he guessed at the bills she would be likely to run up while gossiping with her friends.

'You know why your dad won't let you have one yet, Carla,' Julie reminded her.

'I'll get one soon, when I start working for Paula at the Mill House,' Carla said while Simon drank his coffee and remained silent. 'I don't think I can eat a sandwich.'

'You could take it with you,' Julie told her, 'and I'll fill a flask with coffee in case . . .'

'Yes, if we find Jack, he'll be ready for a hot drink.' Simon was eating at speed as he spoke, eager to get started on his search.

Julie wrapped a couple of cheese rolls in cling film and handed them over to Carla, who was already wearing her

222

hooded fleece. 'Keep in touch, love,' she begged. Then, turning to Simon: 'Do try to keep your speed down in this fog; then you'll be able to borrow your mum's car again, won't you?'

'I will,' he promised. 'Thanks for the coffee, Mrs Bramley.'

'You're welcome, Simon. See you later.'

Julie stood at the open back door watching them go, two tall young people who ought to have been going out somewhere to enjoy themselves rather than into the fogbound countryside on what could prove to be an impossible task. The thought came to her that if they found Jack, it might already be too late. He had been missing now for over twenty hours. Twenty hours' exposure, perhaps lying injured somewhere, could be fatal. She knew that only too well after her many years of nursing.

What would a second tragedy do to Dave? How would he ever manage to survive it?

Since that thought proved too terrifying to dwell on any longer, she pushed it into the back of her mind and went back into the kitchen to find work to do that would occupy her mind and prevent her from imagining the worst – even though she knew that the worst might already have happened.

Twenty-Three

'Where the bloody hell are you, lad?' Matt shouted his rage into the fog and paused yet again to listen. The silence was absolute, and eerie, until the dog at his feet whined. He reached down to put a hand on the creature's head. The thick black hair was damp and flattened by the all-pervading moisture that encompassed both of them. 'I know, lass,' Matt murmured when Brack whined again. 'You don't know where to look for him next, and neither do I.'

The battery in his lamp was growing dimmer and daylight had almost gone. He was weary now and felt chilled to the bone in spite of his leather jacket; yet he could not face going back to the farm and telling Julie that he had not been able to locate Jack. He'd used his mobile a couple of times to check with her whether her stepson was safely home again but each time had received the same discouraging answer. Now, after calling the boy's name into the fog time after time, his voice was beginning to sound like no more than a faint croak – certainly not the sort of strong and penetrating shout that would carry for some distance over this vast moorland area.

He wondered how many of them there were now taking part in this search. So far he had encountered no one else, even though he knew there would be others. There ought to be police on the job by now. Maybe it was too early for that when the missing boy was twelve years old rather than being a toddler, and police officers were thin on the ground in this rural area at the best of times. Dear God, what was going to be the result of this search? Was there going to be a boy still alive, even if injured? Or was there going to be only a body to discover; another tragedy for Dave Bramley to live with?

As this thought crossed his mind, not for the first time since he left Abbot's Fold, Brack let go another melancholy howl that sent a shiver down his back. Dogs knew when their owners were in trouble, especially Border collies. Being a farmer's son and having grown up with such animals, Matt had no doubts about that. The sheep grazing the moor stirred uneasily and moved away at the sound of that howl. Matt's throat felt raw and painful after all the shouting he had done, but still he stumbled on, putting ever more distance between himself and Abbot's Fold Farm. If only a gust of wind, the sort of strong breeze so often to be found on these moors, would come to push away this damned fog!

With this thought still in his mind, and with his eyes sore from the effort of peering ahead in such bad visibility, he and the dog made their unsteady way towards the massive, weirdly shaped rocks that loomed up suddenly and indicated to him that they must be several miles away from the farmhouse now. He was startled when he felt a fierce jerk on the end of Brack's lead.

'What is it, Brack?' he said urgently. 'Where is he?'

Now Brack gave a yelp and began to drag him upwards to where High Moor began to merge with Abbot's Moor. It was time to start shouting again, if he could summon up any sound from his burning throat. He took a deep breath, then let it go in a shout that was agony to endure.

'Jack! Jack! Jack!'

His third attempt was cut off abruptly as Brack almost dragged him off his feet as she raced along yet another sheep track with Matt flashing what light remained in his torch to either side of them. Was that a moan he heard? Or was it just another animal sound distorted by the mist? The weak beam of the light hovered over the dark heap at the base of a tall rock, moved on, then back again as the dog leapt on the bundle and gave vent to a series of joyful barks.

Jack stirred, and groaned as the movement brought him searing pain. He must be in his room at home because there was Brack licking his face and someone placing covers about him. Only there was not the softness of a duvet or blanket beneath his icy fingers but the slippery feeling of damp leather as Matt took his own jacket off and laid it over him. After that came the feel and well-known smell of his own old coat that he wore when he was helping his dad. The voice that spoke to him was vaguely familiar too, but it did not belong to his dad.

'Can you move, Jack? Or does it hurt too much?' the voice was asking now.

'It hurts,' Jack whimpered. 'It hurts a lot.'

'Where? Tell me where?'

'My leg. At the top.'

'I'll need to take a look. To see whether I can carry you or if we must wait here for help.'

The boy was silent, only half-conscious again. Matt saw the odd angle of the damaged leg and guessed it to be broken. 'Poor little sod,' he muttered under his breath as he covered him again – then reached for his mobile phone.

'I'm cold,' was the next thing he heard, so he replaced the phone and slid a hand into the pocket of the leather coat to find the small flask of hot drink, which he helped the boy to sip from the metal top. By now Brack was lying very close to Jack, his muzzle on the boy's neck, his body on his chest. There would be warmth there, Matt knew – warmth that could save Jack's life if they had to wait long for rescue. In the meantime, he must try to keep him awake.

'Do you know where we are, Jack?' he asked as loudly as he could manage. 'I need to let people know, on my phone, so they can come and find us.'

The boy frowned in concentration. It seemed a long time to Matt before he replied. 'I was running after Joe's dog. He ran up on top of Bear's Head rock. I tried to grab him, and I fell. It hurts. It hurts a lot!'

'The paramedics will be here soon, Jack. They'll help. I'll make the call to them now.'

Thank God for mobile phones, Matt thought as he made the call, hoping that the signal was strong enough, to the emergency services. After that he made a brief call to Abbot's Fold and spoke to Julie. Her voice was full of tears when she thanked him for finding Jack. Then he lay down beside the boy and the dog and put his arms about both of them.

226

Fear for Jack's life consumed him when the lad slipped into unconsciousness again. Would there be any point in praying that the boy be saved when he himself had been a stranger to prayer, or belief, for so many years? Since it wasn't for himself, but for this child who was so dear to Julie, he would have to risk it . . .

She must ring Dorothy and Ben at once, Julie decided as soon as the short call from Matt had come to an end, but first she must get a firm hold on her emotions. So she gave her nose a good blow, took a long drink from the mug of tea which had long since gone cold on her, and then let the few words she had been longing to say for many hours spill out of her into the kitchen. 'Oh, thank God! Thank God!'

When she spoke to Dorothy she heard the same thanksgiving uttered. 'I was beginning to be so afraid, Julie, when he'd been missing for so long. You hear of such dreadful things happening to children that it's hard not to fear the worst. What did happen, do you know?'

'It seems he was trying to catch the dog, the one belonging to the old chap who's in hospital just now, and he slipped and fell off Bear's Head rock. Matt thinks he's broken his leg, so I suppose he'll finish up in the cottage hospital too when the rescue people have picked him up.'

Dorothy hesitated, then voiced a new fear. 'If he's been lying there in the icy fog for all those hours, he won't be in very good shape, will he?'

Julie sighed. 'No, but he's a healthy young lad, so we have to hope for the best. I'll be in touch again when there's any more news, Dorothy.'

'Does David know yet?' his mother wanted to know.

'No, he's still out searching for him. So is Carla.'

'Not on her own, I hope!' There was alarm in the grandmother's voice.

'No, she has a school friend with her. A very tall, sixth-form lad who turned up to help with the search. He has a mobile phone with him, so I'll be able to contact them next.'

'I'd better go and tell Ben; he's been so worried too . . .'

So many people had been sharing their concern throughout

227

this day, Julie knew. Friends and neighbours, her colleagues at the health centre – and somewhere out there Dave was still searching for his son and still worrying about him, without a mobile phone that she could immediately have set his fears to rest with. She would go out and buy one for him tomorrow and have no arguments from him . . .

Dave, tramping once more over ground he was certain he had covered earlier, found himself wishing yet again that he possessed a mobile phone so that he could have kept in touch with Julie. Because there was always a chance that Jack was home now, safe and sound. His mother had wanted to give him a phone for Christmas, but having said Carla could not have one he was of the mind that to accept one himself would only set in motion another request for one from her. It wasn't the cost of the phone that worried him; it was the inevitable high cost of the constant calls Carla would make to her friends that he felt he could not afford. Jack had never asked for a mobile. If he had been given one, they might not be going through this present crisis. It was a waste of time to allow his thoughts to travel any further along that road, he reminded himself sternly. Best to follow the track down to the village and use the phone box there to contact Julie.

'Come on, Tyke,' he said wearily, flashing his heavy torch on the steep downward track that would bring him to the village. Tyke walked close to his heels and sat patiently outside the box while he used the phone. His call was answered at the second ring by a tearful Julie who could hardly get the words out as she told him of the call from Matt which had given good news.

'Matt's found him, but he's hurt. A broken leg, Matt thinks, so they'll have to stay where they are until the ambulance can get there.'

'Where are they? Can I get to them?' Dave wanted to know.

'Somewhere near Bear's Head rock, Matt said.'

'Miles away from here!' Dave was in despair when he heard that.

'Don't try to get there, Dave, not now. The rescue team will be already on their way. Just come home. I need you here.'

With that Julie ended the call, leaving Dave to drop his head on to the handset and weep hot tears of relief and exhaustion.

'We're never going to find him, are we?' Carla said with a sob in her throat. 'Something's happened to him, hasn't it? Someone's picked him up and taken him away; some gross man . . .'

Simon put an arm about her and gave her a little shake. 'Hey, you mustn't go thinking that, Carla. Jack wouldn't go with anybody he didn't know. He'll be lost in the fog somewhere, still looking for that dog. That's where he'll be.'

'Why can't we find him then? We've looked everywhere . . .'

Simon gave her another little shake that was also a hug. 'We haven't looked everywhere, not yet. There are miles and miles of open moorland where he could be – quite safe but not able to see his way home because of the fog. By now a lot of people will be out there searching too. I think we ought to give your step-mum another call to see if any of them have found him.'

Already the tall slender sixth-former was releasing her shoulders and reaching for his mobile.

'What if it's bad news?' Carla shivered. 'What would we do? First losing Mum, then our Jack. How would we cope with it?'

'Stop that sort of talk, Carla! Take the phone and speak to Julie, now!' Simon ordered.

For once, Carla did not argue with him. She just stood there and listened to what Julie had to say; then she turned towards him and said, 'They've found him. Matt and Brack have found him, but he's hurt, so they have to wait for the rescue services to get to them. Oh, Simon!'

Simon put his arms about her. When he kissed her, his mouth was wet with her tears. 'I said he'd be OK, didn't I?'

'Thanks,' she said.

'What for? I didn't find him,' he protested, still holding her close.

'Thanks for just being here with me. For trying to help, I mean.'

That was when they both realized that his expensive mobile phone had been dropped in the excitement. They both bent to pick it up, then exploded into laughter when their heads collided.

'Come on, let's get you home before they send out a search party for us,' he said as he took her arm and they began the long walk back to the car.

The fog was still thick around the Mill House when Paula heard Daniel Price's vehicle turning into the drive and coming to a halt. Archie let out a couple of barks, though whether of welcome or warning Paula was unable to decide. She took the precaution of shutting him into the utility room again before she opened the door to Daniel, just in case he made another bid for freedom. Archie had already been responsible for bringing the sort of excitement to this quiet area that they could have all done without, especially Carla Bramley's family.

'The dog's in good voice,' Daniel said with a grin. 'Is he settling in with you?'

Paula smiled back. 'I think so, but I wouldn't trust him yet not to make a bid for freedom if he got half a chance, because he seems to be a real escape artist.'

'He's probably just wanting to get back to his master, if they've been together for a long time.'

'That's why I've been keeping him on a lead every time I've taken him out.'

'You won't have enjoyed doing that in such weather?'

'No, but I've been hoping each time that I might find Carla's brother, because she told me he used to enjoy coming here to barbecues in the garden with her when the American family were living here.'

'I wonder if he's turned up yet?' Daniel was slipping off his suede jacket as he spoke.

'There was nothing on the six o'clock news, but there'll be another bulletin soon. It seems so much worse when the

230

people involved live so close, and when you actually know one of them.'

'I don't know them, but I know someone from the family the boy's grandmother married into. His name is Matt Harper and they have a farm transport business at Nyddford. I was at school with Matt.' Daniel broke off then and said he'd have to go back to his car, as he'd forgotten something.

'I'll go and put the pasta on while you do that. We'll be eating in the kitchen,' Paula told him.

She was standing with her back to the door when he came back. When she turned to face him, her eyes widened with surprise and pleasure. The flowers he was holding were full of the scents and colours of spring. The unexpected sight of them brought a swift rush of emotion to her. It was so long since anyone had brought her flowers. Gareth had not been in the habit of doing that; all the flowers in the flat they had shared had been brought for her by her father from his nursery when he came to visit them.

'Oh, how lovely!' she exclaimed. 'It's such a long time since anyone brought me flowers.'

'I'm afraid they're not properly arranged. I'm not much good at that,' Daniel told her.

'I'm surprised you found the time to buy them.'

He laughed. 'I didn't have far to go to do that. We sell them in the farm shop. Not enough of them to make it viable for us to employ a florist, but sufficient to tempt some of the customers who come to buy the farm produce.'

'Is the farm produce from your own farm?' she asked as she took the flowers and found a tall jug to stand them in.

'From my father's farm mostly, though I do get supplies from other people as well. The retail business is mine.' He was sitting, quite relaxed, in one of the chairs at the large round table, which Paula had set with mats, cutlery and a bottle of red wine.

'You did the same as my dad then: diversified from traditional farming?'

'Yes, quite a few years ago when I saw the way the farming industry was going.'

Paula frowned. 'I don't know whether that was the reason Dad left the farm here or not. He never really said much about it. Sometimes I got the impression it could have been more to do with some sort of family upset. I don't think *his* father agreed with what he wanted to do, so he went to work on a big estate in the south. By the time I was born he had his own garden centre.' She waited for Daniel to comment on this, to add to her own scant knowledge about what had happened perhaps; but he did not do so.

Instead he referred back to her delight with the flowers. 'I would have thought that by now there would have been someone regularly bringing you flowers, Paula. Someone special to you, I mean.'

Paula served up the pasta before she replied. 'There was someone special for a couple of years, but he wasn't into buying me flowers. Dad was the one who brought me the flowers, from his own garden centre.'

They gave their attention to the food and the wine then. It was when she brought the cheese tray to the table and made coffee that Daniel returned to the subject she would much rather have left alone. Archie had been allowed to join them and was lying just behind her chair, keeping a watchful eye on the stacks of cheese biscuits which were so temptingly close. The aroma of freshly brewed coffee was scenting the warm air and Paula was feeling relaxed in the company of the man and the dog who both ought to be still feeling like strangers to her, but were not. So the question that Daniel put to her caught her off guard.

'Tell me more about the man who didn't bring you flowers, Paula. Is he still around?' He was gazing intently at her as he asked that question.

She took her time about answering him. Then, 'No, not any more,' she said. 'At least he wasn't until he turned up here unexpectedly when he heard about Dad.'

'What happened? Or would you rather I didn't ask?' Again his regard was intense.

She shrugged her slender shoulders and stared down at the crumbs of cheese on her plate. 'I suppose it was Dad's accident, to start with. You see, it left him with serious sight problems, so I went back to live with him when he came out of hospital.'

'What about your mother? Wasn't she able to cope?' he asked quietly.

Paula shrugged again. 'She left us when I was still at school, and he never found anyone else, so he only had me. I couldn't leave him to manage on his own. I thought it would only be for a short time, but it didn't work out like that. Gareth got tired of waiting for me to go back to him, and that was the end of our engagement.'

'I suppose when he heard of your father's death he came to ask you to go back to him?'

Paula shook her head slowly, sadly. 'No. It wasn't quite like that. He came to ask me to sell this place and put the money into us buying a restaurant together, as we had been planning to do before Dad's accident.'

She heard his sharp intake of breath, followed by a long moment of silence before he asked another question. 'What did you say to that, Paula?'

'I told him it was not mine to sell; not all of it anyway.'

Now his face was full of distress. 'Oh God, Paula, I feel more guilty than ever now.'

'Why? It wasn't your fault.' She faced him as she told him the rest. 'I could have agreed to sell the place and share the proceeds with you, but since I've lived here I've come to feel that it's the right place for me and that Dad would have wanted me to stay and see if I can make a success of it. Now I'm quite determined to do that.'

'Couldn't he have stayed and worked here with you?'

She shook her head vigorously. 'No, he wasn't willing to do that. He wanted me to go back to London with *him*.'

'So your father's will has spoiled your life?' There was a deep sadness in his eyes as he voiced these words.

Her answer startled him. 'No! It may have changed my life, altered some of my plans, but even without Dad I love living here. It's where I want to stay. So I must make a success of the Mill House; then I *will* be able to stay, won't I?'

Daniel smiled. 'If everything you cook is as good as what

233

I've eaten tonight, you're certain to make a success of this place.'

'Then I'll be able to make sure you get what Dad intended you to have.'

There was a long moment of silence after she said the words. Then Daniel reached across the table and took her hands in his own. 'I don't give a damn about what your father intended me to have, Paula. I have no right to it anyway because I'm certainly *not* related to your father. It seems he was in love with my mother before he left Yorkshire, but she married his older brother and they adopted me. Perhaps your father got the wrong idea about who I really am? That's why I feel so sorry, and so guilty.'

As Daniel finished speaking he released her hands and got to his feet. 'Come on, Archie; let's give you that walk. Then I'm going back home, because I've got some urgent paperwork to do.'

While he was out with the dog Paula switched on the local radio to get the latest news. When he came back she was able to tell him that Jack Bramley had been found and was being taken to hospital.

'I won't stay any longer now, Paula,' Daniel said. 'Thanks for the meal. I'll see you again soon. There are so many things I want to say to you, but not tonight. We need to get to know each other better first.'

He took her hands in his own and held them briefly, but warmly, then went out to his car. She found herself wishing he had not been in such a hurry to leave her. There were other times to look forward to though, those times when Daniel had said they would get to know each other better . . .

Twenty-Four

A ndrea drove very slowly along Beck Lane, fighting her weariness and the fog, which, though slightly less dense now that a breeze was stirring, still made driving along such a narrow road hazardous. The lights from the cottages were barely visible and the glow cast from the overhead lamps was only just sufficient for her to see the edges of the grass verges. Her eyes felt sore and her shoulders tense, but soon she would be home in her manse, and soon Bill, her beloved Bill, would be back to share it with her – back to paint more of his beautiful pictures of Yorkshire villages, abbeys and moors; back to play the organ in this little village church; back to hold her in his arms every night at the end of her busy days. She missed Bill so much, but there were only two more nights to be spent on her own in the big bed where they shared so much joy. The day after tomorrow she would drive to the airport to pick him up, and to give him such wonderful news . . .

This last thought was still lingering in her mind when she entered her home, to an ecstatic welcome from Lucky. As she made a fuss of him in the hall, she saw the red light glowing from her answerphone. Instantly then her thoughts switched from Bill to the Bramleys and the trauma they had been forced to endure throughout this long day. Was there news of Jack at last? If so, was it the sort of news they and all their friends were hoping for? Or was there another tragedy descending on the family at Abbot's Fold Farm?

Her fingers were trembling as she waited for an answer to those questions. It was Julie's voice on the tape. She listened as Julie told her that Jack had been found by Matt and was being recovered by the emergency services and taken to hospital with a broken leg. So her prayers, and theirs, had been answered. Emotion engulfed her. She was still choking back tears when she became aware that there was another message for her.

This time it was Bill calling to assure her that he loved her, and was longing to be back with her. 'I'll see you on Friday, darling. Take care of yourself,' were his final words.

Oh yes, she would do that now she knew for certain that she was pregnant. She would start doing it right now, because suddenly, after having had almost nothing to eat all day, she was absolutely starving. A few minutes later she was curled up on the sofa enjoying a substantial supper of cheese and biscuits, helped by Lucky, who was not often allowed such treats.

'We're celebrating tonight, Lucky,' she told him, 'but we'll have a better celebration when your master gets home. It won't be long now!'

At Abbot's Fold Dave was lying on the old sofa lost in the deep sleep of exhaustion, having told Julie that she must wake him immediately if there was news of where Jack was being taken, whether it was to the cottage hospital at Nyddford or to the larger district hospital at Harrogate. As soon as he knew, he would drive there.

'He'll need us to be there for him because he'll probably be frightened, or at least bewildered,' Julie had said. Jack would also be deeply upset at having caused such a fuss, she knew. 'I'll start to get his pyjamas and toilet things ready to take with us.'

'If you'd rather go to bed, since you didn't get much sleep last night, I can go on my own,' Dave had offered before sinking into slumber.

She knew that it would be best for her to do the driving to whichever hospital they went, and that she wanted to be there to see for herself how Jack was after his ordeal. Her years of nursing warned her that he could be in a serious condition after the hours of exposure he had endured. Dave would need her support if things were not going well with his son. As she went to gather up the things Jack would need while he was in hospital, she paused to stare out of a window into the night sky. Was the fog beginning to lift at last? Were the branches of the trees behind the farmhouse stirring in a rising wind? Her spirits began to lift when she opened the back door and saw that they were indeed moving and the fog was becoming thinner and patchy. So they might be able to use the air ambulance to reach Bear's Head rock instead of having to rely on the more conventional road rescue team.

'Dear God, please let them reach him before it's too late,' she found herself silently praying.

Her thoughts moved on then to Matt. How was he coping with the situation? It was some time since she had taken the phone call from him saying that he had found Jack. He had been out for hours on the search then and he had sounded desperately tired. Dave's reaction, when she had told him it was Matt who had found his son, had left her feeling uneasy. Surely his jealousy of Matt would not prevent him from showing gratitude to the man who had found his son?

Matt shivered as he forced his eyes to open. He must not allow himself to drift into sleep again. It was vital that he remain alert until he and Jack were picked up by the rescue services. The cold wind that was biting into his chilled flesh was beginning to pierce the fog at last. So with a bit of luck the Yorkshire Air Ambulance might be able to reach them soon. It would certainly be able to reach them quicker than any other form of transport. As his thoughts reached that point, he found himself listening for the sound of the helicopter used by the team. He had seen them in action once close to Harrogate District Hospital but had never imagined then that he would one day be praying himself for their help. Jack stirred as he remembered that. Matt spoke urgently to him, trying to keep him from drifting into unconsciousness again.

'It won't be long now, Jack, before someone comes to help us. Just hang on there, lad.'

Jack murmured something he could not quite catch. Brack murmured back deep in his throat and reached out to lick his face. Thank God for the collie; Matt knew that the warmth from the dog who was lying alongside her young master was helping to keep him alive.

'Well done, Brack,' he said as he reached out to stroke her ears.

'Good lass, Brack,' Jack whispered.

'Thanks a lot, Simon. I don't know what I'd have done if you hadn't come.' Carla's voice was soft and slightly slurred with tiredness. The long, long walk back to the car, from the place where they had heard that Jack had been found, had taken its toll of her strength.

'You would have coped,' Simon told her.

'I'm still glad you were here. Will you come in and have a coffee?'

The tall young man pushed back a lock of the thick dark hair that had fallen over his forehead before he answered her. 'Not tonight, Carla. You need to get some sleep now, and I need to get Mum's car back to her. I'd like to come for a coffee another time, though, or to meet you in Nyddford for a drink. Is that on? Or are you . . .?'

Carla smiled. 'Yes, it's on.'

Simon hesitated. 'Only I heard there was this American guy whose dad taught at Nyddford High last year . . .'

Carla smiled again. 'Yes, I do write to Josh Bolton sometimes, or phone him, but we've both got years of study to get through, so we're only friends now.'

'I'll see when I can borrow Mum's car again then and I'll pick you up. OK?'

'OK!' Carla promised.

'Will you be here in the morning, Daddy?' Elliot asked when Tim tucked him into his bed for the second time.

'Yes. I'll be here every morning from now on,' Tim assured him. He had told both the children, after reading their bedtime stories, that he would see them in the morning. Kerry had been satisfied with that promise. Elliot had come

238

downstairs, long after they had thought he was asleep, to make sure he was still there. It had taken Jane and Tim some time to convince him that Tim really was back for good.

'You won't go away again and only come home for tea, will you?' he asked as Tim prepared to go downstairs again.

'No. I love all of you far too much ever to do that.'

Jane, standing in the doorway behind him, felt a lump come into her throat.

'Didn't you love us enough when you used to go back to somewhere else?' Elliot wanted to know next. His eyes were closing as he put this unexpected question to Tim, but he still wanted to know the answer.

Tim felt a rush of moisture invade his eyes. From behind him he heard Jane make a sound that was somewhere between a gasp and a sob. Words seemed to have deserted him for a long, agonizing moment. Then they came with a rush as he gathered the little boy into his arms.

'I never stopped loving you, Elliot, and I never will. I love all of you,' he said.

'Even Darcy?' was Elliot's final sleepy question.

'Even Darcy.'

Tim stepped back then out of the small bedroom and on to the landing where Jane was waiting for him. This time there were no words. None were needed. The long, shared embrace was all that was needed to set their world to rights. Then they looked in at their tiny, sleeping daughter and kissed her before moving into their own bedroom. So immersed were they after that in sharing their love for each other that neither of them heard Darcy creep up the stairs and stretch himself out at the foot of Elliot's bed.

'Dave!' Julie shook him firmly enough to startle him into awareness as soon as she had put the telephone down. 'It's time to go.'

'Go where?' Dave muttered as he stirred into life. He winced as cramp caught him painfully after his few hours of uncomfortable sleep on the elderly sofa.

'To the district hospital. They've taken Jack there. He's having surgery, but we can go as soon as we like.' Julie poured boiling water on the coffee in two large mugs and began to stir it as she finished speaking.

'Thank God he's safe at last.' He was already stretching himself upright as he spoke.

'Amen to that,' she said, with a catch in her throat.

'I don't know what I'd have done if it had been his body they had found.' His expression was sombre as he shared that thought with her. 'After what happened to Jill, when Jack went missing I was beginning to think I might have nothing left to live for.'

A small frisson of shock hit Julie before she was able to subdue the fierce hurt his unthinking remark brought to her. 'It was just as well that Matt managed to find him in time then, wasn't it?' she said quietly.

'It wasn't my fault that I didn't find him myself.' Dave was swallowing the scalding-hot drink at speed as those words came from him.

'You *would* have had someone to live for,' she reminded him. 'You do have a daughter, Dave. Sometimes you seem to forget that.'

'I don't when she's causing me problems, bringing me aggro! Jack never does that.'

'You *do* have a wife too,' she said under her breath as she went upstairs to rouse Carla and tell her that they were going to the hospital at once.

'I'll come with you,' Carla said eagerly.

'You'll need to be quick because your dad is in a rush to get there. So don't keep him waiting. I'll make you a hot drink while you dress.'

Back in the kitchen again she picked up the bag of clothes and toiletries that Jack would need while he was away from home and carried it out to the Land Rover. The fog was clearing fast now and it was just possible to catch a glimpse of a star in the darkness of the sky above it. A great wave of sadness descended on Julie as she stared about her. She was unable to dismiss from her mind those words Dave had uttered a few minutes ago. 'After what happened to Jill, when

Jack went missing I was beginning to think I might have nothing left to live for.'

Did her presence here at Abbot's Fold as his wife mean so little to him? Was she only a substitute in his kitchen, and his bed, for Jill?

Matt slid further and further down on the hard chair he had been occupying in the ward waiting room for what seemed to be hours now. He was bone-weary from lying close to the boy on the damp rock that had been their resting place while they waited for the fog to clear enough for the rescue team to reach them, and he longed to be in his large, luxury bed in his new house. They had told him he could go because the boy's parents would be here by the time Jack came out of surgery, but Matt would not do that. He wanted to stay until Dave Bramley arrived – if only to tell him how worried Jack had been because he had allowed old Joe Robinson's dog to escape from the hayshed. Just to make sure Dave didn't blow his top with Jack for going after the dog and causing all this fuss. It would be just like Dave to do that. He didn't know when he was lucky, and he *was* bloody lucky to have Julie and the boy.

Of course, what he really wanted was to see Julie. He was certain she would come with Dave to see her stepson and he wanted to tell her, if they got a minute alone, how while he had been lying beside the boy trying to keep him warm and awake, he had been thinking of *her*. Maybe he was wasting his time, though. Perhaps she would not come if she had to make an early start on her nursing duties tomorrow. It was already tomorrow, though, and there were footsteps to be heard hurrying along the corridor outside the room – footsteps that echoed loudly in the silence of the very-early-morning emptiness. A moment later there were voices too.

'Will you wait in here, please? Doctor will be along to have a word with you soon. The man who found the boy is still there,' the nurse said briskly before she hurried away.

The other voices were hushed as one by one the Bramley

family came into the room. Only the women were speaking. Dave was silent.

'Hi, Matt,' Carla greeted him as he struggled to get to his feet.

'Matt!' Julie's voice was warm. 'Don't get up, you look all in!' She crossed the small room swiftly to look at him with compassion. 'Thanks for finding Jack.' As the words left her mouth, she was reaching to kiss him on the lips.

Matt sensed rather than saw Dave's reaction, but before anything could be said the door was opening to admit a man wearing a stethoscope round his neck.

'Your son's leg has been set and he's back on the ward now, if you'd like to see him. He's in a private room for tonight; then we'll see how he is tomorrow. Don't stay too long. Only a few minutes, please. He's worrying about something. About his dog, I think. Just reassure him, then leave him to us. Nurse will show you where to go.'

They were on their way out of the room when Julie turned back to speak to Matt. 'How will you get home, Matt? Didn't you leave your car at Abbot's Fold?'

'Yes. I'll need to pick it up tomorrow. For tonight I've booked myself in with an old friend who lives in Harrogate. He's already taken Brack with him to give him a meal. So I'll get a taxi to where he lives.'

Julie made her mind up. 'No. I'll drive you there while Dave and Carla are with Jack. We'll go right now.'

He staggered slightly as he got to his feet. Julie put out a hand to steady him and kept it there to support him as they made their way to where the Land Rover was parked in front of the hospital. They were silent during the short journey across the green acres known as The Stray before coming to a halt outside a tall Edwardian house.

'Thanks, Julie,' Matt murmured as he reached to open the door.

'I should be saying that to you.'

He turned swiftly and caught her hands in his own. 'I'd do so much more than that for you.'

She waited until she saw him walk down the short path and enter the house; then she drove back to the hospital and met Dave and Carla at Jack's bedside. The boy was sleeping, so they left him to it and walked away down the empty corridor.

'Where were you?' Dave said sharply.

'Driving Matt to where he was going to stay the night because he left his car at our place.'

'Couldn't he have got a taxi?'

'He was going to, but he was almost out on his feet, so I wanted to make sure he got there safely.' Julie's voice was sharp.

'So he'll be coming to pick up his car tomorrow, I suppose?'

'Yes.'

'I'll make sure I'm around when he does.'

Was Dave still jealous of Matt, in spite of that thoughtless remark he had made to her just before they had left to come to the hospital? Julie could not make her mind up about that. He was such a volatile character, so much like Carla in that respect. Life with him was never going to be easy, but since she loved him, she must accept him the way he was.

'Oh, I'm so tired!' Carla yawned widely as they reached the hospital exit.

'We all are, but at least now we know Jack's going to be all right.' As he spoke, Dave put one arm round Julie's shoulder and the other round Carla's. 'Now we can go all go home and get some rest.'

Paula was up early so that she could walk Archie before any of the workmen arrived. She was going to miss him a lot when his master was well enough to claim him again; though she would soon have a dog of her own, because Daniel had told her, when he had brought Archie back from a late-night walk last night, that he knew of a dog needing a good home, a black, collie-labrador with a nice temperament.

'She's quite young, only a few months old, but her owners are service people who are being posted abroad. I could bring her to meet you and see how you get on,' Daniel had offered.

'Yes, I'd like that.'

After that she had said goodnight to him as he got into his estate car. As she watched him drive away, she found herself wondering why she felt so sorry to see him go when he had promised to come and see her again soon, and when he was the reason why she had lost half of her inheritance in the Mill House. It was as if she had always known Daniel Price, and always liked him. Yet she had known him for only a short time.

Her reflections came to an end as the plumber's van turned into the drive to remind her of all the many things that were still to be done if the Mill House was to be ready in time for opening next month.

Andrea woke to sunlight streaming through her bedroom window. The fog had gone at last. It would make things so much easier for her as she drove from Nyddbeck to the district hospital to see Jack this morning. She had had a soft spot for him ever since the day when, on arriving home from a nightmare journey through snowstorms a few months after she had come to the village, she had found that he and Dave had cleared her drive of snow and Jack had made her a little snowman to welcome her. Many people who knew him and loved him would be offering up thanksgiving prayers for his safety, as she herself had already. What sort of sweets should she take for him when she went to visit him? She would be able to buy some at the hospital shop.

A new thought came to her then. On other mornings during the last few weeks she had felt so sick and unwell that even to think of sweets would have been unwise. Not today, though. Today she felt fine, and very hungry!

Matt's friend dropped him off at the end of Abbot's Fold Lane so that he could pick up his car from there and start on work which he did not really feel up to because, in spite of his extreme weariness, he had not slept well. He seemed to have spent most of the night feeling his aches and pains, and thinking of Julie. Of course he still wanted Julie with a longing he had never previously experienced, and he knew

Dave Bramley did not deserve her. Yet during those hours he had spent waiting on the fogbound moor with her injured stepson for rescuers to arrive he had come to accept that he must get on with his life without her.

To do otherwise, even if he could manage to persuade her to leave Dave, would cause too much distress for the family at Abbot's Fold and for his dad and Dorothy. Brought up by his parents to be straight-dealing, even though he had gone off the rails somewhat during his late teens and twenties, Matt cared too much about the welfare of Ben and his second wife to risk spoiling it. His father's serious illness had proved that to him. So he was coming here simply to pick up his car and ask for the latest news of Jack; then he would keep his distance from Julie.

It was not going to be easy, though. He knew that as she met him at the farm gate, looking neat and extremely desirable in her nursing uniform.

'I've come for the car,' he said.

'I'm just going on duty,' she replied. 'Take care, Matt; you look tired still.'

He watched her drive away from him as Dave came to speak to him. 'Thanks for what you did,' Dave said. 'I'll always be grateful. I don't know what I would have done if I'd lost Jack, after losing Jill as I did.'

Matt met his gaze, then said what was in his mind. 'You'd still have had Julie, and you're bloody lucky to have *her*.'

Since there was nothing more to be said, he slid into his car, switched on the engine and left Dave to reflect on it.

Andrea bought sweets at the hospital shop and took them to Jack. He was propped up in bed looking pale and rather bored, but his face brightened when he saw the sweets. 'I wasn't sure what you liked, so I bought two different ones,' she explained.

'Thanks. I like them both. I might be able to go home this afternoon, so I'll take them with me,' he told her.

'You've had a rough time, haven't you?'

'They said it was on the radio news about me.'

'So it was. We were all worried about you. All saying a prayer for you.'

'Thanks,' he said again, blushing slightly. 'I was worried about losing Archie.'

Andrea smiled. 'You don't need to worry about him any more. He's staying at the Mill House until Mr Robinson is well enough to be able to leave here,' she told him. 'I'm going to see him next.'

'Will you tell him I'm sorry I let Archie get away, please?'

'I will, but he won't be blaming you, Jack. He'll be glad you are safe.'

'I might not have been if Brack hadn't found me. She's brilliant!' He was opening one of the bags of sweets and offering it to her.

'Thanks, Jack,' she said with a smile.

'Have one for Wandering Joe – Mr Robinson – or two,' he offered then.

'One will do. I don't think his teeth are up to eating many.' She prepared to move on to visit the old soldier.

'He can take his teeth out. Did you know that?' Jack said.

She smothered her laughter as she gave him a solemn 'No!' before leaving him.

With a bit of luck, and God willing, one day she and Bill would have a boy like Jack – a kind, sparky, funny, absolutely lovely son like Jack. They would have him, or her, before the end of the year. This time tomorrow Bill would be on his way home, and she would be waiting at the airport to give him that wonderful news.

She walked on towards her next visit, a tall beautiful woman wearing a dark suit and the narrow white collar which told passing medical staff and outpatients that she was a church minister serving her community. In her hand she carried a single large toffee, a token of friendship between a young boy and an old countryman. It could all have been so different, so tragically different, if Jack had not been found in time. There would have been duties for her then which would have tested her courage, and her faith, to the limit.

Her face was radiant with joy as she took the good news to Joe Robinson, who had trusted Jack with his most valued possession, his dog.

'Hello, Mr Robinson,' she said. 'I've just been to see Jack. He says he's sorry he let your dog run away, and he's sent you a toffee!'

Joe Robinson chuckled until his eyes began to water. 'I'd never blame the lad for that. Archie's always been a bit of an escape artist and he's not going to change now. I'll soon be home to look after him myself.'

'He's being well looked after by a nice young lady who lives at the Mill House, so you don't need to worry about him,' Andrea assured him.

'I was more worried about the boy. Such a grand boy, padre. Sort of lad I'd have been proud of if my missus hadn't been killed during the war. I'm allowed to get up in the afternoon, so I'll go and see him to thank him for the sweet.' He looked at it, resting on the bedside table, then chuckled again. 'I don't think my old choppers will be able to cope with that one. It seems a pity to waste young Jack's kindness, though, so maybe you'll accept it?'

He passed over the sweet in the shiny purple wrapping and Andrea took it with a smile. This was one of the things she loved about her work: the way it brought her so many small kindnesses from the people she was here to serve.

'Thank you for coming to see me,' Joe said as she held out her hand to him. 'God bless you.'

Her eyes were moist as she answered him. 'You too, Mr Robinson.'

Then she was on her way home, driving through sunlit villages where the grass verges were aglow with thousands of daffodils and where roadside fields held skittish young lambs chasing one another. Spring had come to the dale overnight to bring to an end the savage final months of winter. Spring would see Nyddford Church roof repairs completed, and preparations for Nyddford Summer Festival going ahead. The winter had tested her endurance, especially while Bill had been away, but spring was bringing Bill back to her. The thought brought a song into

247

her heart and she began to hum it as she turned into Beck Lane and saw her church ahead of her. It was a song of thanksgiving.